Peculiar Passions

Or,
The Treasure of Mermaid Island

Ruby Vise

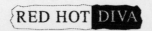

by the same author:
Sweet Violet

First published 2003 by Red Hot Diva/Diva Books,
an imprint of Millivres Prowler Limited
Spectrum House, Unit M, 32–34 Gordon House Road, London NW5 1LP
www.divamag.co.uk

A catalogue record for this book is available from the British Library

ISBN 1-873741-83-9

Printed and bound in Finland by WS Bookwell

Distributed in the UK and Europe by Airlift Book Company,
8 The Arena, Mollison Avenue,
Enfield, Middlesex EN3 7NJ
Telephone: 020 8804 0400

Distributed in North America by Consortium,
1045 Westgate Drive, St Paul, MN 55114-1065
Telephone: 1 800 283 3572

Distributed in Australia by Bulldog Books,
PO Box 300, Beaconsfield, NSW 2014

Prologue

Elizabeth wiped her mother's fevered brow.

"Oh, sweet child," her mother whispered.

"Hush."

"There is something I must give to you."

"In the morning, Mother."

"I will not see another morning."

Elizabeth wanted to contradict her, but she could see from the steely light in her mother's eyes that it was not a good idea. She also knew from the worried looks of the doctor that what she said was probably true.

"Here." Her mother reached inside her nightdress and pulled out a golden locket. Elizabeth had seen it often times before and had marvelled at its clever construction, wondered at its odd shape and what it might hold within.

"It was my mother's – she gave it to me just before she died in the carriage fire and now I hand it on to you, Elizabeth. I was never brave enough to pursue its secret, yet I think maybe you will be."

"Hush, Mother." Elizabeth could see that talking and even a small amount of movement were putting a terrible strain upon her mother's breathing. She unclasped the locket and gently removed it from around her mother's neck. She held it in her hand and gazed upon it – soon it would be all that she had.

She re-clasped it around her own neck, burning with desire to ask more about the mystery, but knowing that she could not.

Her mother smiled. "It suits you well." Her voice sounded as if it came from a great distance. Her breathing suddenly turned shallow and ragged.

The doctor turned to Mary, the family maid. "Go and find your master." Elizabeth knew that Mary would not step outside the house after dark.

"I will go." Elizabeth stood up. She did not feel the need to watch her mother's last moments; she had watched her die slowly over the past four years, while her father drank away their meagre income in one low inn or another. She collected her cape and stepped out into the damp night. Mary, terrified, pulled upon her arm.

"Please, Mistress, do not go. The night is dark and not safe. You cannot go and leave me alone with a strange man."

Elizabeth shook her off and strode out into the street, heading for 'The Jolly Sailor', her father's favoured haunt of late.

1

Girl Meets Boy

Elizabeth stood outside the tavern and listened to the raucous noise coming from within. Her heart was beating fast, but that could have been from the run along the filthy street to get there. She was afraid. In any dark corner, there might stand a man with a knife, ready to relieve her of her purse or her life, and Mrs Wattle, their cook, had warned her of such places as this tavern, warned her she would not escape them with her virtue intact. She took a deep breath and pushed the door open before her nerve failed her completely.

Inside, it was dim and smoky, and the stench of ale and the sweat of men rushed up to greet her. The place was packed with a seething mass of bodies, such as she had only seen in a reproduction of a painting of Hell by Dante. In the centre of this mass was a small, clear space where two men were locked in some sort of wrestling match. One man was fat and bald, while the other appeared to be no more than a boy and a small, skinny lad at that. It seemed to Elizabeth a most unfair pairing: the fat man had the boy in a headlock, from which he was trying and failing to escape. Then suddenly, with surprising speed and strength, the lad landed a series of stinging blows that felled the big man.

A huge cheer went up, the lad was lifted on to a table and someone pressed a jug of ale into his hands. He looked up for a moment and, on seeing Elizabeth, raised the jug to her before taking a long draught. Other heads turned and saw her standing there, and a silence descended upon the place that was more ominous than all the noise had been. A man near the bottom of the steps staggered over to her, reeking of ale and pickles.

"Well, well." He leaned in towards her. "What have we here?" He made to grab her skirt. Elizabeth kicked out– now that she was amongst these men, her breathless excitement was gone. They were repugnant. She felt a burning anger and resentment rise up within her.

"I am looking for my father," she said firmly to the man, who was still attempting to take hold of a piece of her skirt, and took a step down the small short staircase that led into the tavern.

"There is no man in here who could be the father of such a beautiful daughter." The man lunged closer to her, but with a quick slap, she unbalanced him. He fell over a nearby chair and went crashing to the floor, which brought a cheer from the watching crowd.

"What, pray, is your father's name?" the lad standing on the table called out to her. His voice was light and cultured.

"William Harvey," Elizabeth replied. The lad was quite beautiful in the way some young men are, despite having a black eye and one tooth missing.

"I think you will find him over there." The young man pointed to a corner dimmer than the rest and Elizabeth saw her father being hauled to his feet by a tall man.

"Bethy?" Her father approached her, his face red and blotchy, his eyes blurred and unfocused. He leaned heavily on the arm of his companion who, now that Elizabeth could see him better, was obviously of a better class than most in the tavern. The cut and cloth of his clothes suggested he was a man of good breeding and some refinement.

"My mother is gravely ill. The doctor is attending upon her, and the minister. The doctor sent me to fetch you," she said with much feeling. Even if her father had not given her mother much affection or attention in her life, he could at least be there to witness her death.

"Come, William." The tall gentleman led her father past Elizabeth and up the stairs. Elizabeth turned and followed them. At the top of the stairs she looked back once more at the scene in the tavern. The young man on the table blew her a kiss. It flew across the space between. She blushed to the roots of her hair and rushed for the door, gasping for fresh air.

Her father and the gentleman were waiting for her. She ignored them, hurrying on ahead of them through the muddy streets not caring now for her ruined shoes, just wanting to be safely indoors again.

She was exceedingly worried. What would happen to the household when her mother died? New bills arrived almost every day and without the little money her mother made from her embroidery, none would get paid. Large, bullish, rough men arrived some nights, well after the time respectable men did business, and her father would hide in his study. Elizabeth was forced, trembling, to inform them that he was out.

She knew that soon the house would have to be sold to pay off her father's debts, and where they would live after that, she had no idea. The only possible solution to their problems – she shuddered – was for her to marry, to find some suitable husband who was rich enough and tolerant enough to take not only her, but her father and Mary, too. For Mary would surely never find another employer to put up with her flighty ways.

She studied the man helping her father. He was full of ale, too, but was in better command of himself. She wondered what his occupation might be, to be dressed so well but still find his entertainment in such a low tavern. He could be an actor – he was handsome enough, and they were well known to frequent such places – but the cut of his clothes was too respectable. What solace or entertainment he found in her father's company, she could not guess at. Her father, he who had once been physician to the Court of King Charles II, could these days barely string together a sentence.

They were at the house now. Her father, supported by the unknown gentleman, pounded upon the door to be admitted. Mary opened it, saw who it was, and fled back into the kitchen. The minister was there now, and self-importantly called for silence. In her mother's room a single candle burned, sending long shadows up the wall. Her mother, engaged in weak tortuous coughing, lay as pale as the linen sheets, the blood on her lips a sharp, mocking contrast to her pallor. Elizabeth longed to see no more the pained look upon her poor face, the only sign that she still clung on to life. No more; let her rest with God, at peace.

The stranger hovered for a moment in the doorway of her mother's room, greatly interested, but the minister waved him away. Her father went and knelt beside the bed, put his hand on his wife's neck and slid his fingers under her nightgown. It looked such a loving gesture, and for a moment Elizabeth was greatly touched. Until, that was, her father began pulling urgently at the neck of the nightgown, as if looking for something.

"Enough now, William." The good doctor pulled him away.

Elizabeth, angry with her father, yet unwilling to remonstrate with him and disturb her mother, went in search of Mary, to see if she could be persuaded to prepare some refreshments for their guests. The girl was nowhere to be found and, as Mrs Wattle had been given the evening to rest, Elizabeth steadied herself by preparing a dish of tea for the doctor and minister. She found also some cake and a bottle of brandy, to which she knew the doctor was partial with his tea.

She took the refreshments into the withdrawing room and lit a lamp in there. The whole house was cold and damp; Mary had not lit any fires – she was too scared to go into the cellar by herself, and Elizabeth had been too preoccupied to go with her. Elizabeth hoped the doctor and minister would not notice; she could not even be sure there was coal. Her mother had of late been too ill to supplement their tiny income with her handiwork, and the coal bill remained unpaid.

The strange gentleman was still standing in the hall.

"Won't you come into the withdrawing room?" asked Elizabeth.

He nodded his thanks and went and stood in front of the empty fireplace, pulling his coat closer around him. Elizabeth wondered why he was still there. She called the doctor and minister through; it was best to leave her mother and father alone together.

She poured the tea and offered the cake; the gentleman clutched his cup in both hands as if to draw its warmth into his body. The minister and the doctor studied him but neither said anything to him. The minister talked of the funeral and the doctor ate his cake in silence.

Elizabeth had come to know the doctor well on his many visits to her mother. He was a warm man, with kind eyes and a long-suffering wife. He had known her father when they were students and both destined for great things – now he tended the poor and made little or no money from it, while her father drank away the last years of his life, having fallen out of favour with the Court. Thankful she was that because of this past friendship, the doctor charged them little or nothing for his time.

The minister had been a frequent visitor of late, too, but Elizabeth could not make herself like him. He talked of nothing but money and sin, and tried to extract some of each, or both, from Elizabeth's mother on his every visit. He was even now telling Elizabeth how much a decent burial would cost, and her mother not dead yet.

The gentleman by the fire looked annoyed by this; he reached inside his fine jacket and produced a purse fat with coins, the half of which he emptied on to the table in front of the minister.

"Take that for the funeral, if, indeed, there is to be one, and get yourself gone from this house."

Elizabeth was shocked to hear such disrespect shown to a man of the cloth, but was shocked, too, by the number of coins on the table; more money than she saw from one year to the next. The minister was surprised. He stared at the coins on the table, torn between berating the gentleman for speaking so, and his desire to take the money.

His dilemma was solved by a cry from the sick room. The doctor, who had also been staring at the coins, put down his tea and rushed out of the room. Neither the minister nor the gentleman moved, locked in a battle of wills. Elizabeth, however, left them and ran to join the doctor at her mother's bedside.

Her mother's eyes were open and staring at the ceiling, a dribble of blood at the corner of her mouth and her hands clutching the bedclothes in death. The room smelt differently; a smell akin to sulphur now pervaded it. Somewhere in the street outside a dog barked wildly, and her father, broken and crumpled, was huddled in the corner of the room, sobbing like a child.

The doctor sighed and placed a penny on each staring eye; the minister appeared briefly to say a few words over the body and then left quickly with the sound of coins jangling in his pocket. Elizabeth saw the good doctor out and helped her father to his bed. The gentleman was gone, though no one saw him leave and there was another – smaller – pile of coins on the table.

Elizabeth dragged herself up to her own room, and was, this once, pleased to see the sleeping form of Mary already in her bed. Her bed would be at least warm and she was a little afraid, she had to admit to herself, of sleeping alone in a house in which there was a dead body. She undressed quickly then pulled on her nightdress and slipped under the covers, trying not to wake Mary.

"Oh, Mistress Elizabeth –" Mary turned and threw her arms around her "– what will become of us?"

"Hush now, Mary." Elizabeth stroked her head, finding solace herself in the gesture.

"We will be out on the streets."

"No, we will not," Elizabeth rebuked her.

Mary whimpered, and Elizabeth felt sorry for being sharp with her. She put her hand under Mary's chin and tipped her face up to her own. She kissed the soft lips, wondering at the peculiar passions that Mary stirred in her. She wanted to protect her yet, at the same time, she wanted to chastise her, punish her for all her sins and for the sins of the world.

She thought Mary's weakness of resolve and tendency towards anxious fits were a medical condition and they were working together to strengthen her character. Elizabeth had prescribed cold baths and vigorous exercise, but these had left Mary more wretched than before. Now they were trying out a curative method about which Elizabeth had read in one of her father's tracts – a cure for ague of the melancholic humour in women.

Despite her own weariness, she felt Mary might benefit from a session of treatment that very night. She began by administering calming kisses – her mouth over Mary's breathing her own calm essence into Mary, using her tongue to stir their breath together in Mary's mouth, feeling the texture of Mary's tongue with her own to try to ascertain whether the treatment was working or not. By the movement of Mary's body under her own, she could tell it was not working. She would have to resort to more drastic measures.

Mary's hands clutched at Elizabeth, pulling at her nightdress and at her own. Elizabeth knew this was just the start of a fit and, that if allowed to go unchecked, it could lead to Mary damaging herself.

Elizabeth positioned her body on top of Mary's, pinning her to the bed. She had learnt some time back that by holding Mary's breasts she could sometimes alleviate the symptoms. She pulled up Mary's nightgown and grasped one breast in her hand, gently rubbing the nipple with her thumb. Tonight, this seemed to inflame Mary further and she strained under Elizabeth. Elizabeth sighed – she would need to administer the full treatment.

She pushed Mary's nightgown up to her neck, placed one hand upon each of Mary's breasts and squeezed them firmly. Mary's hands flew about, at once pulling and pushing at Elizabeth. Elizabeth released the breasts and, instead, held Mary's arms firmly to her sides to stop her interfering with the treatment. With both her hands occupied, Elizabeth had to use her mouth on Mary's nipples. She sucked and licked first one and then the other, feeling their texture change under her tongue.

Mary groaned. Her mood was turning quite feverish, and she arched her back and turned her head from side to side against the pillow. The fit was gathering strength now and Elizabeth knew it was time to bring it to its conclusion. She released one of Mary's wrists and slid her hand down between their bodies, finding the entrance to the hole in which she believed the seat of Mary's trouble lay. She inserted one finger and then a second; they slid in easily, as they always did. Mary arched her back and pushed her hips off the bed. Her legs began to shake. All these symptoms Elizabeth had witnessed countless times before; she believed they were a physical manifestation of Mary's illness and that she was freeing Mary of them with this treatment. What Elizabeth did not understand was why they recurred so often and why the treatment was always only temporary. She also didn't understand why administering the treatment made her feel hot and excitable in herself; she wondered if by expelling the fit from Mary in the way she did, she somehow drew it into her own body.

Elizabeth had no time to ponder that now. She moved her fingers backwards and forwards, in and out of the opening, bringing the fit to a peak in order to break it. Mary was breathing heavily; her legs where twitching now. Elizabeth moved her fingers faster and faster, trying to shake the fit from Mary, but tonight it seemed reluctant to let loose its grip. Elizabeth had often thought of inventing an instrument that would fulfill the task of ridding women of these fits. It would need to be a little longer than Elizabeth's longest finger and two or three times its girth, and by some force, natural or otherwise, it should vibrate.

Mary's body was twisting, her back arching, her free hand clutching at Elizabeth's back. Elizabeth knew the fit was close to its peak; she increased the speed and depth of her finger movements, using her thumb to rub the stiff little nubbin of flesh at the top of Mary's hole. All at once Mary cried out loudly, her body went stiff like that of someone who had been dead the past few hours, and then it relaxed. The fit was over and Mary was calm again. Elizabeth removed her fingers and Mary sighed and stretched, smiling up at Elizabeth.

"Thank you," she whispered.

Elizabeth pulled her nightgown down, and kissed her on the forehead. Mary would now sleep peacefully and wake calm and refreshed. Mary turned over and had soon fallen into a relaxed slumber. Elizabeth, however, found that she was far from sleep. She was worried about Mary; they could barely afford to keep Mrs Wattle on, and she was a cheerful worker and a passable cook, but Mary was nigh on useless around the house, being too frail or too scared to perform many simple tasks. But where else would she find employment? Who else would know how to quell her fits and restore her to calm as Elizabeth did?

She looked at the ceiling and tried to bring forth a picture of her mother before the sickness had drained her of her strength and courage, before the coughing had left her as weak as an infant and spittled her embroidery with tiny spots of blood. She remembered her with her father, before he fell out of favour with the Court. Their house then had always been filled with visitors of the noblest ranks, and laughter rang out from every room.

Before the Great Fire destroyed that house and they built this much smaller one in its stead, they had a staff of six. That never seemed enough, for Elizabeth had been kept busy doing errands about the city.

She remembered learning to read and write at her father's knee, and being taught also a little Latin, but not being able to tell anyone because many people still believed that only boys should be taught such skills. She remembered going to Court one day with her father and seeing the King, and being so proud.

All these memories brought tears to her eyes. Whatever it was her father had done to fall so out of favour, she had never been told. Whatever it was, it seemed to be the start of their decline, first the Fire and then her mother's sickness and her father's drinking. Now, at the death of her mother, it appeared they would lose everything.

Mary turned over in her sleep and Elizabeth sighed. There was nothing else to do but that she would have to marry. She was twenty, after all, well past marrying age. She had not been wed before now because she was nursing her mother, but it had to be done. Having no other female relatives to help her with an entrée, she would go and see Mrs Tuppins the matchmaker as soon after the funeral as decency allowed. She realised she lacked the merits to make a good match; there was no money and she was no beauty, being too tall and broad of shoulder for the current fashion, not round enough or palely delicate in any way. Her feet and hands were too big, and her skin too dark and ruddy compared to the ivory beauty of the ladies of the Court. Some merchant, she thought, who was often off trading, or a widower, perhaps, who was less interested in adornment and wanted simply someone to manage his household affairs.

She did not like to think of the physical nature of marriage, although she had heard Mrs Wattle talk of it to Mary when they had not known she had been listening, and even seen diagrams in her father's medical texts. She could not imagine what the act would be like, except to be uncomfortable and distasteful.

For some reason, she thought of the lad she had seen fighting at the tavern, and the kiss he had blown her, and she felt herself blush with the impertinence of it. A lad such as himself, thinking she would even entertain the idea of a dalliance with a tavern brawler. If she saw him again, which she sincerely hoped she would not, he would certainly feel the sharp edge of her tongue.

She fell into a troubled sleep, buffeted by disturbing dreams, first of her poor mother's death and then of an even stranger nature. She was on a ship in rough seas and the lad was there. They were fighting side by side under a fluttering flag. Thugs and ruffians threw themselves at her and she cut and thrust with her long sword, driving them through and then tossing them aside to face the next and the next. It seemed there was an endless stream of the most unsavoury characters coming at her, lining up to feel the sharp edge of her blade.

The lad fought beside her, slaying an equal number of men with great speed and dexterity, assisting her sometimes when she seemed to be losing her fight and needing assistance at others. All the time, Elizabeth felt a great need that they win this fight, that more than their small lives were at risk.

2

Girl Meets Girl

Jacqueline touched the locket that nestled between her flat breasts. It was the last thing her mother ever gave her, and had hung around her mother's neck for as long as she could remember, before her mother had taken it and tossed it to her.

"Be brave, my love –" her mother had instructed "– as I never was. Its secret will save you." And then the press gang had dragged Jacqueline off.

It had, indeed, seemed to act as a lucky charm, and so far had protected her against all manner of evils. Scurvy onboard ships, storms that had washed men overboard, the wild men of the West Indies, all had been warded off by the charm of the locket. Besides, she had seen the natives of the Indies wearing such things around their own necks, though theirs were made of rough cloth, not shiny gold, and contained feathers and bones and spices. Hers held nothing more than a lock of her mother's hair and some unreadable inscription. It was an odd shape, too, fashioned to look like half a heart, with the other half missing.

Jack, the name by which she had been known for the longest time, touched it now and felt the fine metal warm under her fingers. The fight she was about to enter into was not much different to any other that she had fought, except that the man was the size of a ship and she hoped that Harry had slipped enough of the sleeping draught into his drink to slow him sufficiently, yet not send him unconscious before she had landed enough blows to explain it.

A space was cleared for them in the middle of the tavern, and the patrons of the tavern gathered around. A few late bets were placed, and not in Jack's favour, for who would bet on such a small lad beating Giant Ted? Jack grinned; all the more money for Harry and her to split later. She was ready. The landlord announced the start and the fight began.

Jack was quick and stronger than she looked, but Giant Ted was stronger still and obviously had a good constitution, for the sleeping draught appeared to be having no effect upon him. Jack let her concentration slip for a second and he grabbed her around the neck. No amount of punching would loose his grip. Jack heard the door of the tavern open and felt the crowd around them turn towards it. Ted was distracted for a moment, and that gave her the opening she was looking for. She twisted in his grip, and landed a series of punches upon him that not only freed her, but also sent Ted crashing to the floor.

The crowd roared their surprise and someone lifted Jack on to a table and passed her a drink. Jack looked for the first time towards the door and the person who had saved her neck. She realised why the rowdies had been so distracted – at the top of the stairs stood a fine lady, tall and strong, dressed in fancy clothes. Such a lady as Jack had never seen in a tavern like this.

Jack raised her mug now as a thank you; not only had the lady distracted her opponent on her entry, but she was now diverting the gamblers from any questions of the money they had so willingly handed over to her mate Harry. Jack saw Harry making a well-timed exit, and so she drank deeply of her ale and hoped Ted wouldn't wake too soon and remember Harry plying him with drinks of a peculiar taste before the fight.

The crowd, in any case, had all but forgotten the fight and were watching this new entertainment in the doorway. Old John Compton was trying to get a feel of the lady's skirt, but was sharply rebuked with a stinging blow to his head. The lady was demanding to know if her father was within, and Old John was right when he said there wasn't a man in the place who could have fathered such a wondrous thing as she.

Jack watched from the vantage point of her table as the lady surveyed the crowd, her eyes flashing like the candlelight they were reflecting. Her cheeks were flushed red, from anger, perhaps, or from the heat of the tavern after the chill of the night outside. Her breasts under her cloak rose and fell as she breathed hard. Jack sensed she was torn between fear and anger at her treatment. Old John made another lunge for her skirt and this time was met with the lady's boot and was sent crashing to the floor. The watching crowd roared their approval, but Jack knew that their mood could turn.

"What, pray, is your father's name?" she called across to the lady.

"William Harvey."

Jack knew of no such man, but this was not a regular haunt of hers. She had noticed an elderly man talking to one of the regulars, a well-known sea captain, Captain Luther, in the back corner.

"Is that him sitting over there?" She pointed in their direction, but the captain had already seen the fine lady and had risen, leading the older man towards the door.

The lady said something of her mother being unwell and they all three hurried from the tavern. The lady did pause then at the door and look back over the heads of the crowd to Jack, still standing on the table. Jack was struck again by how beautiful she looked and could not resist blowing her a kiss. She looked shocked, and left quickly.

Ted was beginning to stir and members of the crowd were turning their attention back to her. She decided it was time to leave before he woke fully and wondered why his head ached so. She called her thanks to the patrons and hurried out of the door. The fine lady and her father were gone into the night, but Harry was there, grinning like a demon.

"You have the money?" Jack asked.

Harry rattled his purse; it sounded heavy. He slapped Jack's back. "Aye, lad. Soon we will be able to retire."

They made their way back to their lodgings. Sweet Anne, Harry's beautiful daughter, would be there waiting for them. She would steal a few coins out of the purse while she thought they were not watching, and, as like as not, sneak into Jack's room after her father was safely snoring and demand of her certain services.

Jack retired soon after they returned, feeling suddenly very tired. She took to her bed and, as was her wont of late, began reminiscing about her life and how strange it had turned out for her.

She had been dressed as a boy from an early age and passed well enough; so well, in fact, that she was press-ganged into the Navy. There, she learned she was missing a vital piece of anatomy. While in the Indies, she was introduced to a native master carver who made for her a wooden phallus; he made it with such skill and care that no woman upon whom she had used it had noticed it wasn't made of flesh and blood.

Sweet Anne was fair and blessed with rosy cheeks and a buxom bosom; Jack loved her as well as she loved her own life. Harry was hoping to match Anne off with some man of money and class, and expressly forbade Jack from entertaining her advances, but she was a persistent wench and went at Jack until she had worn down her defenses. Harry thought of Jack as no threat, being nothing more than a lad; she certainly looked no older than fifteen or sixteen although she was into her twenty-first year.

She had been fifteen when, while quartering in Portsmouth to escape the Plague in London, the press-gang roaming the city had pounced upon her and dragged her away. Her mother had wept and begged; she was ready, even, to give out Jack's terrible secret. Jack had told her to hush and went with the men with as much dignity as she could muster.

Being a seaman was rough and, being so small of stature, Jack was often beaten and punished for crimes other men had committed. The crew around her were hard, and if they were cruel, they had been made that way by the treatment they received from their superiors, not by their own nature.

Jack often sought out the duty that would allow her to climb to the peace and fresh air of the main mast crow's nest, for below-decks reeked with all manner of foul odours. After a time, she came to love the sea and the life thereupon. They sailed six weeks to the West Indies, six long weeks of endless hours with nothing to do but scrub the decks and try to avoid the boatswain's whip. Hours of nothing to do but watch the sea slip away below her and wait for the sound of gulls that meant land was near.

Jack watched the men as she had watched the boys when she was younger, so that she would know how to act like them. She knew there where great differences between the sexes, even before she was aware of the physical differences. They walked differently, talked differently, even the way they ate their food was different. She copied these differences and when she had first met her grandparents, for whom this deception had been planned, they believed her to be the son of her father and had treated her as such. They hired a tutor for her, and lavished upon her all the care and attention they would have had she truly been their grandson and heir.

It had all played out as her mother had hoped, until the press gang had appeared and whisked Jack away, but the lessons she had learnt in her youth she put to good use, and none onboard the ship guessed she was anything other than that which she presented herself to be. Even Harry, who befriended her early in the voyage and taught her how to use her smallness and speed to great advantage in a fight, never guessed her secret.

Her letters served her well, too. She would sometimes read

aloud to members of the crew; they did not care much for Mr
Milton or Mr Pope, but Mr Defoe and his Robinson Crusoe they liked
very much. This won her friends amongst the men, but also brought
her to the attention of the captain, a young gentleman who seemed
almost as surprised as Jack to find himself at sea, and, lacking any
half decent company, promptly made Jack his cabin boy.

The voyage passed more easily in this way, but she still sought
out the solitude and serenity of the crow's nest when she could,
and kept Harry informed and well fed with leavings from the
captain's table.

In the West Indies, Jack saw many wondrous things, all manner
of fruit that smelled and tasted of the heavens and people so
different from herself. Though many of the indigenous people, the
Caribs, had been driven to the hills by early settlers, some
remained by the ports, trading what little fruits and produce they
could come by to newcomers. She watched these people and
found that she could copy some of their words and make herself
understood by them. She soon learned that they were as human as
she was herself, with the same hopes and fears as any of the people
back in England. They were friendly and warm, despite the terrible
treatment they received from her fellow countrymen. She loved
the land on which they lived, so green and abundant, and rejoiced
in the warmth of the sun and the embrace of the coastal waters.

She learned to fish with the local men and was taken under the
wing of the local women, who poked and prodded her and didn't
believe for a moment that she was a boy. It was they who
introduced her to the carver, and who, with no worries for their
immortal souls, naturally and freely, lined up to offer themselves
for her to try out her new member on. Jack had been too shy then
to take up their offers. The carver showed her how to strap it to her
body so that she could use it as a man would use his real member,
and tape it to her leg when it was not in use.

A tapping at Jack's door broke into her reverie. It creaked open on its old hinges and closed again. Sweet Anne was there beside her bed.

"Dear Jack," she whispered, "I am so cold." It was not such a cold night, being May, though it was damp. "Please let me lie with you."

"No, Anne, we should not." Jack knew that Harry would be enraged if he found out. "Your father wants you for a better man than I," she said, but even to her own ears it sounded unconvincing.

"Oh, la, Jack." Anne was in the bed under the covers by now. "No such man exists." She snuggled up close to her. Jack could feel Anne's pert breasts pushed into her own meagre ones, and her sweet breath against her cheek. She knew she should not be doing this, Harry trusted her as a friend, but even as she thought about the unworthiness of one who betrayed her friend, her hands were reaching out to grasp those delicious breasts, to undo the draw string of Anne's nightgown and to plunge her face deep between the two perfect orbs and breathe in the intoxicating scent that was Anne.

Anne, meanwhile, pulled up her nightgown to reveal her luscious thighs to Jack's roving hand. The smoothness of them made even the finest silk seem of poor workmanship. Their texture was of the best bought porcelain and, in the moonlight coming through the window, they looked like alabaster marble.

Jack ran her hand over those thighs and marvelled at their construction compared to her own spindly legs. She came up for air from between the breasts and sought out a nipple with her mouth. Anne sighed and clasped Jack's head closer, then took one of Jack's hands and guided it along her thigh to the rough hair of her pubis. The hair twisted and curled like a man's beard. She led Jack's exploring fingers to its mouth, and such a mouth it was. Its lips were soft and sweet like those on Anne's face, inside it was wet like a tongue and sucked at Jack's fingers as she slid them inside.

She explored it thoroughly with her fingers, feeling the walls and rubbing her thumb round its nose, all the time still sucking on the nipple of Anne's breast. Anne's whole body was responding now to Jack's attentions; she arched her back and rocked her hips, grinding them hard into Jack's hand, forcing Jack's finger deeper inside her. Her breathing was changing, too, becoming quicker. As was Jack's; she loved Anne more than anything else in this world, for she stirred such a peculiar passion within her.

Jack slid down Anne's smooth, pale body and kissed that lower mouth. Anne gasped as Jack's tongue touched her and raised her hips even more to encourage that tongue to enter her more fully. Jack did so, pushing with tongue, fingers and thumb, drinking in the smell and taste of her, rubbing and sucking in time with her own heartbeat, faster and faster as her heart instructed her.

Anne threw wide her arms and tossed her pretty head from side to side. "Now, my love, now," she cried, and Jack quickly raised her nightshirt, unstrapped the wood phallus from her leg and carefully slid it into Anne.

"Oh, sweet Jesus." Anne grasped Jack's hips and pulled her closer. Jack pushed with her pelvis and felt the phallus slide deeper in. Anne's face was radiant in the moonlight, her eyes closed, her lips slightly parted. Jack rocked her hips, sliding the phallus in and out, and using her other hand to rub Anne to even greater stimulation. Anne arched her back to match Jack's rocking; between them, they set up a rhythm, like waves reaching the shore, faster and faster still. All the while, Jack looked into Anne's glowing face, wondering what manner of thought was going through her pretty head to engender such an expression of concentration.

Jack could feel Anne's body tighten under her own, until every muscle and sinew was drawn taut like an archer's bow. Then, with a cry like an arrow being let loose, Anne came to her climax; for a moment, it seemed her whole body was thrown wide open and Jack could see into her very soul.

Jack slid the phallus out and carefully tucked it back into its strapping. Anne sighed and turned over as if to go to sleep. Jack hugged her from behind, wishing they could stay like that all night, but knowing that it was not possible.

"Sweet Anne," she whispered in her pretty ear, "you must away to your own bed now."

Anne stirred and then seemed to fall back into sleep.

"Sweetest Anne," Jack whispered again.

Anne sighed. She reached her hand back and felt along Jack's thigh until she touched the phallus. "Oh, Jack," she giggled. "It is hard again; can we not do it one more time?"

"No." Jack pushed her hand away. "Your father will surely hear us and if he does, both you and I will be thrown on to the street."

Anne sighed again and climbed from the bed; for a moment her nightdress lodged above her hips and Jack had a clear view of the two perfect, white mounds. She sighed – oh, that she could spend one whole night with those sweet buttocks without fear of discovery, but that would never be. The nightdress fell to cover all, and Anne turned and planted one last sweet kiss upon Jack's lips.

"Goodnight, Jack lad," she whispered.

"Good night, my Sweet Anne." Jack watched her tiptoe to the door, listen for a moment and then quietly leave. She sighed again and pulled the covers to her chin. She thanked God for their brief encounter and wondered if it was a reward or punishment, and what she had done to deserve such moments as these.

She turned on to her side and fell into a troubled sleep, where she dreamed she was at sea again, in the midst of a terrible battle. The sea was rough and throwing the ship about; she was standing under a flag and fighting for her life with a long sword and dagger. Beside her was the fine lady from the tavern, who she had all but forgotten. The dream went on and on, man after man presenting themselves for a fight. Jack cut and thrust, driving her sword through one man, stabbing another with the dagger, one moment helping the lady fend off an assailant and the next requiring her assistance to drive off another.

Never had a battle at sea lasted so long, nor been fought in such terrible conditions. The deck under her feet buckled and heaved, yet the oncoming pirates seemed to have no trouble keeping their footing. Every moment it lasted, Jack was in fear for her life. She was also aware that something larger than her life was at sake here. Even as she dreamed, she wondered what it meant and why it was the lady who fought by her side. She felt their destinies were tied together in some way and that their paths would cross again – the Fates would have it so.

3

The Funeral

Elizabeth awoke, drenched with sweat, and exhausted. Her arms ached as if she had indeed been fighting off an unknown number of men with a heavy sword, and when she saw that it was Mary next to her in the bed and not the young lad, she found that she was deeply disappointed. The feeling disturbed her greatly.

It was growing light outside the window. She roused Mary and sent her out for water. She dressed and went herself into the cellar and dug around for the last of the coal; today, at least, the house would be warm for the mourners to come back to after the funeral.

She gave Mrs Wattle some of the coins the gentleman had left and sent her out to buy extra provisions, instructing her to first pay off the debt that they owed the grocer and afterwards use what money was left over. Elizabeth then went into her father's room, and found him sound asleep with a bottle of liquor still in his hand. She would let him rest a little longer, she thought, and hoped that he would wake sober and in a reasonable mood. She dragged the coals to the withdrawing room in a piece of sacking and laid the fire herself. She also stoked up the kitchen fire and set the kettle to boil.

She went into her mother's room and stood for a moment looking at the body; it was quite cold to the touch, but, otherwise, she looked much as she had done when she was alive, except that now she looked at peace and free from pain. Elizabeth thanked God for her release and prayed that she would have an easy journey to Heaven. If anyone on this earth had led a Christian life, it was her mother. Still, she was grateful that an end had come to her mother's long, long suffering; beneath her otherwise dispassionate countenance, Elizabeth grieved.

The minister would have appraised the good women of the parish of their loss, and they would arrive soon to prepare the body. Elizabeth needed to prepare herself first to greet them. Mary finally returned with the water, and Elizabeth washed and changed into her only black dress, made for her grandmother's mourning. There was no time or money to have had another made, and this one was fraying around the cuffs and hem. If she turned them under, however, no one would notice, she hoped.

She left a bowl of warm water in her father's room and shook him gently out of his slumber. He opened his eyes and they, bleary and bloodshot still, fixed themselves upon her mother's locket that she had about her neck. He sobered immediately, and, reaching out as if to grab it, fell from his bed when Elizabeth stepped beyond his reach.

"The locket," he cried, and stumbled to his feet, "I must have it."

"No, Father." Elizabeth was firm. It was the last thing she had from her mother and she intended to keep it. She left the room and returned to the kitchen, where she helped Mrs Wattle to prepare food and drinks for the women and the minister – who had arrived and were now laying out her mother's body.

There was a loud knocking on the front door. Elizabeth waited for Mary to answer it and, when she did not, went herself in her apron, all covered in flour. It was the gentleman from the night before and he bowed low on seeing her. In the daylight and after a night's sleep, he looked very fine indeed. Elizabeth was surprised, and embarrassed to greet him in such a shabby state.

"Captain Marcus Luther," he said, and held out his hand to shake hers. Elizabeth dusted off the flour and held out her own. He took it and held it tightly, looking intently at a point somewhere between her breasts. Elizabeth tried to pull her hand away, but his was a very firm grip.

"A lovely hand, Mistress Elizabeth." His eyes had not moved, his gaze avid and piercing.

"My father is in his study." Elizabeth tugged her hand free, affronted at his familiarity without there having been a formal introduction between them. "I fear he is not receiving visitors."

"It was not him I came to see."

Elizabeth didn't understand. "My mother is dead, sir."

"I know and I am most terribly sorry."

Then she realised he must mean it was her he had come to see. What presumption! "I am very busy, as you can imagine." She was angry, but not a little intrigued also – what would such a fine gentleman as he want with her? He stared intently, still, upon her chest, and Elizabeth realised he looked at her mother's locket.

Elizabeth took it and held it up.

"You marvel at my locket, sir. My late mother gave it me. Indeed, it is a thing of great beauty, is it not? I have never seen its like; it has markings upon it of most unusual design, though I do not know what they represent..."

She stopped; she had said too much, and to a stranger. However, his interest in her mother's locket, at such a time, had seemed a balm.

"I understand." He looked almost guilty, finding his manners once more. "It is a difficult time for you. Here." He thrust into her hand a card. "What time is the funeral?"

"At four o'clock this afternoon."

"I will return before then with my carriage for you and your father." He turned on his heels, his coat swinging behind him, and marched off down the street.

His card was as fine as his clothes; on it was printed in dark-blue ink:

Marcus Luther Esquire,
Captain in the Merchant Fleet
of His Majesty King Charles II.

His address was in the best part of Greenwich. The print was embossed and the card itself was of the best quality. Elizabeth slipped it into her dress pocket and tried to forget about it while she went about the business of preparing for her mother's funeral.

People called intermittently all day, and she entertained them as best she could. Her father remained in his study and refused to come out. By three o'clock, Elizabeth was exhausted; the undertaker was due at any moment, and her father was still refusing to emerge. Mary stood by and watched her as she pleaded with him through the closed door.

"Your mother is ready," Mary informed her. "I sat by her all day and she didn't stir once." Her face was pale and her eyes wide open.

Elizabeth wondered whether Mary might have lost her reason, but did not comment; instead, she clasped Mary to her breast. "Oh, Mary, that this day were over," she sighed. Outside it was raining and grey – fitting weather for a funeral.

The undertaker arrived, tall and pale. He wasted no time, supervising his assistants in the placing of the body in the coffin with cold efficiency. Elizabeth could not watch as he nailed the lid down. She went once again to her father's room and was surprised to find the door open, and Captain Luther in there, helping her father to dress and ready himself for the funeral. He snapped his heels together when he saw her and patted her father on the back.

"There you go, old man."

The undertaker's assistants loaded the coffin on to the funeral cart, and the procession began. The captain offered the use of his carriage, but Elizabeth wanted to walk behind the cart, so her father and the captain joined her there. She felt it wasn't right for this stranger to come with them on this most sad day but, since he had financed the affair, she didn't see how she could refuse him.

There was a modest gathering of onlookers and followers – Elizabeth would have liked to think it was because her mother was a good woman and had many friends, but more likely it was the ample amount with which the captain had supplied the minister which had enabled him to buy the services of so many mourners. Her father's gait was rather unsteady and he had to lean upon the captain; Elizabeth kept her eyes upon the coffin and tried to forget that it was her mother inside it. She concentrated upon the quality of the wood and the craftsmanship of its construction. Besides, she felt that an open display of mourning was undignified and she would have plenty of time to grieve in private.

Near the church, the cart lurched in a pothole and the coffin slid dangerously across it; only the quick actions of the captain stopped it crashing to the ground and spilling its precious cargo. Elizabeth nodded her thanks to the captain; she would have hated to think of her mother lying out on the wet street for all the world to see.

At the church, they carried the coffin inside and Elizabeth and her father took a seat in the front pew. The captain sat in the row behind them and, for that, she was grateful. She didn't know what the tattling tongues of the churchwomen would make of it if he had joined them in the front pew.

The minister preached a long sermon on the perils of sin committed in this life and how they would lead to an eternity spent in hell after death. The mourners shuffled nervously behind Elizabeth; though most, being people of commerce, could not have understood the Latin, the invective and meaning were plain. It was likely, also, that they were bored, and Elizabeth wished that the minister would finish. Her mother had led an exemplary life, tested by God more than most, and never complained. She was given a husband full of promise and then had to watch as he fell out of favour and then drank away his talents.

Her father started snoring beside Elizabeth. She gave him a sharp nudge in the ribs, and he awoke with a start and grunted loudly. The minister stopped mid-sentence and gave him a dark look. Elizabeth decided at that moment that their future rested entirely in her hands, and she would have to take charge of the situation.

She was aware of Captain Luther behind her; she would marry him, she decided. He certainly appeared interested, and was obviously wealthy enough to support not only her but her father and Mary as well. If he was away at sea often, then all to the good; that would leave her free to pursue her own interests. He was handsome enough, though he obviously had the same taste for low inns and cheap ales as her father, but that seemed a small price to pay for sercuity. She had never thought that she would marry, let alone marry for love as her mother and father had done, but at the very least this way she would not end up with a broken heart.

She felt better as she walked from the church again, following the coffin to its final resting place in the family vault. Mary clutched her arm and whimpered like an injured animal as the coffin was slid inside. Elizabeth knew that she would require a treatment again that night after the mourners had gone. She was cheered by the thought, and patted Mary's hand gently.

"Tonight, we will see to this mood of yours, Mary," she whispered. Mary looked up at her, her eyes wide with anticipation.

"Oh, yes, Mistress," she sighed. "I am in terrible need of the treatment." She was calmer after that.

"You handle your maid well, Mistress Elizabeth." Captain Luther was at her side. Elizabeth had not seen him arrive there, and his sudden appearance made her start.

"She is of a delicate disposition. Sometimes she vexes me, but, in our present circumstances, we must bear with what we have."

"And you bear it wonderfully well."

Elizabeth was not used to receiving compliments and felt herself redden. In her limited experience with men, she had noticed that they never seemed comfortable in her presence, as if her height intimidated them. Captain Luther, however, appeared more than comfortable talking to her; in fact, he looked at her with great interest, but he was a tall man himself and did not have the appearance of one who would frighten easily.

The gates of the vault slammed shut, an act that seemed more final than anything that had gone before. Her mother was dead, gone from her forever. Elizabeth felt a swelling of emotion inside her and, determined not to shame herself by showing this in front of the captain, she turned from him.

"Excuse me," she said, "I have to return to the house to prepare for the guests."

"Of course." He bowed. "I have my carriage waiting by the gate, if you would allow me to place it at your service for the journey home." He took her arm and escorted her along the path. Elizabeth kept her head lowered so he could not see how close to tears she was. Mary hurried along beside her.

The carriage was black and most luxurious inside and out; its two horses seemed finely bred, though Elizabeth knew little of horse husbandry.

"You are most kind," Elizabeth said, although she would have preferred to walk back to the house to clear her silly, emotional head.

The captain helped her inside and then settled Mary beside her.

"I will walk behind with your father." He stepped back and directed the driver onwards. Elizabeth looked out at the back window and saw them in deep discussion, and wondered again what a man of learning such as her father and a sea-going man like the captain could possibly have to talk about.

She had little time to ponder such things, though, because Mary had become very excited, it being the first time she had been in such a carriage. Elizabeth had to restrain her from waving out the window to complete strangers they passed in the street.

"Oh, Mistress Elizabeth, such a fine carriage." She ran her hand over the leather seats. "And such a fine gentleman, too." She giggled. "He seems to have taken a fair shine to you." She patted Elizabeth's cheek.

Elizabeth slapped her hand away. "What a lot of nonsense you do talk, Mary. If you don't behave yourself, I will have to strap you to your bed and punish you, instead of treating your ague."

Mary's eyes opened wide again, as if she relished the thought of punishment. Elizabeth wondered at what an odd girl she was.

"Sorry, Mistress," she said after a pause. Elizabeth hoped the matter was closed.

Mary brought it up again, however, after the guests had departed and they were both in Elizabeth's bed.

"Are you going to marry the captain?" she asked suddenly, as they were about to settle to sleep.

"Why Mary, where do you get these ideas?"

"Only Cook said that that was what you'd have to do."

"We will see." This was the last thing Elizabeth wanted to discuss.

"What do you suppose it's like, being married?" Mary was lying facing Elizabeth, who could see she wasn't going to drop the subject.

"Well..." Elizabeth had no idea, except what she had seen of her parents. "I expect it... can be very nice."

"Nice?" Mary obviously didn't believe her. "Cook says all men are animals and only after one thing."

"You shouldn't listen to Mrs Wattle." Elizabeth had spoken to her before about putting notions into Mary's head. "Does the Master seem like an animal?"

Mary paused and Elizabeth thought he possibly wasn't a good example, but she knew so few men.

"No, but the captain might be, after all those months alone at sea without sight or sound of a woman. He will come home and pin you to the bed." As she spoke, she acted out the motion and pressed Elizabeth to the bed, holding her shoulders down.

"I hardly know the man, nor he me."

"He will smother you in kisses." Mary kissed her hard on the lips a few times and then moved to kissing her throat.

"Mary, stop this." Elizabeth protested, but she did not struggle as hard as she might have, for, in truth, she was quite enjoying this game. It would help her prepare for her wedding night, she told herself, and let Mary continue.

"And he will tear at your nightgown –" Mary roughly pulled at the neck of Elizabeth's gown, exposing her chest "– and gaze hungrily on your breasts." Mary sat back a little and stared down at Elizabeth's breasts. "Then he will seize them in his large, manly hands –" she grasped one and squeezed it hard "– and he will take them in his mouth." She leant forward and took the nipple between her teeth.

Elizabeth gasped at the shock of it. She knew she should stop Mary, but her body was experiencing things it had never felt before. She was at once a little afraid and at the same time rather excited. She noticed that her breathing and that of Mary's had quickened.

Mary stopped nibbling on her nipple and continued talking. "Then his rough hands will slide down your body." She traced her hands down to Elizabeth's waist, over her hips and down to the hem of her gown. "Then he will pull up your nightgown –" she jerked it suddenly up to Elizabeth's waist, leaving her exposed, then slapped her hand over Elizabeth's mound "– and put his hand on you."

Elizabeth was breathing hard now. She could feel Mary's fingers in her mound's hair, and was aware of Mary's other hand still upon her shoulder, pressing her down into the bed. Mary now looked hot and was breathing hard; Elizabeth was worried that she might start having a fit before she finished what she was doing. She sincerely hoped she would not, for Elizabeth did not want this to stop.

"He now undoes his belt." Mary mimed that even though she, too, was wearing her nightgown. She pulled it up and knelt between Elizabeth's legs, her other hand still pressed hard into Elizabeth's mound. "Then he produces his manhood." Mary pretended to be holding something large and long in front of her.

Elizabeth wished she truly had something, for she could feel a pressure building up inside of her and wanted something to enter her to relieve it.

Mary was clearly thinking the same thing, for she looked about her to see if there was anything she could use. There wasn't, so, instead she held up two fingers. "And he thrusts his straining manhood into you." She pressed her two fingers inside Elizabeth.

"Dear God." Elizabeth felt the fingers slide into her; her hips pushed up towards them as if of their own accord and the fingers moved deeper into her. Mary's thumb rested just outside the opening and, whenever she moved it, the pressure Elizabeth felt increased tenfold.

"And he thrusts it into you again and again." Mary moved her fingers as she talked, removing them a little and then sending them deeper in. She was by no means thrusting, but Elizabeth rather wished that she would.

"Again and again –" Mary moved them faster "– again and again." Her breathing was now quite frantic, as was Elizabeth's own. She could feel her heart racing and a terrible tension built inside her, until it felt like she was going to burst.

"Again and again," Mary kept repeating as she moved her fingers. "His manhood is throbbing," she panted. "He has dreamed of doing this for all those months at sea. He has wanted you there underneath him, helpless and at his mercy. Again and again." She was now pushing her fingers deep into Elizabeth, and sweat was forming upon her brow. "He has imagined this for days, and run through in his head what he would do to you, and now here he is doing it, again and again."

Elizabeth was no longer watching Mary; her eyes were closed and she could barely hear what it was Mary was saying, her own heartbeat was so loud in her ears. She thought that if something did not happen soon she would burst.

"Again and again." Mary sounded as if she were a very long

way away now. Elizabeth felt she could not breathe; she wanted to cry out, to beg Mary to stop, yet, at the same time, wanted her to thrust harder. Then, suddenly, something seemed to snap inside her and all the muscles of her body convulsed together as if she were having one of Mary's fits. It lasted only a moment, and then waves of relief swept over her, sweet relief, like a blessing from the angels.

Mary had stopped all movement. She, too, twitched as though having a small fit, and then lay down beside Elizabeth and slowly withdrew her fingers. This sent another convulsion through Elizabeth, and she sighed.

"Oh, Mistress Elizabeth –" Mary was close to tears "– it will be awful to be so married."

"Hush." Elizabeth drew Mary closer to her and held her.

"I vow that I will never wed and will stay forever in your service."

Elizabeth put a finger to her lips to stop her saying anything further. She hoped that it would be possible to keep Mary forever in her service. She stroked the girl's hair; for a moment, she had forgotten her stricken plight, but now she started to worry again. Mary was calmer now and even appeared to have fallen asleep. Elizabeth wondered at what a child she really was, for all her seventeen years. She kissed her sleepy forehead, hardly believing that this was the same girl who, a few moments ago, had acted out so convincingly the part of Elizabeth's possible future husband.

Would it really be like that? Elizabeth wondered. Her mother had said nothing to her of the physical relations between men and women. Mrs Wattle made vague and damning comments about the opposite sex, and nothing that could lead Elizabeth to believe that any good could come of it.

Still, she supposed she would find out soon enough. In the meantime, she and Mary would just have to practice further.

4

The Eviction

Jack woke before dawn and climbed out on to the roof. It was raining and all about her was grey. From here, she could see the Thames, thick and brown, only a few small boats on it going about their business at this time of the morning. Although her time at sea had been rough and sometimes even harsh, she missed it, often with an intensity that surprised her. Some mornings she would walk by the river and see the tall ships slipping quietly from their moorings and wonder where they were going and what manner of wondrous things they would bring back.

At sea, she had always been moving, on her way to or from somewhere for the captain, always with some purpose. In London, there never seemed any purpose to Jack's life, just one day following another, trying to find ways of earning money to pay the rent for the next day's board. All the while at sea, the one thing that kept her going was the thought of returning to London to her mother – who had returned to live with her parents once Jack had been taken to sea – to continue her apprenticeship with her grandfather and become a bookbinder as he was, and as her father had been before he ran off to join the Roundheads and fight their senseless war.

She had even thought that one day she might live as a woman, find a husband and have children of her own. But her return met with bitter sadness and deep disappointment. Her mother had died of the Plague, and was buried somewhere on the Black Heath along with thousands of other poor souls, while her grandfather's business lay in smouldering ruins after the Great Fire.

Jack had sought out her grandparents, but they were old and had barely the means to keep themselves, let alone to keep her. Neither did they have a business to which to apprentice her. Other businesses were having a hard time of it, and were wary of a strange lad, as Jack must have seemed, all rough and tanned from being at sea. So she stayed with Harry and earned them money from their staged fights. It wasn't a fortune but enough to let them live comfortably. One day, though, she knew that an opponent would become wise to their methods and threaten to break her neck and then she knew not what she would do.

The rain was heavier now and she was soaked through her nightgown to her skin. The sky was lightening, but they would be lucky if they saw the sun that day. It seemed the perfect day for a funeral; she suddenly remembered the lady from the tavern and wondered how her mother fared, and then remembered the dream. She placed great store by dreams and this one had been so vivid and so strange. She had never been in a battle, though she had heard tales from men who had. It had been such a real dream, as if she had actually been there, and the lady, too. Who was she?

She decided to return to the tavern and see if anyone there might know who the lady was and where she might live. So Jack dressed and set out, smiling to herself at the idea of such a fine lady knowing how to use a sword and dagger and where she could have learnt such skills. Even in a dream, it seemed unlikely.

No one else in the house was about; both Anne and Harry were late sleepers, unimpressed by the joys of a beautiful sunrise. In the street, the vendors were setting up their barrows. Jack splashed through the mud to 'The Jolly Sailor'. Its doors were locked and barred, and Jack could stir no one with her hammering. She wandered the streets close by; the lady could not live far to have come seeking her father alone as she had. Everything still smelled of smoke even these years after the Fire, and a great many houses had not yet been rebuilt, their owners lacking the finance to do it.

Jack could not imagine what it must have been like; her grandparents would not talk of it. Others did not seem to notice the smell, but at times it seemed overwhelming to her, as if the fire still smouldered nearby. It seemed to hang in the air all about, as a constant reminder of the life she had lost due to the Fire.

She was about to give up her search when she noticed Captain Luther standing in the street, staring at the front door of a small but handsome house. Its bricks were new and its windows clean of dust and soot; clearly, its owners had had enough money saved from the Fire to rebuild. The door of the house opened and a woman in her middle years came out and hurried off down the street. The captain made as if to go after her, and then stopped. Jack ducked into a doorway to avoid detection. Soon after the woman had left, she returned with provisions, and soon after her return, some women of the parish went into the house. From their demeanour, Jack guessed that someone in the house had died, and, given the captain's attendance upon the young lady and her father the night before, that this was her home, and that her mother had, indeed, expired. She recognised some of the women as being from St Augustine's; the funeral would surely be held there that afternoon.

She could not wait there all day, watching the captain watching the house. The young lady's loss reminded her of her own, so she decided to visit the place where her mother was buried. She walked out to the Black Heath with the city waking around her, and stopped and bought some flowers from a young gypsy girl, who grabbed her hand.

"Read your fortune, young sir?" Her grip was strong, determined.

"I have no silver to cross your palm."

"No matter." The gypsy looked intently into Jack's eyes.

"You will meet a tall stranger with a head of flames. Jill will wear the britches and Jack the skirt." Jack turned pale and tried to retrieve her hand. "Ill winds will blow you, but good comes, so trow you, and the golden heart finds a true." She finally let go of Jack's hand and held out her own.

"I have no silver," Jack said again.

The girl smiled. "Then kiss me, kind sir," and before Jack could protest, she threw herself at Jack and sealed her lips around hers. The kiss lasted only a moment but left Jack breathless and a little dizzy. The girl laughed at Jack's reaction, and moved off to sell her flowers and fortune-telling to the next unsuspecting soul.

Jack wondered at her reading – she would like to meet 'a true heart'; she had thought her Sweet Anne hers, as unnatural as that seemed. Dressed as she was and living the life of a man, she did not believe she would find her true love amongst the male sex, though she knew a few who did. She sighed and continued on her walk to the Heath.

She scattered the flowers along the path as she walked over the flat expanse, having no grave to lay them upon. A petal here and a petal there, hoping that some would find the spot where her mother's bones were. From here, she could see the river and the small docks that lay on the other side, the docks like the ones from which she had been forced to sail. She wondered again, as she always did, if she had been with her mother and not half way across the world, if she might not have prevented her mother's death. More likely, she would be down there under the smooth turf of the Heath, rotting somewhere with her.

She sighed and headed home. It was past noon now, and the house would be stirring. Maybe she and Harry would catch the midday crowd in some tavern and make themselves a bit of money.

As she approached the house, she heard raised voices within; Harry bellowing angrily and Anne replying in tears. They were in the withdrawing room and, on Jack's entry, they both stopped and turned to her. Anne ran to her and cowered behind her, while

Harry stepped forward with his fist raised as if to strike.

"Be this true?" he demanded, his face red with anger.

"Is what true?" she asked in turn, though she felt she knew to what he was referring. Anne clutched at her arm.

"That you have used my daughter and got her with child!"

"With child?" Jack almost laughed – her wooden phallus was a miraculous thing, but...

Harry lunged at her and grabbed hold of her throat. Anne tried to pull him off, and Jack had to think fast. With a quick blow, she dislodged Harry's grip and threw herself over a nearby table to place something between them. It was not solely due to the effects of the sleeping draught that she won her fights. As she caught her breath, she had time to consider the implications of what Harry had said, and what she could say to explain.

"It is not possible for me to be the father," she said, before Harry could pursue her around the table. She could not reveal the truth of her terrible secret, it would be the end of Sweet Anne and herself.

"As a child, I had a terrible accident," she began, hoping a tale would present itself to her as she went along. Harry wasn't listening. He tried to reach her over the table to once again get his hands on her neck. Anne was not listening, either, but screamed at her father to stop.

Jack continued to talk even as she dodged him, hoping that he would hear what she was saying. "My member was severed from my body."

Harry stopped then and Anne, too, quieted her noise.

"While I was in Jamaica, a master carver created this for me." She reached inside her britches and produced her wooden phallus. Anne cried out and fell into a dead faint. Harry stood and stared at the cunningly constructed instrument.

"But..." he finally said, and looked over at Anne's crumpled form. "I thought..." He turned from flushed red to pale. "But you did...?"

Jack nodded. "We did."

Harry lunged at her again, but his heart was not in it and Jack easily evaded him. Harry instead turned to Anne's limp body and shook her.

"No, Harry," Jack cried out and ran to his side. "Be gentle with her."

Harry turned and stared at Jack. "I think you had better go."

She nodded and went upstairs to pack her few belongings. She tied them in a bundle and crept back down to the withdrawing room. She stopped in the doorway and watched as Harry lifted Anne into a chair, where she was weeping quietly. Harry saw her standing there.

"It seems she has deceived us both, Jack."

Jack nodded again, though she wanted to stay and explain, or even, indeed, receive an explanation from Anne. If she was with child, whose was it? Had she planned to trap Jack into marrying her? But she knew these questions would have to wait for another day. The father and daughter needed to make their peace.

She left the house and wandered into the street: she would head towards the dock and seek lodgings there. As she walked, she thought about what had just befallen her, but more about what would happen to Anne. To bear a child outside of wedlock was a terrible thing; she would be disgraced and reviled. Many such young women had to turn to prostitution to survive. She hated to think of Sweet Anne making a living in some tavern or other, at the mercy of any man who took a fancy to her and had the money to pay.

Jack stopped walking. Maybe she should marry her; there were a lot worse fates she could imagine for herself. Anne was a gentle girl, and she could sew, and kept a tidy house. Jack imagined them together as husband and wife, a child or maybe more running to greet Jack as she came in from a hard day's work at the docks, for she would have to get steady work to support them.

She imagined the wedding; Anne in a floral gown, her round stomach barely noticeable, would take Jack's arm after she had walked up the aisle, and the minister would ask if anyone knew just cause why they should not be joined. Jack stopped her imaginings there. Of course they could not be joined, for she might fool all the people on this earth with her disguise but she would not fool God. Come Judgment Day, she would be judged as a woman, and sent to Hell as a woman married to another woman.

She walked on to the house of Mrs Jacobson, a Jewish widow she knew who had clean rooms and at a fair price. She would stay there until she found a ship sailing, and go wherever it took her, back to the West Indies or off to the East Indies. There was talk that Captain Luther would be off soon, and she had heard that he was a fair-minded man.

A funeral procession approached, and Jack stopped to let it pass. Behind the coffin were a woman and two men, one old and faltering in his step, the other she recognised as Captain Luther. Jack stood and watched, a little shocked; it was as if she had conjured him there by her very thoughts. She looked back at the woman, attracted by her upright carriage and dignity, and realised it was the woman from the tavern, from her dream.

This seemed more than just coincidence; it was as if Fate were pushing her towards her destiny. In the morning she would seek out Captain Luther and petition him for a place on his crew. She could not do it now, at such a sad moment, and she had her lodging to secure.

Mrs Jacobson was a small, round woman well into her middle years – some said she was even as old as forty, though Jack thought they were being unkind. How she came upon the money to set up her lodging house was the source of much idle gossip and scandal-making. Jack had paid little heed to it; she preferred to believe the story that Mrs Jacobson was a respectable widow, doing the best she could under difficult circumstances.

The widow greeted Jack like a long-lost son, and assured her that of course there was a room for her. It seemed she had already heard of Jack's eviction and even knew the reason for it.

"That Anne," she said and tutted. "*Sweet* Anne, indeed." She tutted some more.

Jack was loath to hear hard words said against her lately-loved. "Please," she said.

"Poor lamb." Mrs Jacobson came and stood very close to Jack, the mingled smell of lavender and perspiration nearly overwhelming Jack. "You thought it was true love." She took Jack's hand and patted it. "But you are just a lad; you will learn."

She led Jack up to her best room, overlooking the river.

Jack took to her bed, even though it was only the afternoon still. She didn't want to listen to the idle tongue of Mrs Jacobson. Although she had heard tales about Anne, Jack had stopped her ears to them, thinking they came from jealous minds. Now, of course, she wasn't so sure. Mrs Jacobson was right, she realised; she had given her heart to Anne. No more, Jack resolved; she would never give her heart to another woman.

There was a knock on the door, but before she could say that she wanted to be left alone, it was pushed open and Mrs Jacobson was there with a tray of food.

"I thought you might be hungry." She smiled at Jack. Food was the last thing on Jack's mind at that moment; it did not seem to be much on Mrs Jacobson's mind, either, for she put the tray down on the table and came to the bedside.

Jack thought she looked different; she noticed she had changed her clothes. She now had on a robe of red velvet that seemed to highlight her redder lips and cheeks. She had also let her hair fall free of its ribbons. She smiled again at Jack.

"Poor lad," she said, and leaned forward to rest the back of her hand on Jack's forehead. "You are quite out of sorts."

Courtesy of the dress's décolletage, Jack could see right down the cleavage of Mrs Jacobson's more-than-ample bosom.

"But they say a broken heart makes for a stronger part." Her hand strayed from Jack's head down her body to her inner thigh. Jack was shocked: Mrs Jacobson was a respectable woman, was she not? Her hand had stopped and now rested on Jack's wooden phallus.

"Oh, Jack, you naughty boy," she giggled, then stood up and let her velvet robe slip to the floor, leaving her standing in nothing more than her stays and petticoats.

"No, Mrs Jacobson." Jack gathered the bedcovers to her, although it was Mrs Jacobson who was nearly naked.

"La, my dear, your voice might say no, but your manhood is telling me quite a different tale." She wrenched the covers from Jack's hands and climbed under them beside her.

Jack didn't know what to do. She could not cry for help – this was Mrs Jacobson's own house, and no one would believe that Jack was the innocent one here. She was also worried that the widow might see the phallus, it still being quite light outside. She wasn't sure everyone would believe her tale of childhood amputation and her true and terrible secret might be uncovered.

Mrs Jacobson nuzzled at her neck, her hands roaming wildly all over Jack's body. She had to act before it was too late. She took hold of both Mrs Jacobson's wandering, wanton hands and held them firmly. She kissed her upon the lips, as hard a kiss as she had ever given to Anne, and turned her so as to lie her on her back.

"Oh, Jack." Mrs Jacobson seemed to enjoy this treatment.

Jack reached down and picked her hemp stockings and 'kerchief from where she had dropped them on the floor. She lashed the stockings around the older woman's wrists, then secured them to the head of the bed, not tightly, but enough to remove the curious hands out of harm's way. As an extra precaution, she tied the kerchief around Mrs Jacobson's head as a blindfold.

She expected that, at any moment, Mrs Jacobson might start screaming, fearing for her life as she could well be doing with this rough treatment. Instead, she just sighed often and twisted about, but not enough to loosen her bindings. Jack thought her fear of discovery must be greater than her fear of what Jack might be about to do to her.

Jack sat back and admired her handiwork; Mrs Jacobson looked a picture, tied up as she was, her large breasts straining against her stays. Jack had thought Anne to be buxom, but hers were just pippins compared to these, the smallest of stars to these glorious moons.

She hardly dared to touch them for fear that they might burst, so big and full were they. She pulled the lacing loose until they sprang free of their restraints and placed her hand gently on one and rubbed its nipple. Mrs Jacobson sighed and arched her back. Jack lowered her head to suckle on the huge nipple and Mrs Jacobson gave a little gasp of pleasure. Jack held the breast in both hands now and explored the nipple with her tongue.

The older woman's breathing had increased, and she pushed her hips up and pressed them into Jack's. Jack thought briefly of binding Mrs Jacobson's legs to the bed also, but didn't want to let go of that luscious breast. Instead, she laid the full length and weight of her body down on top of that of Mrs Jacobson to keep her from moving too much.

She moved one hand down the plump woman's body and lifted up the petticoats to explore her lower regions. She found smooth skin and the wiry brush of her mound, which she explored with her fingers, while still sucking on the ever-tightening nipple. The hair was long and curly and led Jack's fingers towards the centre of the mound and the treasure that lay within it.

Jack moved slowly; she was now enjoying herself, knowing that the slower she proceeded, the more pleasure she could bring to a woman, even those who begged her to go faster.

Mrs Jacobson moved her hips again, trying to encourage Jack's fingers to their destination, but Jack resisted. She first found the moist opening with just one finger and rubbed it to and fro, enjoying the contrast of textures between the rough hair and the smooth skin within. She had heard sailors describe their sexual conquests as just that, a conquest. As if they were some sort of victory over a life-long enemy. They described the anatomy of their partners with equal parts of fear and revulsion; the hole into which they rammed their hardened manhoods seemed to instil in them terror, as if it were a dark cave that was the home of any number of unseen monsters.

Jack thought of a woman's opening more like a pool of water into which she could dive. She had seen such pools in Jamaica, bush-clad and deep-emerald green, cool and refreshing after a long, hot walk.

She let her finger slide inside; it was wet in there, and fluid rushed up to greet her finger. She slipped two more fingers in, preparing the way for her phallus. Although it was quite small, she was often afraid of hurting a woman, especially those with little experience of men. It didn't seem that Mrs Jacobson fell into this category, for she opened wide under Jack's fingers.

Jack let go of the breast she was still sucking and untied the drawstring of her britches in which she was still dressed. With that one hand, she unstrapped her phallus. Removing her fingers from within Mrs Jacobson, she wiped some of the fluid from them on to its end, before sliding it gently up into her. Mrs Jacobson cried out as if in pain, but when Jack stopped pushing she lifted her hips off the bed drawing the phallus deeper into her.

"Oh, lad, yes," she breathed.

Jack set up a rhythm, pushing the phallus in and then withdrawing it slightly, Mrs Jacobson matching her stroke for stroke.

The carver who had fashioned the phallus for her had tried to persuade her to have a much larger creation. Jack was shocked by the dimensions he first suggested, not only did she not believe such a thing would fit without hurting a woman profoundly, but also she thought it would hamper her ability to move freely. She knew now that members of such size did exist; she had seen a few in her travels, but they belonged to men much bigger than herself. She felt that she should have one that was in proportion with her slight frame. It had been a wise decision; it hampered her not at all, and no woman had yet complained of its lack of ability to satisfy.

Mrs Jacobson certainly seemed satisfied thus far; her head was flung back, her right hand was upon her mound, rubbing briskly, and her hips were fairly bouncing off the bed, driving Jack to quicker, deeper plunges of the phallus. Jack's landlady was close to reaching her peak; her breathing was quick and ragged, her body covered with a sheen of sweat, and her nipples were puckered so tightly that they looked to be causing her pain. Jack took one between the thumb and forefinger and squeezed it. Mrs Jacobson let out a cry and her body went rigid. Then it twitched mightily and finally relaxed.

Jack slid her tool out and wiped it on her hand before strapping it back in place and tying up her britches once more.

"Oh, lad," the older woman sighed.

Jack untied her hands and removed the blindfold.

"You are a marvel. For one so young to know how to give a woman so much pleasure." She squeezed Jack's arm. She pulled down her petticoats and collected her robe from where she had discarded it.

"Anne was not mistaken in you." She pulled her robe on and, blowing Jack a kiss, left.

Jack sat down on the bed. Anne? Surely Anne would not have tattled about their dalliances and not to Mrs Jacobson, whom she scarcely knew. If Mrs Jacobson knew, how many of the other good women of the parish also knew? Jack wondered how she would now be able to walk the streets thereabouts with all the women looking at her, eyeing her wooden member through her britches. She was filled with a bitter shame at the thought. She had to be away to sea again.

5

The Proposal

The week after the funeral, Captain Luther came calling. Elizabeth's father was still in his bed, having barely been out of it since the funeral, but it was not he whom the Captain wanted to see.

"I know it is soon after the death of your good mother, but I have a proposal that I would like you to consider."

Elizabeth's heart was racing. "You had better come in, Captain Luther."

He came straight to the point of his visit as they sat down to tea in the parlour.

The proposal was, of course, of marriage, but he proffered it in such a business-like manner that Elizabeth was left feeling disheartened rather than elated – or even mildly happy – as she had heard one was supposed to be made to feel by an offer of marriage.

It seemed clear that he found her no more than acceptable and felt that he was doing her a great favour in taking her to wife and her father as an encumbant, which was probably true, but Elizabeth would have liked to believe that he thought something more of her than merely acceptable. After he had gone, taking with him a promise that she would consider the matter, she found herself close to tears.

She knew she would have to accept; she had no other choice, and, plainly, the captain knew it, too. He was no doubt well acquainted with her father's long list of debts and knew the house was close to being taken from them. She paused again to wonder at his interest – it seemed to have shifted from her father to her since her mother's death.

She could make no clear sense of it but she felt, with that sixth sense of a woman, that he wanted something more from them, something more than all his money could buy. She did not think, though, that it was her virtue or her household skills. However, as she sat, pondering her present predicament, another thought, small at first, but then more bold, presented itself at the door of her conscience. As the wife of a sea captain, she might well be afforded the opportunity to set foot aboard his ship. Her spirits lifted a little.

She was uncertain, however, how to proceed. She could not discuss the matter with her father, who had become a virtual recluse, shut day and night in his room, refusing to eat or drink or even allow the curtains to be opened. The good doctor had paid him several visits, but even he could not persuade Elizabeth's father out of his seclusion. Elizabeth tried to carry on as before, but both Mary and Mrs Wattle were fretful and hovered around her, as if seeking some assurance that they were not to be imminently turned away. Assurances which Elizabeth could not give them, unless she agreed to marry the captain.

By the evening she was at her wit's end; she felt as frayed as the cuffs on her mourning dress. Everything was resting upon her shoulders – she was not used to such responsibility and it wasn't only her own future that depended upon this; they were all reliant upon her. She wondered if this was how her mother had felt in the last few years of her life, and wept bitter tears at having been such a burden to her. She swore that she would never be a burden to anyone ever again.

She retired to her bed, only to discover Mary already there. She was too tired to administer any treatment, herself too close to tears.

"Please, Mary –" she begged "– not tonight."

"No," Mary said, more firmly than Elizabeth had ever heard

her speak. "Tonight I will treat you."

Elizabeth had never considered this possibility before. She had never felt in need of the treatment, but maybe it was the very thing to clear her mind and bring about a clarity of thought in which she could make the right decision. She did not know if Mary was capable of administering the treatment – it required a dedicated hand and some dexterity – but, before she knew what was happening, Mary was pushing her back on to the bed.

Mary first took off her shoes and then rolled down her stockings, the touch of her warm hand sending shivers over Elizabeth's skin. Mary unlaced the black dress, removing the bodice and then the skirt. She even took the clasp from Elizabeth's hair and spread her locks out on the pillow around her head.

Elizabeth watched Mary; her movements were precise, as if she had been planning this for some time. She did everything with a look of great concentration, as though she were trying to remember what to do next. Once she had Elizabeth arranged to her liking, she carefully lifted her mistress's petticoats and rolled down her cotton stockings. These were exactly the actions Elizabeth had performed on Mary countless times in the past, and she had not thought for a moment about the effect they might be having upon her maid. Now that she was the recipient, she felt a mounting frustration in her body, as if all the small tensions of her life were being drawn into one and concentrating themselves in the centre of her being.

Mary gently kissed her forehead and eyelids and then placed her lips over Elizabeth's and kissed her passionately. Elizabeth was a little taken aback at first; it felt so strange to be receiving the kisses rather than administering them, but the feel of Mary's tongue against her lips and then against her own tongue when she opened her lips served to increase the tension she was feeling, which she knew to be a good thing.

Mary's hands, meanwhile, had unlaced her bodice and were

rubbing at her nipples. This, too, added to the feeling; in fact, she found herself wishing Mary would rub them harder. Mary's lips left hers and Elizabeth, for a moment, was sorry to have lost them, until they attached themselves to one of her nipples and started their clever sucking and licking there. This had an effect similar to that which she had felt when Mary was acting as her husband; it made her want to arch her back and push more of her breast into Mary's mouth. She rather wished that Mary had two mouths so that she could kiss both of her breasts at the same time.

Elizabeth then became aware of Mary's hands working their way down her body, inch by slow inch, migrating towards her centre, the seat of the still-building tension. She tried to urge them on to greater speed by lifting her hips from the bed. She remembered Mary doing thus as she treated her, and knew now what the cause of it was. She wanted so desperately for Mary's fingers to be inside her that she had to clutch the bed sheets to stop herself taking Mary's hands and putting them there. She realised now why Mary so often grabbed at her hand during her treatments.

Mary's mouth had moved to her other breast and it responded by sending goose-bumps all over Elizabeth's body. Mary's hands were now tracing circles on her mistress's inner thighs, occasionally brushing against her mound, making it strain towards them for firmer contact. Then, suddenly, Mary plunged her fingers deep inside Elizabeth, making her gasp with the shock of it and dig her nails into the mattress.

Mary moved her fingers inside Elizabeth, and her thumb over Elizabeth's little bud, back and forth, gathering momentum, as was the tension within Elizabeth. Gathering itself together like some caged animal ready to spring, coiling itself tighter and tighter until she could barely breathe. Mary moved her fingers faster and faster. Elizabeth didn't know if she could stand much more. If the fit did not break soon, she thought she might burst. Mary added another finger and then another. She was breathing heavily, too, sucking on

Elizabeth's nipple, pulling at it with her teeth.

Suddenly the fit broke. Elizabeth felt her body buck under Mary, and her legs jerked uncontrollably. The whole of the inside of her seemed to explode outwards; for a moment it was so intense that it felt almost like pain. Then that feeling passed and was replaced by one of tremendous relief. It swept over her like a tide of warm, refreshing water. Mary lay down beside her and held her tightly until the sweet release of sleep carried her off.

In the morning, things seemed clearer, not only in Elizabeth's mind but in the world in general. After weeks of rain and mist the sun was now out and shining brightly. The trees were coming into bud, and it felt like spring might soon burst upon the earth once again. If she had to marry someone, and she did have to marry, it might as well be the captain, who was obviously rich and whom she at least knew. Better that than marry a complete stranger who was not so well monied.

She decided to reply in person, and since it was such a glorious day, she set off to walk to his address in Greenwich. The streets seemed less grim than they had done of late, and the river was full of boats going about their everyday business. The house, when she found it, was very fine indeed; a modern building built of brick upon three storeys, with no timber, as was the style since the Great Fire (although the fire had not reached this far along the river). He must be a man who liked to keep abreast of the fashions, and could afford to.

When she rang the bell, the door was answered by a handsome young footman in a smart uniform.

"Is Captain Luther within?" she said as grandly as she could; she was now doubting the wisdom of arriving unannounced and so soon after the proposal. To be confronted with such obvious wealth left her feeling a little unsure of herself.

The footman ushered her into the library and, as she waited, she wondered again what it could be apart from love that the captain wanted of her. She did not have long to wonder because suddenly he was there, directing her to a seat and ordering tea from the maid.

"You have come with an answer?"

She nodded.

"I had not expected one so soon."

Elizabeth felt herself start to blush: she had been over-hasty, then.

He must have seen her blushes. "But I am pleased, or will be if the answer is yes."

She nodded again. "It is."

He rose from his seat and came towards her. "You have made me a very happy man." He clasped her two hands in his and gazed upon her smiling face.

Elizabeth was unnerved by his passionate response; she had not expected such an open display of pleasure after the way he had coolly made the proposal to her; maybe she had misjudged him. For she noticed that his gaze was directed not upon her face, but lower than that – at her breasts.

They settled on a date, one month hence. The captain would have liked it to be sooner, but Elizabeth wanted to observe a decent period of mourning for her mother. There was also much to do before the day, and they discussed the expenses of it. He would help her sell the house to pay off her father's debts, and any outstanding after that he would cover from his estate. Her father was to have a room in the captain's house and a small income; Elizabeth could bring Mary with her and Mrs Wattle, too, if she wished, although the captain already had a cook and a full kitchen staff.

Elizabeth returned home in the captain's carriage at his insistence, feeling rather relieved and excited. She broke the news to her household over lunch, insisting that her father join them to hear it.

"No, Bethy, you mustn't," was her father's response.

She was surprised – he and the captain had seemed such good friends, and after all the captain had done for them, she felt he was being terribly ungrateful.

"His intentions are not what they seem." Her father became quite agitated. "He is a sailor, a treasure hunter, no more."

Elizabeth lost her patience. If he had been more temperate in his life, then she would not be in this position. "Either I marry the captain or it will be the workhouse for us all. Which would you prefer, Father?"

He looked at her, shocked by the tone of her voice.

"But I..." He looked about the room in some confusion. "Your mother will know what to do." He shuffled from the room.

Elizabeth was stunned. She put her head in her hands. Her mother would have known exactly what to do, but she wasn't there anymore, and her father, it seemed, was losing his reason, having lost his life's anchor. It was up to Elizabeth to make the decisions now and she had decided. She sighed and stood up. Once she was married, everything would be all right; the captain could make all the hard decisions and leave her free to...

She stopped and looked around the familiar room. Free to do what? For a moment her mind was blank, without her mother to care for, what was she to do? Look after the captain and his house, that is what she would have to do; as his wife that was her duty. Much relieved, she went to find her father. He was sitting in her mother's old room, staring at the empty bed.

"She is dead, Father," she said as gently as she could. He looked at her and then returned his gaze to the bed.

"I know," he said in a small, sad voice that nearly brought tears to her eyes.

"We will manage." She patted him on the arm in a way she had often seen her mother do to comfort him. "The captain will help us."

*

55

The captain found a buyer for the house and they got a fair price for it. The money covered most of her father's debts, but Elizabeth was dismayed to see how many men came forward when word got out that they were settling his bills. He denied most of them, but it was clearly his signature on the pieces of paper that were proffered.

They moved in with an aunt of the captain, Mrs Mathers. She was a stern-looking widow, but she was kind and showed much forbearance with Elizabeth's father, who was now insisting that the house had been stolen from him and that the wedding must not go ahead. Elizabeth was embarrassed by these assertions, especially when he made them in front of the captain or Mrs Mathers, but both ignored his outbursts, and Mrs Mathers became expert at directing his attention off on to other matters that distressed him less.

If Elizabeth ever took to wondering if there might not be a touch of truth in her father's warnings, she had just to spend an hour or two in Captain Luther's company and her fears were laid to rest. He was always the perfect gentleman, with interesting and amusing stories about his life at sea, and he was generous beyond measure. If it had not been for his constant staring at her bosom, Elizabeth would have been a very happy bride-to-be.

In preparation for the forthcoming wedding, Mrs Mathers proved a gem. She organised the church, the dressmakers and the milliners, and arranged for flowers to be purchased and delivered. If Elizabeth queried the cost of anything she would just wave her hand and say, "The captain can afford it." Or, "You are worth every penny of it, my dear." She over-ruled any suggestion Elizabeth made that would have reduced the cost, especially with the dressmaker.

Not only was Elizabeth having her wedding dress made, but half a dozen other dresses besides for her trousseau. All were of the best material, and with the finest buttons and bows. This entailed almost daily visits from the seamstress to be measured and fitted, tucked and lifted. At first, Elizabeth felt uncomfortable with all the attention, but the seamstress was a sweet young woman called Rose, whose laughter bubbled from her as prettily as her blonde hair curled around her face, and whose eyes were a wide, innocent blue that seemed at odds with the ample cleavage that she displayed.

One day near to the wedding, Rose arrived unannounced, seeking Elizabeth's opinion on a piece of lace. It was a fine piece, and would have graced any of the dresses she was making. The rest of the household members were all out, Mary on an errand and Mrs Mathers and Elizabeth's father off on a long walk. Elizabeth made them some tea and wondered why Rose had thought to come all the way from Lambeth to ask her about one piece of lace, but she was glad of the company.

The talk turned to the wedding and Elizabeth could not help but express some worries about what might happen after the ceremony was over. Rose, who was herself married, confessed that she was not at all enamoured of the mechanics of sexual intercourse with her husband. Elizabeth was quite shocked to hear this.

She was even more shocked as Rose went on to discuss, in some detail, the first night with her husband. Elizabeth found herself getting rather agitated as she started to describe it. She watched Rose's pretty mouth as she told how her husband had disrobed her roughly and then run his hands over her body.

"As a groom would a horse," she said, and sighed a sigh that lifted her pale bosoms to the top of her dress and let them settle again.

Elizabeth found herself imagining Rose's body unclothed, the roundness of her belly, the breasts free and as soft to touch as two ripe peaches.

"He took one breast in each hand and weighed them as though they were fruit."

Elizabeth felt herself blush; she wondered if Rose could read her thoughts.

"Then he grasped my buttocks as if to test their firmness." Rose's voice was now husky. "He threw me back on to the bed and undid his britches." Rose stopped and looked at Elizabeth, who saw she was shaking slightly, as if about to cry.

"I was so afraid," she whispered and crept closer to Elizabeth. "And then..." She could not carry on for the tears. "Oh, Mistress Elizabeth, he hurt me so."

"Hush," Elizabeth took her in her arms, "hush there." She patted Rose's head, breathing in the scent of apples and fresh linen that Rose seemed to always have about her. Her words had no effect upon Rose, who cried as if she would never stop. Elizabeth knew she could not send poor Rose out into the street like this; she also knew that neither Mary, nor Mrs Mathers and her own father, would be back for some hours.

"Come." She led Rose to her own bedchamber. "I have a treatment that will relieve you of this state in which you find yourself. I have been practicing it from some time now on Mary, my maid, who also suffers from this affliction."

Rose looked at her curiously.

"It is somewhat unorthodox and will not hurt you, but I have found it to be very effective. I first read about it in one of my father's medical journals."

Rose was now looking at her in amazement.

"We could try it if you like."

Rose did not say anything but nodded her head in agreement, her blue eyes now even wider and dry of their tears.

"I promise I will not hurt you," Elizabeth whispered as she turned Rose around and started to untie the laces of Rose's dress and loosened those of her stays.

"You need to be able to breathe easily." Elizabeth explained. Rose stood very still and silent, while Elizabeth turned her again and laid her gently on to the bed. She leaned over and kissed her on both cheeks.

"Are you ready?" she asked. Rose, again, did not say anything but nodded her assent, her eyes following Elizabeth's every move.

"If at any point you wish me to stop, you must tell me." Rose nodded again. Elizabeth took a deep breath – it was one thing to do this to Mary, whom she had known all her life, but to do it to a near-stranger... She found that her hands were trembling and her heart was racing. She was doing this for Rose, she told herself, as a cure for her melancholia. She touched Rose's soft cheek and Rose leant her head into Elizabeth's hand and looked at her most pleadingly, though for what she was pleading, Elizabeth could not tell.

Elizabeth kissed Rose gently on the lips, those petal-like lips for which she surely was named.

"Rose," Elizabeth whispered, feeling an ache start within her. "Oh, Rose." She kissed her harder, feeling those delicate petals part to allow her tongue entry to the softness beyond them. While her tongue explored this new territory, her hands followed the soft curves of Rose's body down to the hem of her dress and then back up under the folds of its stiff material. She found the fine silk of Rose's stockings and then the smooth skin above them.

Rose was sighing now between kisses. Elizabeth moved down to kiss the smooth whiteness of her neck, while her hands sought to find the seat from which Rose's woe emanated. She slid her hand up Rose's thigh. Her skin was as smooth as satin, and the hairs that surrounded her mound were soft and as curly as those on her head.

Elizabeth watched Rose's face as she traced her finger in circles ever closer to that moist centre. Rose was watching Elizabeth too, her eyes wide but all evidence of fear gone. As Elizabeth reached the wet opening, Rose closed her eyes and sighed. Elizabeth sighed too, for although she was doing this to relieve Rose of her present melancholic passion, she had to admit that it stirred in her some of her *own* peculiar passion.

She slid her finger into Rose and the seamstress let out a little groan. Elizabeth knew this to be a good sign. She rubbed her finger backwards and forwards over the button above Rose's soft, wet opening, feeling it expand and change texture under her administrations. Rose was moving her body to aid this; she clasped Elizabeth's back as if to urge her to rub harder and faster. Elizabeth was not sure if this would help or hinder the treatment, but Rose's fit seemed to be coming to a peak.

"Dear God," Rose called out, then: "Mistress Elizabeth, please."

Elizabeth was rather taken aback, Mary did not utter a word during her treatment, but she supposed women were all different, and Rose certainly seemed to be close to her peak. Elizabeth slipped another finger in and Rose greeted it with a cry that sounded almost like triumph, her face was now flushed and her lips, that had been pink, were almost scarlet. She looked so beautiful that Elizabeth had to lean forwards and kiss her, still rubbing the bud as fast as her finger would move, and so hard now that she feared she might do some damage. Rose suddenly threw back her head and, with a jolt that took over her entire body, her fit broke.

Elizabeth held herself very still until Rose regained her composure. She opened her eyes and looked at Elizabeth with such a look as Elizabeth had never seen before. It was the sweetest look of love and thanks. Rose wrapped her arms about her and held her as if she never meant to let her go. They stayed like that for some time, until Elizabeth started to worry about Mary returning. She did not think that she would take too kindly to finding the pair of them thus.

"Do you feel better now?" she asked, even though she knew the answer.

Rose smiled and nodded. "I am much recovered, thank you."

"Then probably you should go. My aunt will be returning shortly."

Rose sighed again and sat up, smoothing down her petticoats and skirt. "We will be able to do this again?" She said this without looking at Elizabeth.

"Do you suffer these fits often?"

"Oh, all the time." She gazed up at Elizabeth, her blue eyes wide.

"Then it may be necessary to readminister the cure."

Rose grinned broadly, and Elizabeth was amazed at the transformation in her – once again, the treatment obviously had worked.

6

The Escape

Jack was exhausted. Mrs Jacobson came to her every evening, demanding her attentions. Sometimes Jack thought it would be easier to labour all day at the dock to earn money to pay her rent than to see to Mrs Jacobson's needs, for not only did Mrs Jacobson seek her favours, but Mrs McNally and Mrs Richards also, along with other respectable wives of the parish, and all on Mrs Jacobson's recommendation. Mrs Richards even requested to be bound and blindfolded, as Mrs Jacobson had been, and Jack felt she should agree, even though it was dim and there was little risk of her seeing the member.

Most of the good women who came to her had husbands, Jack knew. She wondered why they risked the frequent trips to Mrs Jacobson's, for surely their husbands were not fools and would one day find them out. Mrs Jacobson never spoke of her husband on her almost nightly visits. She just stretched out, held fast to the headboard, her eyes closed, and waited for Jack to attend to her. The other women did speak of their husbands, most complaining that they did not understand them, or that they did not bed them often enough and when they did, it was over far too quickly. Jack found all this rather diverting, for she had heard the sailors on her ship make exactly the same complaints of their wives.

At first, Jack enjoyed these various encounters, marvelling at how different all the women were. Not only in their bodies, but in how they took the wooden phallus. Some took it all, hard and fast, some she need barely touch with it. Most of all she marvelled at how differently they reached their climax. Some, like Mrs Jacobson, had a long, slow build-up and then an explosive peak; some cried out loud enough to wake the whole street, while some merely sighed.

Jack was at first pleased that the women came to her and that she could find different ways to bring each what they wanted from her. But over time, their appetites seemed to increase, so that they wanted more and more from her, and more often. She could not walk down the street without some good woman pressing a coin into her hand and trying to procure an appointment with her. She also learned that Mrs Jacobson was charging the women admission to her house.

She dared not go into any of the local taverns after one of the women's husbands cornered her.

"Lad, you board with Mrs Jacobson. What is it they are doing in there, all our wives, that is so interesting that they are not home long enough to cook our meals for us?"

Jack blushed to the roots of her hair and claimed no knowledge of what the women were about.

"I will stake my life it is some womanly magic thing." The bewildered man shook his large head. "I wouldn't be surprised if they weren't all of them witches." He laughed, but it was a sad sound. "At least they come home happy." He walked off scratching his head.

Of Harry she saw nothing, nor of Anne. They had moved out to Deptford, and it was said that Harry was working on the docks there. It was also said that Anne was large with child, and that the father could be any number of men.

Jack started looking for a ship on which she might find a post. As hard as life was at sea, it seemed preferable to her present one. Captain Luther was not, after all, sailing in time, but she heard from dockyard gossip that her former commanding officer,

Captain Mathers, was heading once more for the West Indies and he would most certainly take her on again. But then came the news that his departure was delayed by a month, and Jack did not think she would last another month at Mrs Jacobson's. Instead, she found herself a position on a naval vessel which was sailing to Jamaica, taking the new Governor for the island to his post. They were departing in one week, and the captain was glad of an experienced cabin boy.

Mrs Jacobson wept when told the news of her imminent departure. Jack was much taken aback, for she had no idea she would take the news so. She knew it was not the thought of losing income, for Mrs Jacobson had always been very generous to her, if a little demanding in return.

The news of her departure spread rapidly. Other women approached her in the street and begged her not to go. Her last week in London was an especially busy one, and she saw as many as four women in one night. One of the women she never minded seeing, and thought she might even miss, was one Nelly Gwynn. She had heard it said that Nell was the most beautiful woman in all of England, and Jack had to admit she was a pretty girl. But she thought Anne had nicer eyes and her blonde curls were softer then Nell's auburn tresses. Jack also remembered the woman she had seen in the tavern, asking for her father. She had been taller than both Anne and Nell and there was a touch of fire in her eyes and hair that Jack had liked.

They also said that Nell sang quite beautifully, and even acted upon the stage. Jack had never seen her, but she imagined it to be true, for she sighed some sweet notes as the phallus worked its magic.

On Jack's last night in London, Nell made one final visit, bringing with her a companion. Although the figure was dressed as a woman, in heavy coat and veil, and hovered in the corner of the room well out of the light, Jack suspected it to be a man. She was ill at ease with having a third person present, fearing it might be a trap of some kind. She also wondered how much they had paid Mrs Jacobson to allow him entry.

"Come, Jack." Nell threw herself on to Jack's bed. "My companion will cause no fuss." She smiled, and Jack had to admit she had a winning way about her.

"She must stay by the door and look away," Jack ordered.

"Well," Nell said to the figure, who reluctantly backed to the wall and turned to face it, "no peeking, now." Nell laughed.

Jack lay down beside her and kissed her gently on the cheek, but she was much distracted by the companion.

"Could she not wait outside the door?" she asked.

"No," said the figure in a decidedly deep voice. "I mean no." The tone was made lighter, but it was still that of a man. "I will not look – see." The figure put its hands over its eyes.

Jack was not convinced, but Nell pulled her closer and kissed her neck, running one hand dangerously down Jack's body and using the other to place Jack's hand on her delicious breasts. They might not have been as large as Mrs Jacobson's, but they were so perfectly shaped that Jack soon forgot about the companion, and diverted all her attention to the exploration of Nell's lovely body.

Jack loosened the ties on Nell's stays until her breasts were free; one fitted perfectly into her hand. She rubbed her thumb over one dark nipple before taking it into her mouth and sucking it. She was rewarded with a sharp sigh from Nell. With her free hand, Jack searched for the hem of Nelly's dress and slipped her hand beneath it, fighting her way through the layers of petticoats to slide it up over the long legs; she marvelled at the fine silk of her stockings.

Jack had never felt such material, and wondered at what wages an actress must earn to afford such obviously expensive undergarments. None of Jack's other women had near as fine wear, even those who had wealthy husbands. Jack thought they must surely cost half the King's treasury, so fine were they.

Under them, Nelly's legs were even smoother and firm. Jack could have spent all night running her hand over those thighs, marvelling at the suppleness of both the wonderful flesh and the grand silk. But Nell was arching under her, pushing her hips towards Jack as if to remind her of the phallus strapped there and the job it was to perform.

Jack reluctantly let the nipple slip from her mouth and, using both hands, reached under Nell's skirt. The layers of fine petticoats hampered Jack's progress, which, rather than frustrating her, only added to her excitement. She did not want to raise them over Nell's pretty head, as she did with some of the women, for she loved watching Nell's face as she reached her climax. Instead, she crawled up underneath them, thinking to pull them down. The smell in there was wonderfully intoxicating; it invited closer attention. Jack buried her nose in Nelly's hole and breathed in the tantalising aroma.

Nelly tensed and her breathing quickened. Jack was delighted that such a small act could have such an effect. She pushed her nose in deeper, and Nelly emitted a low groan that Jack felt right through her own body. She extended her tongue to taste some of the moistness she could feel around her nose. Nelly groaned louder and pushed her hips forward, causing Jack's tongue to slide deeper in.

The feeling of soft wetness around her tongue was delicious. Jack wanted more, so she inserted two fingers deep into Nelly and rubbed them backwards and forwards. Nelly was rocking her hips, her breathing quite frantic, she pulled up her skirts so she could see what Jack was doing. Her thighs closed around Jack's ears and one hand pressed into the back of Jack's head to stop her pulling away. There was no need for the hand, however; not even an act of God would have induced Jack to stop what she was doing. The feeling of the soft, wet flesh against her tongue, like a thousand maidens' lips, and the rough flesh pulling at her fingers was intoxicating. She had no thought of unstrapping her phallus; her tongue was doing its work for her, lapping at the nectar of Nell's very essence.

Nell writhed under Jack's administrations, her head thrown back, her bare chest rising and falling as if she were short of breath. Jack reached up around the petticoats and took one of Nell's breasts in her free hand, squeezing it hard. Nell's breath was coming in sharp gasps, closer and closer together, growing higher in pitch. Jack hoped she would not climax too soon, for she wanted to stay as long as she could in that damp, soft place, flicking her tongue so fast that it felt like it was not moving at all, sliding her fingers in and out with equal speed.

Jack could feel that the climax was close; Nell's whole body seemed to have expanded under her and now it was closing up again, tensing by degrees, as if gathering in upon itself. Suddenly, the climax exploded into a thousand tiny tremors, starting under Jack's tongue and radiating out though all of Nell's body. Nell cried out at the same moment, a cry of such pure tone and volume that Jack felt sure they would have heard it all the way to Richmond.

Jack reluctantly removed her tongue and fingers, causing more little tremors, and emerged from under the skirts. Nell smiled at her, glowing in the aftermath, and looking even more beautiful than usual.

"Oh, my dearest Jack," she sighed, "I will miss you."

Jack had forgotten her imminent departure, and now wondered if it was such a wise thing. She lay down beside Nell and thought that she would happily sleep with any number of Mrs Jacobson's friends if it meant she could have moments like these with Nell. She hugged Nell to her and smelled the sweet perfume of her hair. Maybe she had been too hasty in her plan to leave. She kissed Nell lightly on the lips, and heard a noise behind her. Looking up, she saw Nell's companion sitting on a chair at the end of the bed. She jumped off the bed and felt for her dagger.

"No, Jack." Nell put her hand on Jack's arm to restrain her. "He wished only to watch."

Jack leant forwards and tore off the veil; under it was revealed the face of a man, dark-haired, and with a false beard.

"I told him of your wondrous skills and he wished to see for himself."

Jack paused, the dagger half-raised; there was something disturbingly familiar about the man's face.

Nell smoothed down her petticoats and skirt and indicated for Jack to relace her stays. Jack complied with trembling fingers. "And were you diverted?" Nell asked her companion, laughing.

"Exceedingly," he said and looked hard at Jack. "If I did not already know that he was departing, I should have to banish him."

Jack could not tell if he spoke in jest or not. "I... I..." She did not know what to say. She tried to concentrate on the laces and ignore the soft warm skin beneath them. It did not seem an appropriate moment to say that she had changed her mind. She had an idea from whence she knew his face, but could not bring herself to consider it seriously, as it seemed too preposterous.

"Not even to use your member, and still bring her to such heights, that is some skill indeed."

"I think it should be taught in schools," Nell laughed. Jack sat back, having finished the task of relacing the stays. Nell got off the bed, lifted her skirt to adjust her stockings, then smoothed them down again.

"Come then, my love." She took her companion by the arm. "Let us repair to my house and see if you have not learnt anything." She winked at Jack.

The man looked at Jack hard as if trying to decide something. Then, he reached into the fine, velvet pantaloons he wore under the dress that ill-fitted him, and drew out a fat purse.

"I trust you will like the West Indies, because I am afraid you must remain there and not return to this kingdom, at least while

I am alive." He tossed the purse on to the bed then turned and left with Nell. She cast a look over her shoulder that seem to say she was sorry and that she had not expected this, or at least that was what Jack hoped the look meant.

Jack sat on the bed and looked at the purse. Her first instinct was to chase them down the stairs and throw the damned thing back at him, but she realised that would not be without risk. She weighed the purse in her hand, and gauged, in amazement, that there was enough money in it to buy her an apprenticeship with a bookbinder, or even her own binding business. What of the sea? She could buy her own ship. She could spend the rest of her life sailing the oceans of the world, discovering wondrous new lands and hitherto unknown peoples and treasures.

She emptied the purse on to her bedside table, the coins glittering in the candlelight. She could buy a whole island, by God, and plant bananas and pineapples and sit for the rest of her days surrounded by golden sands and swaying palm trees. Or she could... Suddenly, she felt very sad and lonely, and clutched the locket around her neck. If only her mother were still alive, the two of them could afford to live the life they were supposed to have had.

Then she remembered how she had earned the money, and swept it off the table on to the floor. It was dirty money; she couldn't keep it. She flung open the window with the intention of throwing the coins out into the muddy street. She picked up a single coin and held it up to the light; the King's head shone back at her. The King's head. Her heart beat rapidly.

Jack heard footsteps on the stairs and a huffing and puffing outside her room. The door swung open. She quickly put down the coin and stood in front of the pile on the floor.

It was Mrs Jacobson, very out of breath and looking very excited. "Oh, la, Jack, my dear; pray you... our strange visitor... you know who He was, do you not!"

Jack nodded.

"To think He was in my house. Wait until I tell..."

"You must not tell," Jack said sternly.

"But, Mrs Richards..."

"No one," Jack said firmly.

"Mrs McNally, she will not breathe a word."

Mrs McNally was a worse gossip than Mrs Jacobson.

"No." Jack stamped her foot to make her point. "He has bid me go, never to return." Perhaps it had even been a jest, but it suited Jack's purposes well enough.

"But..." Mrs Jacobson was about to say something more and then stopped. "Never to return! Oh, Jack!"

She threw herself into Jack's arms, nearly toppling them both out at the window. "My Jack, my little Jack. You must come back, I could not bear it if you never came back."

Jack tried to fend her off – she did not wish Mrs Jacobson to see the money and her shame.

Mrs Jacobson had other ideas, though; her hands roved over Jack's body, down her legs, and they came, as they were wont to do, upon the phallus.

"Oh, my dear, you want me. Even after her, you still want me." She pressed kisses on Jack's lips. "Tell me I am as beautiful as she; tell me, Jack."

She pulled at the ties on Jack's britches and ripped at her own gown. Jack tried to hold her off.

"Jack?" Mrs Jacobson noticed she had not answered.

Jack could not lie, but knew she had to say something. She looked down and saw Mrs Jacobson's large breasts pressed against her own.

"You have a grander bosom than she."

"Oh, Jack!" The widow threw herself once again into Jack's arms, overwhelming her with kisses and caresses.

"You must excuse me." Jack managed to push her away. "I need to relieve myself."

Mrs Jacobson stilled her advances.

"If you were just able..." Jack shooed her out of the door, and she went, reluctantly.

Jack scooped up the money and replaced it in the purse, hiding it amongst her clothes. She would think on what to do with it once she had pleasured Mrs Jacobson. She peed into her chamber pot, and threw its contents out the window.

Mrs Jacobson re-entered as she heard the pee hit the street below; she laid herself straight down on the bed and spread her legs, pulling her huge breasts from inside her gown and holding them together. "Better than that Nelly Gwynn," she said, and rubbed her thumbs over the vast pink nipples. "I shall tell Mrs McNally so."

She was already wet when Jack entered her, and it took very little work to bring her to her climax, for which Jack was grateful. She was tired and confused and needed time alone to think. Mrs Jacobson cried out Jack's name as she came, and cried afterwards, holding Jack in a suffocating embrace before she finally fell asleep on Jack's bed.

Jack sat and looked out of the window. Tomorrow she was off again on her travels, off to sea. She would be free of these women; she would once again be able to sit in the crow's nest and feel the fresh wind on her cheeks. And when they reached Jamaica, she would seek out the crystal-clear pools in the running rivers and jump from waterfalls. She would taste again the fruits of the island and fish straight from the sea, and feel the heat of the sun warm her to her very bones.

There was little she felt sad about leaving, her mother's resting place, certainly, but as long as she had the locket she would carry always her mother with her. Anne she would miss, too, though she was gone off to make her own life with her unborn child. A hard life it would be, too, for a woman with a child born out of wedlock.

That gave Jack an idea; the money she would give to Anne, or some of it, anyway. She realised that she would need some, if she were never to return to England. As quietly as she could (so as not to wake the now-snoring Mrs Jacobson), she emptied half of the coins into an old sock and stowed them with the rest of her clothes in a bundle. The other half she left in their fine purse, ready to give to Anne. As she bent to pick up her bundle of clothes, however, the purse brushed against Mrs Jacobson, who reached out and clasped it to her breast. Jack tried to retrieve it, but the sleeping woman held fast to it.

Jack sighed and gave up the struggle; perhaps it was best where it was. Mrs Jacobson had certainly been very kind to her. She could afford to set herself up in early retirement.

Jack left the house quietly; no one stirred or noticed her departure, and that was how she wanted it. She walked through the dark, empty streets and in her mind she said a farewell to all the familiar things. She walked out to the Black Heath and, once again, stood on the earth under which her mother was buried; holding the locket, she offered up a prayer for safe passage. Then she walked to Greenwich and the ship waiting at the wharf. She, the *St Michael*, was smaller than her last berth, but she still looked a fine sight to Jack. Her captain was Sir Robert Holmes, and Jack had heard good report of him.

She stole aboard and climbed up the main mast to the crow's nest. The night was clear for once and there was a full moon. The stars were picked out of the black night like jewels placed there by some benevolent God to guide sailors on their way. Tonight, though, it seemed they were there purely for Jack's pleasure and entertainment; she found the Plough and the Bear before she fell asleep, rocked by the gentle motion of the Thames.

When she woke again, the sun was over the yard arm and the ship was being readied to sail out on the high tide. Below her, men were stowing supplies, with the boatswain and the captain, Sir Robert, overseeing them. Some fine furniture was being winched aboard, watched by a very worried gentleman. Jack climbed down from her perch and landed lightly on the deck next to the captain.

"Permission to come aboard, sir. A good day for sailing," she remarked.

Sir Robert turned quickly, reaching for his dagger, but stopped when he saw it was Jack.

"I took you for a stowaway, boy."

"I started my watch early, sir." Jack pointed to the crow's nest. She noticed the boatswain looking thunderously at her, but Sir Robert laughed.

"You are not late, then?" he asked.

"Never sir, but I don't expect favours for my extra hours."

"I should think not, ye unmannered knave," the boatswain snapped, casting Jack another dark look.

"Get yourself to my cabin and make sure it is shipshape, and then go and see if His Majesty's Governor is in need of anything."

"A sleeping draught, by the looks of him," Jack said, and scampered off before either man could reply.

The ship may have been smaller than she was used to, but the captain's cabin was far more spacious. Jack stowed her bundle under the narrow bed at the front of the cabin. There were maps laid out on the table with instruments of navigation. Captain Mathers on her last ship had given her some instructions as to their uses, and Jack was keen to learn more.

As she bent over the maps, she heard much shouting and banging from above, so returned to the deck to see what was going on. A harpsichord was hanging half over the ship, half over the land. One of its ropes had broken, leaving it dangling most precariously. If they tried to lower it they risked damaging both it and the deck and yet they could not leave it there for fear that its other ropes would break.

Jack climbed up the winch and shinned down the broken rope;

she wrapped it round her ankle and then lowered herself and grasped a corner of the harpsichord. It was heavier than it looked, and the rope round her ankle slipped a little, but then held. With her acting as the rope, they were able to lower the instrument safely into the hold.

As Jack was untangling herself from the rope, she heard a familiar voice.

"So, up to your old tricks again, eh?" It was Harry. Jack was prepared to run or even fight, but Harry made no move towards her. Jack nodded, remembering the numerous times on the last voyage that she had been called upon to fasten sails that had been torn loose in high winds.

"We are sailing together again?" It was more of a question than a statement from Jack.

"If this is your vessel, too." Jack noticed how much older Harry looked and how sad; she burned with desire to ask after Anne, but felt Harry would take offense.

They stood for a moment in silence, the question hanging in the air between them, then Harry spoke: "She deceived us both, Jack." He looked close to tears.

"The child is to be a mulatto. She told me, after more nights of bluster and tears, that the father is that African who worked the docks, and now she has gone and married him. They went off to Plymouth to settle there." Harry looked at Jack, tears collecting in his eyes. "Oh, Jack, my Sweet Anne."

Jack was shocked by this revelation; her Anne, run off with another man. She would have married her willingly and taken the child as her own, had it not gone against all nature and God's teaching. But she, it seemed, had been in love with another throughout their encounters, had been using Jack just for sport. Jack, too, found herself close to tears.

Still the African had seemed like a good man, and Jack wished them well. Anne's life would be a hard one, married to an African with a child of their two races. She remembered the coins that she had wanted to give her, and decided that she should have those which Jack had reserved for herself; Anne would have more need now of the comforts that money could buy.

"I have a means of easing her way in the world," she told Harry, and went to the cabin to retrieve the sock which held the coins. She wrapped them, sock and all, in a 'kerchief and returned to the deck, wondering how she could get them safely to Anne. A crowd had gathered to see them off. It was a larger crowd than usual, made up of a good many women, all straining to see on to the ship. Jack noticed Mrs Jacobson among them, and Mrs McNally; in fact, it seemed most of the women whom Jack had serviced were there.

At the front of the crowd was Nell, looking glorious in the sunlight and receiving a good deal of attention from the men, including the captain and the Governor.

"Jack," she called, and waved as she saw her emerge. Jack was pleased to see her there – she could be trusted to deliver the money to Anne. Jack ran down the gangplank to greet her.

The men all turned to see whom it was Nell greeted so warmly. Jack fancied she saw surprise on their faces.

"I am so sorry, Jack," Nell said. She took Jack's hand and held it. "I would not have brought him if I had known; he can be so..."

"Regal," Jack suggested lightly.

Nell smiled, and her whole face lit up.

"I don't mind." Jack squeezed her hand. "I am younger than he and likely to live longer; I will return when he is dead." She wasn't sure whether she too was jesting now. "But Nell, I have a task for you." She explained, and Nell promised to seek out Anne and give her the money, though she protested a little.

"But it was meant for you, my love, so you could settle abroad."

"I will not need it," Jack said, hoping it to be true. She jumped back onboard the ship which was nearly ready to get underway.

Below her now, the other women were calling out her name

and waving their handkerchiefs. Jack was embarrassed by this behaviour, and wished for a speedy departure. The other sailors nudged each other and looked slyly at Jack. Harry emerged and gazed in wonder at the scene.

"It seems y'are going to be missed, Jack," he said, nodding towards the crowd.

Jack shrugged and felt herself start to blush; surely the tide was high enough now to set sail? Mrs Jacobson had pushed her way to the front and was waving the fine purse above her head.

"Cooee, my dear, you left this."

"Keep it," Jack shouted back; she wanted no more to do with it.

"No!" Mrs Jacobson tried to throw the purse, but its strings were around her wrist. As she swung it, it hit Mrs McNally on the back of her head. Mrs McNally spun around and was about to slap her friend, when she noticed what the object was, and how full it was of coins. She tried to wrestle it off Mrs Jacobson and, in the tussle, the purse split and coins went flying everywhere. The entire crowd then joined in the scramble to grab as many as they could.

Jack watched the drama unfold before her in amusement. The women did not notice the ship being cast off, and moving away from the wharf and for that, at least, Jack was grateful. As the distance behind the ship and the dock increased, so Jack relaxed, and even Harry cheered up enough to smile. Sir Robert shook his head in puzzlement and the Governor went below to check that his harpsichord was securely stowed.

Jack noticed a woman standing at the back of the crowd away from the mêlée, looking directly at her, or so it seemed to Jack. It was the fine lady from the tavern, and Jack started to wave to her, as though bidding farewell to a long-lost friend, and then remembered that she did not know the lady at all, except to have seen her twice and to have dreamed of her. Jack felt lonely again, as if she were, indeed, losing a very good friend. She shook her head and hurried below to begin her duties as the captain's cabin boy.

7

The Wedding

The wedding was set for the sixth of June, and Elizabeth found herself looking forward to it, although she would miss Mrs Mathers; she knew that her father would miss her even more, for they had formed a fast friendship. Elizabeth wondered if they too might not, in time, wed. No one would ever replace her own dear mother, but Mrs Mathers seemed to make her father happy, and she would not deny him that which would ease his remaining years.

Mary, too, had settled into Mrs Mathers' household surprisingly easily and had become close friends with one of the maids there, a strapping lass called Heather. Elizabeth often saw them together about the house and Mary came less and less often to Elizabeth's bed for treatment sessions. Elizabeth was at once relieved at this, as she felt it indicated some improvement in Mary's well-being, but also unaccountably jealous of Heather and the amount of time Mary spent with her.

Mrs Mathers, seeing how well Mary fitted into her own household, even offered to keep her on if she did not settle in the captain's house, which was well staffed. Elizabeth was reluctant to let her go; she thought she might get lonely in that big house, especially when her new husband was away at sea.

She was dismayed to learn that he intended to sail the week after the wedding. Dismayed and a little relieved. It would give her time, she thought, to get used to the idea of being Mrs Luther without the encumbrance of her husband's presence.

Rose called to see her most days, on some pretext or another, and if no one was about, they would have a treatment session. Elizabeth found that Rose stirred in her the same peculiar passion that Mary had done, and she looked forward to these sessions very much.

In the seemingly endless, empty hours between Rose's visits, she tried her hand at embroidery, but her fingers seemed too large for the tiny stitches and it reminded her of her mother and therefore saddened her. She also tried painting, but the brush refused to convey the scene in front of her on to the paper, and her attempts at playing the spinet or singing sent everyone rushing from the room. In short, she could find nothing to fill her hours now that she was at leisure and had no sick mother to attend to or house to run.

She wondered how other women in her position managed; she had met some, also married to sea captains or to rich merchants, through Mrs Mathers' kind introductions, and they seemed nice enough, although their conversation consisted of nothing more than clothes and hair and idle gossip of the most scandalous nature. Elizabeth found their company both intimidating and tedious and soon started declining invitations on the grounds of prior engagements or ill health.

She began to take long walks early in the morning, before the rest of the world was awake. She knew it was not entirely wise to wander the streets unaccompanied, even in respectable Greenwich but, apart from the enjoyment she took from the exercise, the possibility of encountering danger was half the attraction. Also, she loved the river, with its teeming life and, most of all, the wondrous ships. As a small child, she had often accompanied her father down to the riverside at Greenwich to watch the tall ships, like great water dragons, moving slowly passed, out to the open sea and adventure. As she grew, her love of the great ships and the sea never wavered, but only increased, and she had often wished she were a boy, so that she could join the Navy and seek her fortune as a brave Lieutenant or Able Seaman.

One morning, she came upon the river as a ship was about to set sail. There was a crowd of women waiting to see the ship off. This was not unusual in itself; oftentimes, the wives of sailors came down to wave their 'kerchiefs and wish their husbands "bon voyage". But this crowd was different, in that the women all seemed rather too well dressed for sailors' wives, and were all calling out the name of one man only: 'Jack'.

The sailor to whom they seemed to be directing their calls was a mere lad, who rightfully so was looking rather shamefaced. He disappeared from sight and then reappeared a few minutes later. On his reappearance, a fracas broke out amongst the gathered women; something was flung about, a purse it must have been, for it ruptured, spilling coins all about. The women fought each other off to gain their share of the fallen loot. While they were thus occupied, the ship slipped its moorings and moved away from the dock, the lad standing on deck shaking his head.

There was something familiar about the boy and it was not until he was almost out of sight that Elizabeth realised she had seen him before. He was the lad fighting in the tavern, and then again on the day of her mother's funeral. He looked up and seemed to see her, though from such a great distance, it was hard to tell. He raised his arm as if to wave to her and then changed his mind. Elizabeth remembered her dream as the ship sailed out downriver and dwindled, and she suddenly felt as if she had missed something of vital importance.

She went down to the wharf; the women were dispersing, looking battered and bruised, many of them in tears, each clutching a coin or two. Lying on the ground were the tattered remains of the purse; on a whim, she picked it up and slipped it into her pocket. What she thought she could do with it she had no idea, but it seemed connected to the lad in some way, and she felt closer to him for having a piece of it.

*

The wedding day dawned bright and clear, and Elizabeth was up with the sun, watching it rise through the trees from her bedroom window. Mary had stayed with her that night and had cried bitter tears at the thought of her Mistress Elizabeth getting married; no amount of the treatment would still the tears. Elizabeth told her to hush, but was secretly pleased that Mary felt so. She assured her that she had no intention of sharing her bed with the captain except when absolutely necessary. She wondered if her husband would want relations on the wedding night and supposed, reluctantly, that he would. She was not looking forward to it with any relish.

Mrs Mathers helped her to dress, and Mary ran around fetching and carrying things. Rose came too, in case the dress needed any last-minute alterations. But the dress was beautiful, and Elizabeth nearly cried when she saw herself in the glass. Rose put a touch of powder and rouge on her cheek and, with a hot poker, tonged her hair, which curled fetchingly back off her face. Rose had tried to persuade her to wear a wig, as was the fashion amongst the ladies of the Court, but Elizabeth thought them silly; a captain's wife needed no such frippery. She supposed them to be uncomfortable, besides, being of such large and unnatural proportions.

They all stopped and stared at her reflection when it was done. Elizabeth would not have recognised herself, for she looked almost beautiful. Her strong shoulders, hidden by the sleeves of the dress, were softened, and her small breasts pushed up to give her a delicate cleavage. Her healthy complexion was given a ladylike pallor by the powder and her lips looked like two small rosebuds.

Mary started wailing then, and Rose, too; even Mrs Mathers shed a tear at this wondrous transformation. They gathered tight around her and hugged her and Elizabeth felt a surge of love for them all, which was quickly followed by a great fear at the prospect of marrying.

Her father entered the room, and all the women composed themselves. She noticed Mrs Mathers, especially, stood straighter and smoothed her hair and pinched her cheeks on his arrival. He had come to inform them that the carriages were ready.

She and her father set off in the Captain Luther's finest carriage, which the servants had decorated with ribbons and rosettes. Mrs Mathers followed in her own carriage, allowing Mary and Rose to ride with her. It was only a short ride to the church; Elizabeth would have wanted it to be much longer. She found that she was shaking as she descended from the carriage and had to lean on her father's arm, much as he had done on the captain at her mother's funeral.

"Oh, Father," she sighed, but he was too busy watching for the arrival of Mrs Mathers to notice her distress. The walk up the front steps of the church took all of her willpower, for every instinct told her to run from there. Once inside, however, it seemed easier, for there was no means of escape. The captain stood by the altar, looking very fine in his dress uniform, the buttons polished to a sharp shine, the hair of his forehead oiled into curls and his light beard trimmed close to his face.

He turned as she entered and looked twice at her, as though he could not believe her to be the same woman to whom he had been engaged. This made Elizabeth smile and the sun shone through the stained-glass window of the small church, making everything about her glow, as if with an inner light. The captain smiled in return, and Elizabeth thought that maybe everything would be all right after all.

If she had to marry, and she knew that she must, then one like the captain was ideal. He had always been very courteous towards her; he was rich, good looking and would be absent for long periods with good cause. Elizabeth could think of no better qualities in a husband. If, in the past, his attention had all been upon her breasts, he was now looking her over from head to toe and seemed pleased with what he saw.

Elizabeth noticed, too, that her father's step was steadier than it had been for a long while, and his posture more upright. So different from the last time they had been in their former parish church together. How different their circumstances were now in this, and how quickly they had changed. A month ago she was worried where they would find their next meal, and here she was now, their future secure, worried about nothing more than whether she would like married life or not. She chided herself for being so shallow, and marched purposely towards the captain and the altar.

The church was barely half full; she had only her father as family, and the captain, also, seemed to have few relatives. The minister was a round, jolly looking fellow who conducted the service in a light-hearted manner without once mentioning sin or money. Elizabeth found herself wishing he had been their own minister before, so he could have conducted her mother's funeral. She repeated her vows, trying hard not to think about what she was actually promising to do. The captain repeated his, not looking at her, and then, when they were declared man and wife, he took her hand and looked intently at her bosom or possibly, it now occurred to Elizabeth, her locket.

They walked back down the aisle together and out into the sunshine. There were children waiting to throw petals at them; Elizabeth was pleased and surprised that the captain had thought of such a small detail. He, in turn, threw coins for them to scrabble after.

They rode back to the captain's house together. Alone in the carriage, Elizabeth had no idea what to say to her new husband. Her new husband seemed equally at a loss, so they drove along in silence. Elizabeth saw people in the street stop and watch as the carriage went by; she knew they would be impressed, for the carriage was a fine one, and she and the captain looked grand sitting there together. But she could not help but envy them, out there on the street, free to do whatever they pleased.

The wedding breakfast was in the formal dining room, and only her father, Mrs Mathers, the captain and herself would be attending. Mary went with the other servants, who were having a special meal in the kitchen. None of them spoke; Mrs Mathers made a few brave attempts at conversation, but the captain did not seem interested, and Elizabeth found she was too agitated to say much. Mrs Mathers did not seem to notice or, if she did, she did not mind. She chattered happily about other weddings she had been to and how good the food was. Elizabeth watched her father as he sat listening intently and gazing upon Mrs Mathers' cheerful face.

She was dreading the moment when they would leave, and she and the captain would be alone for the first time as man and wife. Luckily, Mrs Mathers seemed in no hurry to go, and even suggested bringing the servants up for some impromptu dancing. The captain agreed and sent for them. They came and danced, and one of the grooms sang a few songs in a surprisingly good tenor voice.

Elizabeth thought the staff looked a little sullen, as if resenting being dragged from a much better party downstairs. Mary was with them, and she looked the most resentful of all. She was partnered in most of the dances by a tall young man. Elizabeth noticed the Captain watching them carefully and wondered if he found Mary more attractive than herself, being of a more delicate nature.

Mrs Mathers clapped and called for more at the end of each dance; she even encouraged Elizabeth's father up for the gavotte, and Elizabeth had to admit that they made a fine couple. Her new husband, however, refused to move from his seat, despite all Mrs Mathers' considerable persuasion and, for that, Elizabeth was grateful. She danced badly, always taking too long a step, and often treading upon her partners' toes.

Each moment of the evening seemed to last forever, weighing

heavily upon Elizabeth with the dread of what was to follow. Yet it seemed only a moment before the servants were told to return belowstairs, as Mrs Mathers was leaving and bidding them a good night. She hugged Elizabeth and kissed her on both cheeks. Elizabeth wanted to cling to her, and beg her not to go.

Mrs Mathers seemed to sense her fear: "I know my nephew to be a fundamentally decent man, my dear, and although this is a marriage of obvious convenience to you both, I hope it is not without love." She kissed Elizabeth on the forehead and descended the steps to her waiting carriage.

Elizabeth stood and watched it disappear into the night, very aware of the captain beside her. Her father bade them a good night and retired to his room.

"Come, Elizabeth," her husband said and, barely touching her elbow, guided her back inside. He led her up the stairs to the master bedroom and left her there to change. Laid out on the bed was a new nightgown, made of the finest silk, and a beautiful gold locket with a ruby set in it. Elizabeth stood and looked at them, trying not to see the bed beneath upon which they lay. She ran her hand over the nightgown and marvelled at the smoothness of the material. She recognised the lace at the neck as the sample Rose had shown her on that first, special visit. It was too fine a thing for her to wear; she imagined Rose's body in it, feeling the silk shift against her skin, as she ran her hand up underneath it along Rose's thigh.

The door behind her opened and Elizabeth jumped, her heart racing at being caught thinking such thoughts. It was not the captain, however, but Mary come to help her change. Elizabeth felt so relieved, she almost broke into tears.

"He sent me," Mary said sullenly. "And told me to be quick about it."

Elizabeth imagined her husband, standing in the hallway, barely able to contain his lust for her.

Mary began undressing her. Elizabeth was acutely aware of Mary's hand so close to her skin. She imagined the captain's hands there, waiting to knead and press her breasts. She found her breathing had quickened and, blaming the tightness of her stays, instructed Mary to unlace them. She sighed with relief when they was off, and Mary had moved to untie the skirt and many layers of petticoats.

As the last petticoat fell away, leaving Elizabeth standing in just her stockings, Mary started to remove those too, but Elizabeth stopped her. The touch of Mary's hands against her bare thighs was too much.

"I am able to manage now," Elizabeth said as gently as she could. Mary shrugged but looked none too happy. She lifted the silk nightgown over Elizabeth's head, and let it slide down her body. Elizabeth was shocked by the softness of it, like hands caressing her.

"Oh, Mistress." Mary was staring at her, looking as if she was about to cry.

"You had better go now," Elizabeth said firmly. "Please," she added in a softer tone. "And thank you." She meant for everything; the practices they had done in preparation for this night as well as the help undressing, and she hoped Mary knew that. It was hard to tell, for the girl turned and left without saying a word.

Now that the moment was almost upon her, Elizabeth had the overwhelming urge to cry. She knew she must not, however, for she imagined that what would follow would be akin to a battle, and she must show no signs of weakness. Almost as soon as Mary had closed the door, it opened again. Elizabeth thought it was Mary returning, and was about to scold her when she realised it was the captain. He stood in the doorway and looked her up and down. Elizabeth wanted to cover herself with her hands but forced herself to be still. He had also changed, and now wore a dressing gown of fine silk and slippers.

"So," he said after he had finished his perusal. "It fits you well."

Elizabeth nodded; she know not how to reply.

"That seamstress who made it – she knew your measurements by heart, it would seem."

Elizabeth would have smiled at that, had she not detected an underlying threat in her husband's words.

"Come." He indicated the bed and marched over to it, pulling back the covers, and saw the ruby locket there, unmoved.

"You do not like it?" He sounded cross.

"No, no..." Elizabeth stayed where she was. "It is beautiful; it is just that I already have one." She clasped her hand around her own as if to protect it.

"I do not like that one." He pointed at it. "I want you to wear this one."

There was something about his tone, an agitation, that made Elizabeth realise he was lying. She did not want to fight with him on their wedding night, but she would not give up her locket, the deathbed present from her beloved mother.

"You know it was a present from my dying mother. I will not give it up." She tried to sound firm, and not betray the anger and panic that she was beginning to feel.

"Not even if your husband commands it?" His voice was low, threatening.

Elizabeth squared her shoulders. "No," she answered.

The captain paused for a moment, looking at the locket lying untouched on the bed, as if trying to make up his mind about something. After a moment, he shrugged.

"As you wish." He picked up the locket and tossed it from the bed as if it was of no value at all. He climbed into bed, and indicated that she should join him.

Elizabeth walked as steadily as she could to the bedside, she found that her legs were shaking as if she were chilled, although the evening was mild and the room well heated. She did not believe that the captain felt so little for the new locket after trying to force her to wear it. She sat on the edge of the bed for a moment, hoping to still her treacherous limbs, then she swung her legs on to the bed and lay down on her back. She remembered the rehearsal she and Mary had done for this night; she closed her eyes and waited for him to leap on top of her, tearing at her nightgown. Nothing happened for a long time. She opened her eyes. She felt the captain shift his weight upon the bed, and closed her eyes again, but still nothing happened.

Elizabeth opened her eyes and saw the captain lying facing her, looking at the locket.

"You will not be parted from it?" He reached out one finger and touched it gently. She shook her head.

He sat up suddenly. "I am away to sea in one week." He said it as if she did not already know. He looked at her hard, as if he were about to tell her something, but then changed his mind. He climbed down from the bed and went to the window, standing looking out into the night. As Elizabeth watched him, her eyes began closing and she realised how very tired she was after the strains of the day. She had seen the sun up and it was now well past set.

She must have drifted off to sleep, for when she awoke, the captain was gone and sunlight was coming in through the window. The other side of the bed was clean and smooth; the Captain had not spent the night beside her.

Elizabeth did not know whether to be relieved or disappointed. She thought he was probably punishing her for her stubbornness. She rang the bell to summon Mary to help her dress, and noticed, as she did so, that something was missing. Her hand went to her neck; the locket was gone.

A terrible rage started within her. She ran to the door and through the house, wearing only her nightgown, not caring if the servants saw her. She flew down the stairs to the library, the captain's habitual haunt, and threw open the door. He was not in there. She proceeded to cast open the doors of every room that she passed and then slammed them shut again, searching the house for her thieving husband.

She found him in the dining room, sitting alone, eating his breakfast as if nothing in the world could be wrong. He looked up as she burst through the door.

"Elizabeth, good morning," he said, as if she were merely late for breakfast.

"Give me my locket!" she demanded.

He frowned.

"Give it to me this instant!" She thrust out her hand.

"And what shall you do if I do not?"

Elizabeth would have done anything that sprang to mind.

"You are my wife now. Your property is mine," he went on calmly.

"I will leave this house and never return!"

The captain laughed. "Where would you go?"

"Anywhere that honest people dwell, people who do not steal valuable tokens in the middle of the night like petty thieves."

That seemed to touch him, and he lowered his eyes. "It is there." He pointed to a second place setting that Elizabeth had not noticed. The locket was sitting in a bowl. She rushed over to it and, with shaking hands, secured it around her neck.

"Sit," he commanded. He summoned a maid to take her to change into her slammerkin. When she returned, and they were settled and alone again, he himself poured the tea into two dishes and passed one to her. "I have a confession to make," he said.

Elizabeth was not sure she wanted to hear it.

The captain began. "My father was a jeweller. It was he who made this locket and one other. The two fit together and, between them, they hold a great secret; I believe, as have many before me, that they contain a map to an island where a great treasure lies buried."

A treasure map! Elizabeth felt a moment's excitement. To discover treasure, that would be a wonderful thing.

"He made them for a certain Royal personage; she gave them to two of her ladies-in-waiting. One was your grandmother, who gave it to your mother and she to you."

Elizabeth listened to the tale as it unfolded. She was enthralled by it, and held the locket close to her as the captain told it.

"My father told me this story when I was but a child; though he mummeried it, making it out to be a mere cat's paw of a fable, I believed it and resolved to find the lockets and make my fortune on the sea with them. I traced one locket to your mother. The other I have not been able to find; the daughter of the second lady-in-waiting seems to have had no daughters of her own, and died of the Plague. She is probably buried in some foul grave with many others, together with the locket, so I fear it is lost forever." He paused and looked at Elizabeth.

"The locket holds on its casing one half of a text. I have spent this past night studying it and am none the wiser for my troubles."

Elizabeth remembered her mother's word as she gave it to her; that she herself had not been brave enough to pursue its secret, but she thought Elizabeth might be, and she grew more excited.

"I must confess, the locket was the reason for the proposal of marriage," he continued.

Elizabeth knew she was no great catch, and that he could have secured for himself a much better match, but to have him say it, in so many words, upset her. She felt a desire to leave him just as she was, in her slammerkin, taking with her no more than those simple possessions with which she had arrived. The captain had, however, not finished.

"But seeing you yesterday, dear Elizabeth, I will own that my heart was touched by your appearance, and seeing how dearly my aunt holds you in her affection, I now entreat you to forgive my deceitfulness and hope that we can live together, if not as man and wife, than at least as friends."

Elizabeth did not know what to think of this confession. She was at once angry and secretly pleased that he had owned up to his deception. She was confused also; it seemed to her that the confession still lacked a few details.

"Will you not say something?" he asked anxiously when she was silent for too long.

"I am pleased to learn the history of the locket," she said carefully. She paused and looked the captain squarely in the eye. "What I do not understand is why you took the locket and now give it back to me. I can only surmise that there is something more you want from me and, once you have attained this, then you will evict myself and my father."

"No," he said, rather too forcefully. "Your tenancy here and that of you father is assured. I married you to give you that security."

"But the marriage has not been consummated." Elizabeth felt herself start to blush as she said it. The captain, too, looked embarrassed.

"That is of no matter," he said quickly.

"What more, then, do you want of me?"

He paused and toyed with the spoon beside his plate. There was clearly something more.

"I had hoped to examine the locket, gain its secret and return it to you before you awoke, so that you would be none the wiser." He looked up at her for a moment and then back to his spoon. "However, as I said, I was unable to extract any information."

A thought struck Elizabeth, one that greatly amused her. "You mean you could not open it." The locket had a secret catch, but one that any infant girl child would have been able to discover if her curiosity were great enough.

The captain looked at her in surprise. "That is not what I said."

But it was too late, for she had seen the truth in his eyes. She laughed. The captain did not look at all amused, but Elizabeth carried on laughing. A sea captain unable to solve such a simple thing as a locket catch!

The captain rose from the table and stalked to the window. He stood with his back to her, his hands clenched in fists by his side.

Elizabeth stopped her laughing; for the first time in a long while, she felt she was in a position to take control over her own destiny. An exciting proposition presented itself to her.

"Very well," she said to his tense back. "I have something you desire and you have something I want. I suggest we strike a bargain."

8

Pirates Ahoy

Jack could not have wished for a better start to the voyage. The weather held fine and the winds fast for the first week. The captain was a good sort and the First Mate almost cheerful. The boatswain, however, was a bitter, angry man and seemed to have taken strongly against Jack, for some reason. Fortunately, Jack's duties as the cabin boy kept her out of his way for the most part. The captain, learning of her interest, took time to explain the art of navigation and was surprised at how quickly Jack learned.

"You should not be a mere cabin boy," he said as he watched Jack plot their course one day. "Not that I'm complaining, d'ye see – it is good to have you onboard. But you should join the Navy proper, go for a commission, now that you have grown and come of age."

Jack laughed and shrugged; she had been of age for many a year now, and not grown an inch in all that time. Harry was the only person she had known long enough to notice that she did not seem to grow, and he said not a word.

When she was not needed by the captain, she spent her time playing cards with Harry and some of the other crew below decks. She had forgotten how dull smooth sailing was and found herself longing for some rough weather. The other sailors did not share her sentiments, and seemed quite happy to sit doing very little for days on end.

The Governor spent much of his time in his cabin, ordering his manservant about. He was not a good traveller and, even in this fair weather, looked green about the gills and could not be far from his chamber pot. Jack spent some of her time carrying and fetching for him, checking that his furniture, and in particular his precious harpsichord, was unharmed. He was not an easy man to please, finding fault in most things. Jack wondered how he had obtained his commission, and how he would carry it out on such a young and as yet uncivilised isle as Jamaica.

The crow's nest was still her favourite place, and it was from there that she watched the coast of England slip away for what she believed would be the last time. And it was from there she watched the rest of the ship go about its business, hidden from the boatswain's malevolent gaze. She could sit quietly and feel the wind on her face and the sun in her eyes.

She climbed there whenever her duties allowed her to, and relished being on the sea again, free of the obligations she had felt in London. She had to admit that she missed the good women. The feel of their skin under her hand, their smell, even the noises they made as she used her phallus on them. Sometimes when she was feeling lonely and in need of cheering up, she imagined they were there with her. She closed her eyes and dreamed she was touching Anne's rosy cheek, Nell's lustrous thighs and Mrs Jacobson's wonderful breasts. She could almost feel these women around her, moving as she worked her phallus on them. She held fast to her phallus and imagined them sighing for her, calling out her name and then climaxing one after another until they melted into one glorious, enormous, satisfied being.

One day, when she was delivering the meals to the Governor's cabin, she entered without waiting for a reply to her knock. What she saw before her made her blush to the roots of her hair. The Governor and his manservant were locked together in an embrace. The manservant was standing, his britches down around his ankles, while the Governor was on his knees in front of him with the other man's member in his mouth, sucking on it hard and noisily. Jack was so astonished that she could neither flee the scene nor avert her eyes. She stood, frozen to the spot, watching as the Governor continued his ministrations, unaware of her presence. The manservant was fully aware that Jack was there, having seen her enter, but he was apparently too close to his climax to utter a word. In fact, as Jack watched, his face reddened and his body convulsed and he cried out wordlessly.

Jack withdrew at that moment, freed by the noise and sudden realisation of what exactly it was she had been witnessing. She shut the door quietly and leant against the wall. Of course, she had heard of such men, but had thought them to be all of poor birth and lacking in education. To happen upon the future Governor of Jamaica in such an act – well! Jack shook her head: it was none of her business, and had not she herself broken more laws of nature than that?

She straightened up and stepped loudly upon the floor to imitate approaching footsteps, then she knocked hard upon the door and waited for a response. It came quickly; she entered and placed the tray on the table. The Governor was seated at his desk, reading from a large volume, although Jack noticed he held it upside down. The manservant was on the opposite side of the cabin, dusting a small shelf.

The Governor barely acknowledged Jack's presence. The servant, however, caught her eye, his own eyes wide, pleading silently with her to forget what she had just seen. Jack nodded and, suppressing a smile, ambled out of the cabin.

She had no intention of telling anyone of the scene she had witnessed, nor use the information in any way. But on a long, fair sea, you took your entertainment where you could find it, and once Jack was over the initial shock, she found the whole thing vastly diverting.

More diverting still was a change in the weather; the fine days turned quickly into rain and then strong winds blew up from the east. The sea rolled the ship about as if it were a toy, and the winds tore at the sails. The crewmen were on double their watches – eight hours in place of four – and sleep was in short supply.

On the fourth day of the storm, Jack was below, trying to snatch a few hours of sleep, when she hear a banging on the cabin door. It was flung open and Harry stood there clutching the frame, wet through to his skin.

"The fore topsail will take no more, we are close to losing it and none above has the courage to get it down."

Jack scrambled from her bunk. Because of her agility and fearlessness, she had often been called upon to cut the sails down in a storm on their last voyage, with Harry roped to her below. The weather had not been so wild when they had performed these daring acts before. Nevertheless, as Jack staggered on to the deck, she could see that they were, indeed, in great danger of losing the sails.

"Come," she shouted to Harry as she tied a rope around her waist and tossed the other end to him. She climbed the fore port rigging to the nearest flapping sail and, within minutes, was soaked to the skin.

The ship was rolling wildly, so that one moment she was being flung hard against the rigging and the next she was swung away from them with equal force. She hung on as best she could, remembering the sailors she had seen being tossed into the ocean, and not fancying a watery grave.

The fore topsail was thrashing about, torn already in many places from the force of the wind. She knew she must gather it in quickly before the cold crept into her fingers and robbed them of their grip. She climbed quickly when the ship's pitching allowed her to, and then, when she was within an arm's length of the canvas, she reached out to grasp it. A sudden gust slapped the sail into her face with the force of a charging horse.

She lost her hold, and found herself flying through the air. The sail again whipped towards her; she grabbed it and clung on for her very life. It carried her out over the raging water and then back above the deck. There was a terrible ripping sound and Jack plummeted several yards, heading for the water again.

She flailed desperately, and managed to grab the rigging as she and the sail flew past.

A great cheer went up from below. She had not managed to salvage the whole sail, but there would be enough there to patch and use again.

She climbed back down to the deck. Harry gathered the freed sail from her. He said not a word, but Jack could tell he was relieved that she was safe. Her heart was still beating fast in her chest and her hands were rubbed raw from the sheets. Her face was swollen from where the sail had hit her, and she longed to return to her bunk, but her work was not finished, for the other sails needed reefing.

These she managed with much less drama, working alongside the other hands but, by the time she returned to the deck, she was shaking with the cold and exhaustion. The storm had abated somewhat, the winds had eased and the sea calmed. Even the cloud seemed to be clearing. Off in the distance, Jack thought she saw another ship, and, despite her weariness, she climbed once more into the rigging for a better view.

It was, indeed, a ship, and a very fine one too: a Cromster, a little smaller than their own, but with sixteen guns, and she was sailing full speed towards them off the starboard bow.

"Ship ahoy off the starboard bow," she shouted down to the deck. She stayed where she was and watched the ship approach. She wondered why a vessel in these waters should be armed to the top of her poundage. She could see from the speed it was making that it carried little cargo. If it were a trade vessel coming from the Americas, it should have been packed to its gunnels. It was then that she noticed the flag it was flying.

She hurried down the rigging. "Captain," she shouted before she reached the deck, "I think they are pirates."

Sir Robert studied her. "We are too far from land."

"All the same, sir."

He called for his glass and looked at the approaching ship.

"Man the guns!" he shouted when he brought it into focus.

"Man the guns!" The cry echoed around the ship.

They were in no shape to stand to and fight; the crew were exhausted by the ordeal of the storm and, though they had greater fire power, neither were they in any condition to try and outrun them.

Jack ran below to fetch her sword and dagger. As she tucked them into her belt she remembered her dream of fighting pirates, and wondered if this had been an omen. However, there would be no fine lady at her side in this battle.

Back on deck, she could see that the pirate ship was much nearer and heaving to. The captain was ordering the crew about, readying them for the fight. He looked at Jack.

"You want to fight too, lad?" he laughed, but Jack was quite serious. "Very well. If you wish to be of service, take the Governor to the hold and hide him there until we have seen off these villains. He would earn them a handsome ransom, so see to it that he remains safe."

Jack would have liked to be set a more daring mission, but the captain had moved on to issuing orders to other members of the crew. She ran below to the Governor's cabin and rapped loudly on the door. She had not the time to wait for a response and entered. The Governor, who had been in his bunk throughout the entire storm, appeared too ill to move. Jack was taken aback by how thin and pale he looked.

"The captain wants you below," Jack informed them.

"The Governor is too ill to be moved." The manservant stood in Jack's way.

"Nevertheless, he will come below with me." Jack had no time to argue. She could hear shouts from above. She pushed the manservant aside and went to the Governor's bunk.

"I said..." The manservant pulled at her shoulder, but at that moment there was a loud report and the ship rocked violently.

"We are about to be boarded by pirates," Jack hissed at him. "Help me to get him to the hold."

The manservant needed no second telling. Between them, they carried the Governor to the hold and propped him up behind the harpsichord. There was more shouting from above, and another explosion that sent a shudder throughout the hull of the ship.

Jack was worried for the Governor. If they found him, they would surely kill him or, worse, take him as a hostage and demand ransom. If he looked more like an ordinary sailor, maybe they would spare his life. Sitting slumped as he was he looked more drunk than ill. That gave Jack an idea, and she left, quickly returning with clothes she had taken from the crew's quarters and a liberal ration of rum from the stores. The clothes were vile and stank, with many days' sweat on them, but they fitted after a fashion. She liberally dosed the Governor with rum, and splashed some on his clothes to support the thought that he be a drunkard. The alcohol actually roused him a little, but only long enough for him to complain of his new attire. She brought also a change of clothes for the manservant and turned her back as he reluctantly donned them.

The sounds from above had increased – more shouting, and it was coming nearer. Jack hated being below when there was the prospect of a good fight on deck, but Sir Robert had charged her with the safekeeping of the Governor, so she would remain where she was and do her assigned duty as best she could. She gave the manservant her dagger, who told her that his name was James Winters, and that he had no idea how to use a knife at all.

Above them was much crashing and more shouting, a fight in full cry. Jack sent up a silent prayer to preserve the lives of the captain and crew, Harry especially, though she knew him to be a fine swordsman and one who would give even the fiercest pirate a good seeing-to. Another explosion sounded and the ship pitched wildly, throwing them all about the hold. From the shouting that followed, Jack knew the hull must have been breached and that they had to get out before they were drowned.

She and James dragged the Governor up the stairs again. They were met near the top by a savage-looking fellow with an eye patch and a wild head of hair. He laughed when he saw the motley trio.

"Rats up from the hold?" He lunged at Jack, who was nearest. Jack parried with her sword and reached for her dagger to run him through, only to remember she had given it to James. James noticed her panic, and thrust the dagger towards her. At that moment, the ship pitched again, and James reeled. By happy chance, the dagger pierced the pirate's leg. He fell past them, screaming and clutching his injured limb. Jack jumped down after him, finished him off with her sword and retrieved her dagger. She also relieved him of his sword and passed it up to James.

There was another pirate before them now but, on seeing his slain companion, he backed off. He was a stout man with a scar across half his face. His eyes flashed and he grinned, sizing them up, clearly thinking they were merely lucky to have killed his mate and would not be so again.

"You should have stayed down there," he spat through blackened teeth. "I hear drowning's a pretty death." He brought his sword down with surprising speed, as if to slice Jack though the middle. Jack met the sword with her own and, by flicking her wrist sharply, she dislodged the pirate's sword. It was a trick Harry had taught her. The pirate roared his frustration and, grabbing his dagger, made to lunge at Jack. Jack swung to the side and pushed James and the Governor out of the way. The pirate went tumbling down the steep stairs into the belly of the ship.

The ship rolled again, giving Jack no time to enjoy her victory. She climbed the last few steps to the deck, calling James after her. As Jack put her head up, her reflexes, ever her friend, saved her once more. She ducked as a blade flashed above her.

"Sorry!" It was Harry. "I saw the rascals go below; I thought you was them returning." He pulled Jack up on to the deck and helped James and the Governor climb up. Just as he was straightening up, a pirate of huge stature launched himself at Harry, and they fell to the deck. Jack danced about them, ready to put in her sword, but the two combatants writhed about so much, she could not be sure of not striking her friend.

Besides, she had her own fight. A small, wiry lad jumped in front of her and presented his sword. He looked to be no more than sixteen years and, despite trying hard to look fierce, he had one of the sweetest faces Jack had ever seen. She was loath to kill someone so young, but knew that if she did not kill him he would surely kill her. She raised her sword in answer to his but, before they could engage, the ship gave an almighty lurch, and they were both sent flying over the rail and into the water.

Jack landed with a splash and reached out about her for something to keep her afloat. She had learnt to swim while in Jamaica, but there the waters were as warm as a bath; here, they were as cold as London in winter. She saw some planking that had been blasted from the side of the *St Michael*, and pulled herself on to it. Looking about her from the vantage of her improvised raft, she spied the lad, thrashing about in panic. She reached out with the handle of her sword and pulled him aboard. He collapsed, coughing and gasping, very like a newly-caught fish.

Coughing herself, Jack saw a body she thought she recognised in the water close to, floating face down. She slipped off the raft and swam to it. It was Harry. She dragged him back to the make-shift raft and pushed him up on to it. He coughed once and then lay still.

Their ship was nearby and sinking rapidly, its stern high in the air. Men were climbing up beyond the forecastle, clinging to the railings. Jack saw James there, and the Governor. The pirates seemed to have all returned to the safety of their own ship. She could hear their cheering, but could barely see them for all the smoke.

Jack pulled herself again on to the raft and watched as the *St Michael* gracefully surrendered herself to the sea. She watched as the men lost their precious grip and disappeared into the water. She had kept her eye on the Governor and the manservant and manoeuvered the raft around to where she had last seen them. To her relief, they both bobbed back up to the surface, fighting to stay afloat. Once again, she left the safety of the raft and pushed first one and then the other up on to it.

There was little room, and the weight of the four bodies threatened to sink the small section of planks. Jack stayed in the water, holding on to the side. The pirate lad had begun to recover himself and, although very scared, helped Jack steer the raft towards the pirate ship.

"Jack," James hissed. "We cannot go there; they will surely kill us."

"Better a quick death at their hands than a slow one with the sea monsters."

James was the first one up the ladder the pirates had lowered over the side of their ship. He was met with a fist in the face and the flat edge of a sword over his back as he fell to the deck. Jack lifted the pirate lad up so he could reach the ladder, and waited for him to reach the top. His appearance was greeted with cheers of approval and only when he beckoned her up did she risk the climb, hauling the Governor up after her. Harry was sufficiently recovered to climb himself, for which Jack was very grateful – she could barely hold the Governor, and he was a man of very small stature.

The pirate crew was gathered, and eyed Jack and the Governor with suspicion. Jack had heard endless tails of pirates and expected to see a much fiercer assortment of men than those she now faced. They were rough, truly, but not fearsome and obviously not invincible in battle, for she had felled two of their number. In fact, they looked not much different from the crew of her former ship, lately sunk.

"So?" A tall, well-dressed man stepped forward and addressed her. "What have we here?"

"That's the one what saved my life, Cap'n." The pirate lad pointed at Jack.

"Indeed."

Jack was not comfortable with the scrutiny. She doubted the Governor's disguise would fool anyone for very long, and she prayed that James would not regain consciousness soon, for the first word out of his mouth would betray him as a landlubber. Harry was leaning heavily on the railings, and Jack noticed for the first time that he was bleeding from a large wound in his side.

"What have you to say for yourself?" The captain was quite a young man and from an area in the north of England, from the sound of his speech. Jack wondered if he were a pirate of great renown, then realised that he had been addressing her and waiting for an answer.

"I was loathe to see him drown," she said. "A sorry end for any sailor."

"But you would have run him through."

"If he had left me no alternative." Jack did not want to boast, but she had been brought up to tell the truth, if only in the small things.

The captain and crew laughed.

"You think highly of yourself for one so young." The captain took a sword from one of his crew, and Jack thought her end had come. Instead of running her through with it, he tossed it to her. Jack realised that she had lost her own sword somewhere in the water.

"Let us see if your sword play is half as fine as your words."

He drew his own sword and presented it to Jack. She was wet and cold, exhausted from her swimming and the battle before it. She could barely force her fingers to close round the unfamiliar handle of the stranger's sword, but she knew this was the most important fight of her short existence. Her life and the lives of several others depended on her. So, she swung the sword once in front of her to get the feel of its weight and action. It was heavier than she would have liked, but she did not have time to worry about that. The captain lunged at her and she parried quickly. The captain lunged again and Jack jumped out of the way, spinning as she did, and brought the sword over sharply above the captain's head. He barely got his sword up in time to block the blow. He nodded his approval at the move and then lunged again. Jack stepped back and to the side; she was near the main mast, and wondered if she might use it to her advantage.

She worked the fight towards it, letting the captain think he had the upper hand. She felt the mast at her back and the captain laughed, thinking he had her there. He lunged hard, as if to pin her by the heart to the mast, but she ducked out of the way, kicking out as she did, and left the captain sprawled on the deck, the sword embedded in the wood.

The captain reached for his dagger but it wasn't there – lost in the preceding battle. Jack crouched beside the mast, her sword in one hand, her dagger in the other. For a moment, everything was completely still and silent. Jack did not take her eyes off the captain's face but she could not tell his thoughts. The crew were mute and still, as if not sure what to do. Jack could have, at that moment, run the captain through, but she knew she would not have lived long to enjoy her victory. The fight had been about proving her worth, not killing the captain, though she knew that he would not have hesitated to kill her if she had given him the opportunity to do so.

She saw him nod, and felt someone take her from behind and hold her fast. She did not struggle; she was too worn through, and knew there was no use in it. Her eyes stayed on the captain's face. He would be embarrassed to lose the fight to one he thought so young. If he had did not have good command of his crew, this would be fatal for Jack. She prayed that he was a fair-minded man, and fond of the lad she had saved.

The wait seemed interminable. The silence stretched out eerily around her, and all she could hear were the creaking of the ship's timbers and the wind rattling the gaffs. The captain slowly rose from the deck, stepped up to the mast and removed his sword. Only once he had returned it to its sheath did he turn to Jack.

"If only more of your crew had fought as you do, you would still have a ship." He took the sword from Jack's hand and put the tip of it to her throat. Jack tried not to flinch at the feel of the cold metal on her skin. If this was how her life were to end, she wished it to end with as much dignity as she could find.

"Take them below." The sword was whipped from her neck so fast that Jack could not tell whether she had been cut of not.

She was bundled down the stairs, and then down again. She was pushed hard into the hold and stumbled against something in the dark, falling to the floor. Harry followed with the Governor, and the still-unconscious James was slung in after. The hatch was closed and they were alone.

Jack was chilled to her bones and weary beyond anything she had known before; even so, she could not sleep. Harry moaned. Jack felt her way over to him and examined his wound as best she could in the dark. She ripped a strip from her shirt and bound it up, trying to stop the slow trickle of blood which seeped therefrom.

The Governor whimpered like some injured animal. Jack told him to hold his noise if he wanted to get out of this alive, and then examined James. He was still breathing, seeming more asleep now than unconscious. Jack curled up beside him and tried to banish all thought of what might next befall them. She fell into a fitful slumber.

9

The Deal

The compromise Elizabeth proposed involved her going to sea. Yes, she had set her *mind* on going to sea. Of course, her husband wouldn't hear of such a thing.

"Women onboard a ship bring bad luck."

Elizabeth laughed – fustian! A silly superstition. They were wont to say the same about women in the theatre and now all manner were performing and the world had not stopped turning. No more theatres than usual had burned down. She would dress as a boy, of course; she was tall enough and broad across the shoulders. She had no need to stay here in England, for Mary would be well looked after, as would her father. Elizabeth knew she would go mad left alone in the big house, with no one for company but the chattering wives of the other sea captains.

Her husband stomped about the dining room, shouting at any of the servants who dared to show their faces. Elizabeth sat and held the locket, the key to her new future. She was elated by the idea of going to sea, excited and fearful at the same time, more alive than she could ever remember feeling.

"We will say I have been taken ill and had to –" she paused to consider, then continued "– go to the new spa at Bath to take the curative waters."

"No."

She was thinking of what she might wear, having long envied men the freedom their britches gave them. She could see herself learning to handle a sword, and suddenly remembered the dream of the pirate battle.

"Then I will join another ship, and my locket and I will go to sea with them."

Her husband regarded her with total disbelief. Elizabeth clicked the secret catch on the locket, let it spring open, and then shut it again quickly as the captain rushed to see its contents. He banged his fist upon the table, making the remaining breakfast covers jump. Elizabeth did not flinch; she knew he would have to give in to her wishes presently. She had something he coveted very much indeed. He knelt in front of her.

"This plan of yours is madness, my dear. It can lead to only one thing, a violent and bloody death for us both. Surely you would not wish that upon yourself."

Elizabeth knew that the alternative would be a long life of tedium and thwarted dreams. Her mother had said it herself; Elizabeth was the one who would discover the secret of the locket. She felt it was her destiny, and more than anything else of which she might be sure, she was sure of that.

"Captain Montague sets sail in one week also. I hear he is looking for a cabin boy." She smiled sweetly at her husband.

"No!" He took her hand and pleaded, but his eyes did not look up into hers; once more, they fixed upon the locket, as if they could look nowhere else.

"The junior footman is nearly my height, I could wear his clothes."

The captain sprang to his feet. "I forbid you!" He strode from the room, and Elizabeth heard the heavy front door open and then slam shut. She sat still for a moment, feeling the excitement rise within her, but wondering if she might not have provoked him beyond recall.

Mary came hurrying into the room, looking distraught.

"Oh, Mistress, are you well? The maids last night were telling me the captain has a fearsome temper, and I heard shouting."

"As you can see, I am perfectly well," Elizabeth said as calmly as she could. "But come, I need you to help me dress." She realised she was still in her slammerkin. They returned to the bedroom together.

In the more familiar surroundings, Mary relaxed. She smiled at Elizabeth. "And how did you fare last night?" she whispered and giggled. Elizabeth knew she would want to know all. She could scarce tell her the truth, that nothing had happened. She took Mary by the shoulders and threw her back on to the bed.

"He took me thus," she said and laid her body on top of Mary's. "He kissed me tenderly and looked into my eyes with a most deep affection." She kissed Mary on the lips, feeling their soft warmth. She slid her tongue along Mary's teeth until they opened and Mary's tongue came out to greet her own. The two tongues played their own game of kiss and chase. Elizabeth broke off.

From deep within her she felt an anger rising, an anger that she had been denied the sweet pleasure that should have been hers by the man who was supposed to give it.

"Then he grasped my breast and pulled firmly upon my nipple." She did so to Mary with one hand, and with the other, pulled up the skirt of Mary's dress. "His hands were hungry and swift." She reached under Mary's petticoats and cupped her mound. Even without inserting a finger, she could tell that Mary was wet and wanting her. Mary's breathing was shallow and fast and her eyes wide, watching every move that Elizabeth made.

"He asked me if I was ready for him and I nodded, too excited to utter a word. Then he unbuttoned his britches and, with one hand, produced his manhood. It was so beautiful, Mary; I could scarce stop myself from reaching out to touch it." Elizabeth found herself close to tears; all she had hoped for on her wedding night, all she had dreamed and feared and longed for had come to nought.

"But he could contain himself no longer." Elizabeth continued, angry at herself for harbouring such foolish notions and angry at Mary for engendering them. "He thrust his straining member into me." She thrust three fingers up inside Mary, and Mary gasped with their sudden entry and force.

"Again and again, he thrust into me." Elizabeth pushed her fingers as hard as she could in and out of Mary.

"Again and again, deeper and deeper, until I thought I would burst." Elizabeth was crying now, tears flowing down her cheeks, but she still did not stop. Mary was writhing under her, gasping and moaning, clutching at the sheets. Elizabeth thrust her hand in and out, her thumb brushing against the round button of flesh that Mary loved her to touch so much.

Mary's breathing was now high-pitched and short. Her body was gathering itself in, and Elizabeth knew that the fever within her was about to break. She thrust one last time, adding her little finger and pressing her thumb hard into the fleshy button. Mary cried out, howling like some wild animal, and her body bucked. Then she lay still, with little shudders running though her body. Mary was crying now, too, tears running down her cheeks and forming pools in her ears.

Elizabeth removed her fingers, which sent more shuddering throughout Mary's body, and then lay down beside her and held her tightly. Their tears mixed, salt rivers running together.

"He slept on the chair," Elizabeth managed to say when they were both quieter. "He did not even kiss me." Mary stroked her hair.

"The servants say they were surprised he married. He is not a woman's man."

Elizabeth sat up and looked at her. She did not understand.

"They say he is... a boy's man."

Elizabeth stood up. "But why then..." She was about to ask about the marriage, when her locket bumped against her chest. She sighed.

"The junior footman is his present favourite."

Now Elizabeth's mind became clear. She remembered the way he had watched him dance with Mary. So, his look *had* been one of lust, but not for Mary as she had thought at the time. Elizabeth was angry again. Her tears dried up at once, and she began to plot a terrible revenge. A marriage of convenience would have suited her well, if the captain had been man enough to suggest it. She would have agreed, but he had made pretence, with vows of love and promises of a happy wedded life. Well, she would pay him out for his cowardly deception. She would take advantage of his absence and put her plan into immediate action. Her mind was made up.

"Mary, go and find the junior footman and tell him the captain wishes to see him, and bring him up here."

"But the captain is out, and the others say he will be gone all day. He always is when he is in a taking."

"All the better. Now go, and be quick about it."

Mary left, but sulkily. Elizabeth hoped she do as she was bid. She went to the captain's dressing room and selected one of his frock coats and a pair of britches. They were too large for her, but with the curtains drawn and the lamps low, she hoped they would do. She pulled the britches on and felt the rub of the material between her legs. She took a step and stopped; she could not walk, as she normally would, with small steps. She took another step as a man might do; legs wider, stride longer. She smiled to herself. It felt most right, so much more natural to her. She put on the coat; it was far heavier than any of her own bodices and shawls, and the tails came past her knees and swung and she walked. She would have liked to swagger around the room, trying out these new clothes and how they made her feel, but she had work to do and very little time in which to get it done. So, she drew the curtains, sat down and, with her husband's dagger, set about carving what she hoped would be the instrument of her salvation.

She had only just finished her work when there was a tapping at the door. It was too heavy to be Mary's. With her heart racing, she went to the door and opened it, positioning herself behind it so she could not be seen clearly.

It was the junior footman.

"Stay where you are and face about," she ordered in as close an imitation of her husband's voice as she could fashion. He did so.

Elizabeth stepped out and closed the door. "Don't turn around," she said, and tied a length of material around his head covering his eyes. He tried to protest but she bade him keep still. Once the blindfold was secured, she led him back into the bedchamber to the edge of the bed, and directed him to take down his britches. He did so, and bent over before she had to tell him to, reaching out to grasp the posts of the bed to hold himself steady. Clearly, he had done this many times before. Elizabeth then picked up the instrument upon which she had been working. From a thick candle, she had fashioned a manhood, as close as she could remember from the diagrams she had seen in her father's journals. It appeared to be impossibly big, its diameter almost as wide as her wrist, and she worried that it might not be of her husband's size, do some damage or even melt once inside the human body. But it was all she had to hand, and she was curious to see if it would do the job for which she had fashioned it.

She approached the bare bottom and was struck by its hairiness. Other bottoms she had encountered had been smooth and as bare as the faces to which they had belonged.

"Please, Master," the lad whispered. "Please, I am ready."

Elizabeth thought this to be an impertinence and slapped his bottom for it.

"Yes, Master," the boy sighed.

Elizabeth took a deep breath and laid one hand upon his now-red bottom. She held the wax manhood in her other hand and inserted the tip into the lad's hole.

"Oh, yes, Master," the boy panted.

Elizabeth pushed and the manhood slid in deeper.

"Oh, Master, you are so big today. That feels most good."

"Silence!" Elizabeth slapped him again. She found that she was perspiring, and her hands were shaking slightly. Her breathing had quickened and so had that of the lad. She moved the manhood in and out a little, and the boy groaned. She moved it faster.

"Oh, yes, Master!"

His knuckles were white against the bedposts in his effort to remain still.

Elizabeth increased the speed and depth of her thrusting. She could not have imagined how excited she would feel, to have this level of power over another human being, and for them to be enjoying it.

"Again, Master," the boy was saying, and, for a moment, Elizabeth could not guess his meaning so she slapped his up-turned bottom.

"Yes, Master," he groaned, "yes, Master."

Elizabeth pumped with the manhood harder and faster and, when she thought it necessary, she slapped the bottom hard. The boy could no longer keep himself still, but was moving with Elizabeth, so as to force the wax manhood deeper into himself. He put a hand down upon himself as well. Soon, he cried out and collapsed on to the bed.

Elizabeth removed the wax phallus, and was pleased to see that it had maintained most of its shape. She was distracted by footsteps outside the door and remembered her task.

"Now it is your turn," she said to the lad, who was still slumped against the bed.

"But, Master..."

"I wish for you to enter me."

This had obviously not happened before.

"Master..." He sounded unsure and excited at the same time.

"Truly." Elizabeth was growing impatient; she was worried that her husband had returned and she would not have enough time in which to complete her plan. She rolled the boy over and pulled him on to the bed. He reached out a hand to touch her, and she slapped it out of the way.

"You are not to touch, or I needs must tie you to the bed." She noticed that his penis, which had been loose and languid, regained some of its size. "So, that would please you?" she asked.

"Yes, Master."

Elizabeth heard footsteps again, and decided there would not be time. "Then I will not do it. Lie back." She pushed his body down on to the bed. She took off her britches, and knelt above the boy, one knee either side of his slim hips. His penis appeared to have recovered its full size. She grasped it in one hand and the boy groaned.

"Oh, Master, I have longed for this but did not dare hope..."

The footsteps stopped outside the door. Then she heard two voices, her husband's and Mary's. She guided the boy's penis up into her, and then lowered her body to take more of it inside. It felt a little uncomfortable at first but she moved around until it was not. The boy was concentrating hard, moving his hips, setting up a rhythm as she had done with the wax phallus.

"Oh, yes, you are so moist. Am I like that for you?" The lad reached for her waist to steady her, and as they touched, he pulled away as if she were too hot. "Master?" He paused in his rhythm. Elizabeth took it up, raising and lowering her body until the boy had forgotten his question.

"Oh, dear and gracious God!" the boy cried out, close to his climax.

"Not yet," she whispered in her own voice. She reached forward and removed the blindfold. His eyes flew open and he gazed upon Elizabeth with a mixture of wonder and horror, joy and dismay, but he was so close to his climax he did not want to stop and, with a wild grunt and great shudder, he came.

At that very moment, the door was thrown open and the captain stormed in. He marched up to the bed, then stopped straightway when he saw who it was Elizabeth had underneath her. The lad tried to get up but was trapped between Elizabeth's thighs, his penis still inside her. Elizabeth was still breathing hard from her efforts, and the sight of her apoplectic husband staring at her excited her more than she thought possible. She rubbed herself rapidly as he looked on, and in a matter of seconds reached her own peak and came. Her body filled with miraculous waves as relief washed over her.

"So, husband," she said to the still-motionless captain when she had recovered her breath, but remained sitting above the boy. "I thought I would see for myself who it was who pleasured you more than your wife." She raised herself, and let the boy's penis slip out of her; it made a loud sucking noise. She climbed off him and stepped off the bed. "He is rather entertaining."

The junior footman was hunting around the bed for something with which to cover himself. His eyes were full of terror. "I did not know," he muttered, "I thought..." He would not look at either of them.

"Get out!" The captain shouted at him, and pointed to the door. The lad fled, dragging with him the cover off the bed. The captain watched him go and then turned back to Elizabeth.

"As for yourself..." He looked threatening. "I... I..."

"What, pray?" she asked, not caring what he thought of her. "You would not have me." She pulled his jacket close around her. "Nor will you give me what I want, but now you can see I am perfectly capable of taking that which I desire. Mary has made some enquiries and I am to leave with Captain Montague next week." It was a lie but the resultant effect was all she could have wished.

"No!" The captain struck the bedpost with his fist. Then he said again, "No," but with less force this time. He sank on to the bed and held his head in his hands. Elizabeth almost felt sorry for him.

"Then you will not get your treasure." She turned as if to leave.

Mary was there, hovering by the open door; behind her, a few curious members of staff peered over her shoulder.

The captain looked up and noticed. "Get them out of here!" he roared. "And close that door."

After the door closed there was a long pause. Elizabeth held herself very still, hardly daring to breathe.

Finally, the captain spoke, in bitter and defeated tones. "Very well. You may come to sea, but I warn you now, it will be hard. You will have no maid, there is little water for washing, and the food is poor at its best, rotten at its worst. There are rats in every cabin, including the captain's, and if they discover you to be a girl I will feign ignorance and watch with pleasure as they throw you overboard, after doing whatever they fancy with you first!"

Elizabeth shuddered at the last of his warnings but she would not let anything stop her. She had won the right to go to sea; her excitement would not let her hear anything more.

"We sail in six days." The captain stood and left.

She did not see him again until she boarded the ship.

The next days passed in a whirl of activity. Elizabeth let it be known that she was not well and was leaving for Bath. Only Mary was told the truth, and she wept bitter tears at the thought of losing her mistress. She clung to Elizabeth and begged her not to go, howling about how she had heard stories of the monsters that lived under the seas and the things they did to sailors. She repeated tale of pirates and ghosts that the cook had told her to scare her, until Elizabeth grew so tired of her that she sent her away early to Mrs Mathers' house, who had agreed to look after her and Elizabeth's father in her absence. It took some persuading and much explanation over why Elizabeth was not taking her with her but, in the end, Mrs Mathers had to agree that perhaps she would not be the best nurse for someone who was gravely ill.

Elizabeth did not relish having to lie to people she loved and who trusted her. She felt especially sorrowful about lying to her father, whose eyes filled with fear as he stood by her bed and held her hand. She longed to tell him the truth, but knew he would try and stop her, for the adventure she had set her heart on was a strange and dangerous one and she knew not how long she would be away or, indeed, if she would ever return. So, she hugged her father harder than an invalid in her condition should have and then sent him away.

The morning they were to set sail, she left the house in the captain's carriage, wrapped in rugs, with her face powdered to cover her glowing good health. The carriage set off for Bath, but then turned and headed for Deptford where the captain's ship was preparing to set sail. In the privacy of the carriage, she untied the bundle of clothes Mary had stolen from the junior footman. She had dressed in front-lacing stays so that she could now undo these herself. She found the length of material she had requested from an unsuspecting Rose. It was a fine, soft Chinese silk, its colour close to the colour of her own skin. This she bound around her breasts for, though not large, they were fuller than any lad's chest would be. Once they were bound, and the silk tied off, she pulled on a loose cotton shirt with long sleeves. She loosed the ties of her skirt and petticoats and slipped on the black, knee-length britches. Once again, she felt the strange sensation of material between her legs and the freedom of movement this allowed her. She wanted to shout and laugh as she kicked off her skirt.

There were some cotton hose and short leather boots. The boots were too big, and so she tore some strips off one of her petticoats to fill their toes. To complete the outfit, there was a short heavy jacket, not as smart as the one she had worn, but it fitted the part she was about to play. The clothes felt so good on her, so right. She felt as if she had been wearing them all of her life, or certainly should have been.

To complete the conversion from gentlewoman to cabin boy,

she cut her thick, red hair with the little dagger Mary had insisted she take with her. As she watched the curls fall to the floor of the carriage, she could not stop the tears welling up inside her. Whether they were tears of joy or sorrow, she could not tell, and she did not let them linger long. By the time she reached the docks, she had recovered herself and was able to slip from the carriage with a smile and jaunty step.

"Cabin boy Eli Smith reporting," she told the boatswain, who was ticking off his list at the bottom of the gangplank of the *Juno*, Martin's commission.

The man barely looked at her. "Captain's cabin, then," he said, and she fairly skipped aboard, revelling in the freedom of movement that not wearing stays and layers of petticoats gave her. She saw her husband in conversation with some men by the wheel. She sauntered over.

"Cabin boy Eli Smith reporting for duty, sir," she said, and saluted her husband.

He looked up and, for a moment, he did not recognise her. Then his eyes clouded over.

"Get into the cabin, Smith, and do not come out until I tell you that you may!" he snapped at her.

She saluted again, keeping in the laughter that was bubbling up inside her until she was out of sight. The ship was bigger than she had thought it would be, and it took her a few wrong turns before she found the captain's cabin. She was impressed by its size and decor. Before she had time to explore it properly, her husband was there.

"For the love of God, madam," he hissed at her, "Change your mind, I beg you! Give me the locket and leave the ship. Only disaster and despair will come of this."

Elizabeth smiled and shook her head.

"I could have you killed in your sleep, take the locket and throw your body overboard and no one would be any the wiser." Elizabeth had thought of this.

"Except your mother."

"My mother?"

"I was not so foolish as to bring the locket with me. I committed the lines of it to memory and left the locket itself in your mother's care, with instructions that if I do not return, it is to be destroyed." Only part of this was true. Elizabeth had committed the locket's contents to memory, but had found she could not bear to leave it behind. She now wore it strapped between her breasts.

The captain, however, believed her story, and he stomped from the cabin. Elizabeth hugged herself; she had never felt so free. She wanted to climb to the top of the main mast and shout out her joy.

She went back on to deck. The crew were busy; some were stowing the last of the cargo, others were standing by, ready to cast off, while others were standing to the sheets, as she heard them call the ropes, ready to haul away and unfurl the sails. A small crowd had gathered to see them off. Elizabeth remembered the last ship she had seen set sail and the lad, Jack, standing on the deck. They had been bound for Jamaica, too. She wondered for a moment if they might meet there. She smiled to herself and found that she would quite like that.

The ship cast off her moorings and was moving down the river on the tide. Elizabeth had never send the river looking as beautiful as it did now. With the sun on the water, and Greenwich slipping past them, she wondered for a moment if she might truly be suffering with an ague, to wish to leave it all behind. For a moment, she doubted herself and her mission, but it was too late. They were off and there was no turning back. She closed her eyes and turned her face to the sun and prayed as she had never prayed before.

10

A Pirate's Life

Jack slept on and off and could not tell how long they were kept in the hold. She thought they would all perish there from thirst and hunger. Neither the Governor nor Harry were well and, but for the pirate lad sneaking down some rum, they might have lost both.

After an unknown number of days and nights, the hatch above them was thrown open and Jack was called out. She stood blinking on the deck in the bright sunshine.

"Are you hungry, lad?" The captain stood by the helm, smiling broadly. Jack nodded. Her stomach was painful for lack of food. "Would you like to eat?"

There was nothing Jack would have liked more, but then she thought of her companions still in the hold. "If my shipmates may, also," she said.

The captain raised an eyebrow. "And if the meal were only for one?"

"Then I should share it," she answered without hesitation, and meant it.

"Indeed." The captain looked around at his crew. "Do you think he lies?" He asked no one in particular.

"No." It was the pirate lad whom Jack had rescued who answered.

"Would he make a good pirate?" The captain directed this question at the lad.

"We know he can fight," one of the older hands answered, as if to remind the captain of his sword fight with Jack. Jack was sure he did not need reminding.

"Would you like to be a pirate?" The captain turned back to Jack, smiling.

She had heard of decent, honest sailors turning to piracy, but had never thought of it for herself.

"The wages are a share of the loot should we capture any, and your own time is your own time."

She had her dream of buying some land, but she knew it was only a dream, and what did she know of growing crops? The sea she did know, and the thought of sailing around the warm seas of the Indies for the rest of her life was a tempting one, especially if the alternative was to be put overboard. However, she did want to know that she had a choice in the matter; having once been press-ganged, she did not wish to be again.

"And if I refuse?"

The captain shrugged. "We only take willing volunteers. Well?" he prompted when Jack did not answer.

"The alternative being death?" Jack needed to know.

"Don't be so stubborn, boy." The captain was losing his patience. "We would put you ashore somewhere and you could do what you would."

"Very well," Jack said, and then added, in case the captain had not understood her, "I will join."

The captain still looked a little annoyed.

"I like to know that I have a choice," Jack said to explain her reluctance.

"And your mates below?"

Jack laughed at the idea of the Governor becoming a pirate. "Harry might, should he live, but the other two, they are not good sailors."

"No." The captain held out his hand to Jack. "I'm Captain Silk."

Jack gripped his hand. "Jack," she said.

"Welcome aboard, Jack." He slapped her on the back. "Food, then?"

Harry, weak but on the mend, was fetched from the hold. He was only too keen to join up with Jack. A space was found in the crew's quarters for them, and hammocks were set up in the hold for James and the Governor to make the rest of the journey more comfortable. The Governor was less than grateful.

"Do they know who I am?" he demanded.

"No," Jack said with more patience than she felt. "That is why you are still alive and will soon be free."

James was concerned by their decision to join the pirates. "The Governor means to wipe the region clean of pirates. You will end up hung or worse."

"But rich," Harry laughed, his colour and strength improving as he ate.

They learned that were only a few days off the coast of Jamaica, and the Governor and James were kept below deck. Jack visited them every day, taking rum and rations. The Governor had taken quite a liking to the rum, which was as well, for it kept him quiet, though somewhat maudlin.

Jack managed to copy a map of the island for James so that they would be able to find their way to civilisation once they were put ashore. They were rowed in one morning at dawn, and Jack wondered if she would ever see them again. She doubted anyone would believe the Governor was who he claimed to be, soused as he was when he left the ship, but James seemed to have everything under control. Jack prayed that they would be safe. She had developed quite a fondness for James, even if she could not warm to the Governor.

Life on the pirate ship was not so very different than it had been on any other ship. Brass still needed polishing and sails mending. Jack and Harry made themselves useful, and Jack found that wherever she happened to be, Pip, the cabin boy, was usually there, too. When he followed Jack up to the crow's nest one day, however, Jack's patience began to falter.

"Yes, Pip, what need ye?" Jack asked.

"I'm not the captain's boy, you know."

Jack looked puzzled.

"I mean to say, I am his cabin boy, but not his 'boy'."

Jack still did not comprehend.

"I could be your boy." The lad reached out his hand and touch the wooden phallus through Jack's trousers. "Do not say you do not know what I mean. You are hard for me already."

"But I..." Jack started, but was not allowed to continue, for the lad had started kissing her with firmer kisses than the women had bestowed upon her. His hands played up and down her phallus, and he rubbed his own hardening manhood against her leg.

Jack pushed him away, though she did not want to offend her new friend. "Pip, I have never... "

The lad looked at her in astonishment. "But your..." Pip pointed to her phallus.

Jack thought of all the times it had led her into trouble. She could have told Pip the same story she had told Harry and Anne, but she did not know if he would so easily believe her.

She sighed. There appeared to be no other remedy. "You will have to show me what to do."

Pip smiled shyly and laughed. He was a pretty boy, with blonde hair, bleached lighter by his time at sea. His face was fresh, rosy cheeked, and the skin under his shirt was as smooth and hairless as any girl's. He undid his britches and dropped them to reveal a small, slim penis, fully erect. He turned and presented Jack his bottom, also smooth and hairless.

There was little space in the crow's nest and Jack did not have the heart for what she knew Pip wanted her to do. She moved her phallus so it lay between her legs.

"There is not enough room here," she said, and pulled Pip's britches back up for him. "And it is too open a place," she added, though, in truth, no one would be able to see them from the deck. "I have lost my will."

Pip turned and looked hard, but could not see the phallus. He sighed. "But you will. I could..." He tried to kneel before Jack, but there was no room.

"No, pray you."

Pip looked very disappointed. "Come down to the cabin. The captain will be on watch all night and we could do it there."

"I am on lookout here." It was not exactly a lie, and Pip had to believe her; why else would anyone climb all that way?

"Later?" Pip asked.

Jack sighed again, and Pip took it for regret. He kissed her again. "Later then," he said, and climbed down.

Fortunately for Jack, their arrival in Port Royal prevented the need for further play-acting.

They said you could smell Port Royal before you could see it but Jack knew this not to be true. In the summer, when the day was still, it could stink to the very heavens but, with a breeze and good shower of rain, the noxious haze always cleared quickly away. The jagged red mountains on the other side of the harbour stood out like old men's teeth, while the Blue Mountains shimmered in the distance. It was a town that Jack had grown to love and had not thought to see again.

The captain called Jack to his cabin as they were preparing to dock. Jack was worried that Pip had said something, or that she would not be allowed ashore. She was surprised to see Harry already there, getting drunk on the pirate's good rum.

"Your friend Harry tells me you two have a secret."

Jack thought she was surely done for; the captain would not

believe the tail of accidental amputation and would discover that she was a girl. She glared at Harry, who was smiling happily with the bottle of rum still in his hand. She wondered that he would give her secret up so easily.

"You may be more useful to us than I at first thought."

Jack tried to keep her face still but the thought of what he might request of her made her feel bodily ill.

The captain did not notice her discomfort. "There is a man on the island who claims to never have lost a fight."

"A fight?" Jack was so relieved she nearly fell over. She looked at Harry again. She should have known he would not have betrayed her, not for a bottle of rum, anyway.

"Harry says you are a mighty fighter."

"And he told you of the sleeping draught?"

The captain laughed. "Ingenious. I could wager our last haul and double it, if you are game for the venture?"

Jack would have agreed to most anything, she was so relieved. "If Harry can make some more of the draught."

"When he sobers up." The captain gave Harry a slap on the back and Harry slid from his seat on to the floor. "We will go and see this man, then."

Harry was not sober until the next morning, so Jack spent the first night in Port Royal onboard. She was eager to see if the town had changed much; she was sure it had, for it was a good few years since her last visit. She wondered if the carver was still there, and the two prostitutes, Agatha and Beatrice, to whom Harry had once taken a liking.

She roused Harry early, for that was her favourite time in the town, all the excesses of the night shut away behind closed doors. The day was not yet too hot, and the mountains were clear before the haze settled upon them.

Her first steps ashore were uneven, and she felt in the pit of her stomach the sickness she had forgotten. It was as if the land bucked and rolled underneath her.

Harry laughed on seeing her stagger. "Still got your sea legs on, lad," he shouted, shattering the quiet of the early morning. Jack smiled, for she could see him, too, struggling to walk on the land after so long at sea.

The port spread out, with neither planning nor reason, from the tip of the peninsula, and was now even encroaching upon the mainland. Harry and Jack wandered the silent streets, trying to get their barings. There were many ships moored at the docks, which made the quiet of the morning seem even more eerie. They found the Governor's mansion, standing ostentatiously behind its high fence. Jack thought for a moment about alerting someone within to the Governor's plight, before remembering she was now a pirate and, despite her efforts in rescuing him, she and the rest of her new crew could well hang for their part in his capture.

They returned to the ship around noon, when the heat of the day and the smell became too much for them. Other crew members were returning with various souvenirs of their night, a good many with black eyes and new scratches or tattoos. Some had fruit and vegetables: all had sore heads.

"Remember these?" Harry waved a bunch of bananas at Jack. She remembered them from her very first trip. There had been a lot of jokes about their shape and possible uses. Jack had not fully understood the joke, but a lot had happened to her since then.

They napped away the afternoon and, in the evening, went ashore once more to watch the fight. The captain arranged to meet them at the tavern later on. The undefeated champion was called the 'Mountain Man'. Harry laughed at such a name, but Jack knew that, in the warm climes of the West Indies, some men could grow very big indeed. They stopped at a tailor's shop on the way to have new clothes made. The tailor had materials from all over the world, some as smooth as a woman's skin. Jack felt them between her fingers and wondered what it would be like to wear a garment made of such material. There were dresses hung up, awaiting collection, for some well-to-do prostitutes, no doubt. Jack admired their fine lace and vibrant colours. She suddenly found herself longing to try them on, to see what she would look like in the clothes of her true sex.

Harry caught her looking and, misunderstanding her, laughed. "Soon enough we will see beautiful women again." He slapped Jack on the back.

They found the tavern the 'Mountain Man' fought in and, though it was still early, there was already a crowd. A fight was in progress between two men, one African and one white.

"He is not a mountain, the Africk," Harry said, as they settled into seats near the fighting space. Jack watched carefully; she and was neither impressed by the man's bulk nor his fighting skill. He, it seemed, was not the Mountain Man, for another man stood up for the next fight, and he was, indeed, by far the largest man Jack had ever seen. Standing with his head nearly touching the ceiling of the tavern, his girth was four or even five times that of Jack's.

"Well." Harry sat back in his seat. "It will take a mighty draught to knock him off his stride."

Jack could only nod in agreement. Not only was he of gigantic proportions, but he was also surprising quick around the floor. He dispatched three fighters of reasonable size and strength in a matter of minutes. Jack was impressed but, more than that, she was terrified. Harry had been watching the fighter so closely and intently that he had not touched his ale.

They watched three more fights, all as short as the first. Harry pointed out that he did not often stop to drink between the bouts, and the only thing Jack saw pass his lips was some milk given to him by his master. She also noted that, while there were a few women about the place, these did not distract him at all, as they did some fighters. The only time he momentarily lost his concentration was when a young man scampered across the space.

The last fight they watched ended with a sickening crunch, and the Mountain Man's opponent was carried quickly from the floor, his head dangling at a most unnatural angle. Captain Silk joined them in time to see this happen.

"Is the wager still on?" he asked, as if he expected the answer to be in the negative.

"I think you might lose your booty if it is," Jack said.

"Maybe so." The Captain did not look too perturbed.

"No," Harry said. They both looked at him in surprise.

"He would make eight or ten of Jack," the captain declared.

"A wager not to win, but to stay say five minutes in the fight with him." Harry appeared to be serious.

Jack took a deep breath; none of the fights they had seen had lasted close to that long.

"You would still get good odds on that." Harry seemed serious.

Silk looked at Jack. "Do you think you could do it?"

Before Jack could answer, Harry interrupted. "With my aid, he could."

"We will place that wager, then?" The question was directed at Jack. She was not sure what Harry planned. She trusted him; he had never let her down before, but... She looked over at the Mountain Man; he was so very large. She shrugged.

The captain took that to be a yes, and made off towards the fighter's master before Jack could stop him. He fell into conversation with the other man. They both turned and looked over at Jack.

"Stand up, lad," the captain called, and Jack did so.

The master laughed, and many in the place turned to look at Jack. The Mountain Man looked, too; he did not laugh, but looked deeply concerned, Jack thought. There was some further conversation, and then the man's master turned to address the tavern. An expectant hush fell amongst those gathered.

"Captain Silk here has just wagered his latest haul against his lad –" he beckoned Jack down on to the floor, and there was the sound of surprise and some laughter "– to stay in the fight five minutes with the Mountain Man."

The buzz that had started turned into a roar, and Jack worried that a riot might break out.

"Tomorrow night, last bout." The master stamped his stick, as if that made it official. The captain came over and slapped Jack on the back. "You heard the man," he said, and laughed. The place had exploded into a mass of shouting and furious stamping, not much of it in her favour, Jack thought. She looked over at the dark-skinned fighter; he looked as worried as she herself now felt, and she wondered what he could possible have to worry him. She would not show what she was feeling; she smiled and waved at the crowd, flexing her meagre muscles for them. The rowdies laughed in good humour.

Jack hoped that Harry had a good plan in mind, for it would take nothing short of a miracle for her to survive this fight with her neck intact.

11

A Cabin Boy's Life

Elizabeth loved the life at sea. She knew she was protected from the worst hardship by her position in the captain's cabin, but even when the seas were rough, and the crew rougher, she still loved it. Her husband sulked for a good week into their voyage, not looking at her or even speaking to her. But the sea air seemed to soften his demeanour, and she proved herself to be useful about the cabin and in the galley.

One bright morning, after they left the coast of Spain, Martin unfurled his waggon of maps of the Caribbee Islands and invited her to join him in the study of them.

Elizabeth looked upon the maps in wonder. There were so many islands, each beautifully figured, with trees and rocks and small dwellings placed about them. She wondered if they could truly look as strange as they were drawn. Seeing the maps, she was now convinced that the lines engraved on the inside of the locket were those of an island, but incomplete. The rest must be in the lost half of the locket.

Martin left her looking over the maps. She dared not take out the locket for fear that this was some sort of trap, and he would return suddenly and seize it before throwing her overboard. It seemed to Elizabeth an impossible task. She did not know if what she had in the locket was half the outline of a small island or a piece of a large one.

After several hours of study of the maps, she went up on to the deck to enjoy the sun and light winds. The crew were all about their various jobs, cleaning and mending, the carpenter sawing away to replace some damaged boards, while some were up in the foremast rigging, trimming the sails to give them maximum speed.

To avoid getting in the crew's way, it had become a habit of hers to climb up to the main mast crow's nest. From there, she had a view of everything going on below her. The hands working, the sea rushing past the bow of the ship, the blue sky above her and the horizon in every direction as far as she could see, empty of everything.

Later in the day, she entreated her husband, with much persuasion, to instruct her in the use of sword and dagger.

"It will be of great use if we are set upon by pirates," she argued when he stormed against the notion.

He was a surprisingly patient teacher and she was a very able student. She loved those lessons and wondered at the speed with which she gained competence. It even felt, at times, that she had been born to hold a sword. Her hands and mind seemed to know instinctively when to lunge and when to parry. She was reminded of her dream, fighting the pirates with the lad from the tavern, and wondered if at some other time, in some other life, she had not been a sword fighter.

Her days soon fell into a routine. In the mornings she would study the maps, carefully putting aside those that were somewhat similar to the lines engraved in the locket. In the afternoons, she would continue her lessons in the art of sword fighting. At first her husband taught her but, as her skill improved, he passed her over to his First Mate, a tall young man named Peter Finch.

Peter cut a dashing figure. Not only was he tall, but also well built, and he had a liking for brass buttons and shiny buckles. He had been a solider, but preferred the freedom of the sea and merchant ships. He was an excellent swordsman, having a long reach and fast reflexes. He provided Elizabeth with exercises to practice on her own; tossing coins in the air and then catching them upon the tip of her sword was one such. He would time her with his watch while she carved her name on planks of wood. He made her carry barrels across the deck and swing from the rigging to strengthen her arms and stomach. For her legs, he would make her walk with her feet in two buckets, filled with spare blocks and rope.

Elizabeth loved these exercises. She loved the feeling of her body becoming stronger and faster. She felt as though she was becoming as God had intended her to be. Where she had been clumsy at the womanly arts of needlework and painting, she discovered that she was very good at the manly arts of sword and dagger play. After only a few weeks, she was already able to offer Peter fair sport.

The crew watched her lessons with great interest, and cheered her on in her fights with Peter, for he was not popular amongst the crew. This seemed to win her their respect and where they had initially been distant and even a little hostile towards her, they now became warm and friendly. She was invited to join their card games and often was able to win herself a ration or two of rum.

Martin viewed her growing confidence with some suspicion and much reservation. He now applauded her growing skill with the sword, but warned her against becoming too familiar with the crew. He was convinced that they would discover her to be a woman.

Apart from this concern for her, he paid her little other attention. Elizabeth had hoped that, once at sea and her dressed as a boy, he might become interested in her and they could consummate their marriage and become a real husband and his wife. But the captain was preoccupied with the running of the ship and showed her no more interest than he had done before.

Elizabeth was deeply disappointed; she missed Mary and their treatment sessions. She missed Rose, too. She longed for someone to whom to be as close as she had with them. She had her carved candle with her, wrapped carefully in muslin. On some nights, she would take it out and hold it as she lay in her tiny bunk. She stroked it gently and touched herself with her fingers. She imagined Mary was there with her, and that she was using the candle on her, inserting it into her to break her fit and bring her to that calm place.

She wondered if Martin heard her breathing quicken, and what reason he gave himself for the sighs that escaped her clamped lips. She wondered if he missed his junior footman, and if he had found a replacement amongst his crew. If he had, he never brought him to the cabin, which Elizabeth rather regretted, for she thought she would like to watch and see if there were anything she might not learn from such an encounter.

She remembered the junior footman, and the excitement she had felt sliding her candle inside him. She wondered if there were someone amongst the crew who would let her do that to them. She was sure men were prone to fits, too, though perhaps not as often as women, but she thought she would like to help them as she had helped Mary.

The ship made good headway, not being heavy-laden with cargo, and having favourable following winds. They caught the tail-end of a storm some days out from Jamaica, and Elizabeth had her first taste of a rolling deck. The waves crashed over the bow and the sails were ripped by the strong winds, barrels rolled around the decks, and Martin had the helmsman lash himself to the helm. The storm's fury lasted less than twelve hours, and passed leaving the sky as blue as Elizabeth had ever seen it, and the ship with only minor damage amidships.

Despite her husband's orders for Elizabeth to remain in the cabin, she had helped the other hands where she could, tying off sheets and battening down the hatches. She was once nearly washed overboard by a wave breaking along the port side, but managed to grasp the railings and pull herself back on to the deck. The whole experience excited and enlivened her as nothing else in her life had so done. She slept that night feeling happier than she could ever remember. She was sure that this was the life she was born to live.

They docked in Port Royal two days later. Elizabeth had never seen so many ships in one place, and of such differing types: there were brigantines, barkentines, a gay little sloop with red sails, some hoys and a large, stately galleon – the biggest dragon of all – which, she later heard, with shining eyes, had arrived that very morn from the Spanish Main. She little knew that she herself was also on the Spanish Main, and was being gulled by the grinning sea dogs who spied her innocence straightway. She was used to seeing ships berthed in an orderly fashion along the wharves of the Thames, and having them named by type for her by her father when she was small. Here, they were docked in no apparent order, some double-, even triple-berthed.

It was mid-morning and hotter than Elizabeth had ever felt. The docks were nearly deserted, with men lying about in the shade of ramshackle buildings, trying to stay as cool as possible.

A stench emanated from the town beyond the docks, the like of which Elizabeth had never experienced, even near the Thames. Martin gave her dire warnings on all the evils that lurked in the town: robbers and prostitutes, con men and pick pockets. He told her not to leave the ship. He had some matters of business to see, to while the rest of the crew were free to go ashore, knowing he would face mutiny if he tried to keep them onboard.

Elizabeth sought out Peter, and found him still in his cabin.

"Why are you not yet gone ashore?" she asked.

"The town will sleep 'til sunset, then I will go and get me fill." He smiled in a lecherous way Elizabeth had not seen before.

"They say 'tis a sinful port."

"The most in Christendom." He rubbed his hands with glee. "There are women here who will take ye to Heaven or straight to Hell's depravity, whichever is your meat and drink." He grinned at Elizabeth, and she tried not to redden under his gaze.

"Have ye yet been with a woman, Eli?"

"Yes," she answered truthfully.

He laughed as if he did not believe her. "I can take you to a woman who will beat you to with an inch of your life and then suck your manhood so hard that you will think you have gone to Hell and been touched by dark angels." Peter had his hand upon his crotch. "It makes me hard just to think on it."

Elizabeth did not think she would like a lashing, nor a woman sucking on her candle, but only to be with a woman again, that would be wonderful.

"Or are you one of the captain's boys, eh?" Peter winked knowingly.

Elizabeth shook her head more ruefully than she intended.

"Ah, but you would like to be." Peter took her hand. "You are a pretty boy, and a quick learner. Maybe I could offer you lessons in another kind of sword play –" he directed her hand to his britches "– while we wait for the town to awaken." He pressed her hand hard against his bulging member, which seemed to grow under her fingers.

"A pretty mouth for a boy, too. The captain is a fool." He leaned forward and kissed her with hard lips and a thrusting tongue, while rubbing her hand back and forth over his ever-enlarging phallus. Then, with his hand on her head, he pushed her to her knees.

Elizabeth was surprised by this turn of events, but she was curious, too. She had never seen a penis at close quarters, and wondered if her candle was a good likeness of the real thing. She started unlacing Peter's trousers and freed the straining member. It was long and thin, like its owner. She touched its head and watched in amazement as it moved and jerked of its own volition. She ran her hand along its length, feeling its texture and shape. She examined its head and traced its folds with her fingers.

"Oh, Jesu," Peter groaned, and pushed her head closer to it. She realised he wanted her to suck it, as he had described the prostitute doing. Tentatively, she touched the tip with her tongue. It smelt and tasted hard and metallic, not at all like a woman's warm, welcoming aroma. Peter groaned and forced her head still closer. She took the tip in her mouth and sucked upon it gently.

"Oh, God," he gasped and pushed his hips forwards, sliding his member further into her mouth. She continued to suck, looking up at Peter's face. It had upon it the same look of concentration that Mary had often worn during their sessions. His eyes were closed and his hand upon her head was no longer pushing, but stroking her hair.

"Ye bitch," he said, but with no malice. "Ye whoreson." He appeared to be close to tears. He removed his hand from her head and began squeezing his ballsac.

"Ye'll not hurt me – suck it hard." He was scarce able to breathe now, and did not seem to be speaking to Elizabeth, but to some phantom lover he imagined to be on their knees in front of him.

Elizabeth watched in fascination as his squeezing increased in speed until she could barely see his hand moving. Of a sudden, he jerked backwards and his manhood slid from Elizabeth's mouth, and a ribbon of liquid spirited from the end of it. He slumped back on to his bunk. Elizabeth was surprised to see his manhood quickly lose its hardness and shrink in size. She would have liked to touch it again, to feel its texture in this new shape but did not wish to waken Peter, for it seemed that he had fallen asleep.

She left quietly and went back to her husband's cabin. She took her candle out of its wrapping and looked at it. Rubbing her hand along it, she was surprised at how true to life it felt. It was fatter than Peter's, and shorter in length, but she knew they must vary as their masters' own bodies varied. She longed to take it ashore and try its efficacy upon some woman. Let them take Peter's member into their bodies and then Elizabeth's waxen copy, and see if they noticed a difference. She rather thought she had more experience with women than Peter had, and she would therefore be able to give a woman more pleasure than he.

Her husband returned some time before sunset, looking very pleased with himself. He had procured some more detailed maps of the area and, from the smugness of his manner, Elizabeth guessed he had also found himself a lad.

"Was he good?" she asked tartly, emboldened by her encounter with Peter.

"Who?" Martin blushed, his guilt showing in his eyes.

"Whoever you sought relief with while your wife remained a prisoner here, hoping against all hope that you would return and use her as a husband should use his wife."

He glowered at her. "I did not ask you along on this voyage. If you are not careful I will turn you off the ship here and see if you can make a living in the port. I wager you would not get many takers."

"Oh no?" Elizabeth was angry now.

"No!" He stood with his hands upon his hips. "Shall we see, then?"

Elizabeth stood up and prepared to leave the cabin. "Peter was happy enough with my services."

The captain's face turned purple. "You whore!" he shouted, and lunged at her.

Elizabeth put her recent training to good use for the first time. She stepped sharply out of the way and, with her foot, tripped him and sent him flying on to the table that held the maps, scattering maps, instruments and all. She leapt on to his back.

"Whore, am I?" She closed her hands about his throat. He struggled under her, but she thrust her thighs into his waist, winding him. "At least I seek equality in my partners, not some poor lad who knows no better."

Martin thrashed about. Elizabeth reached out for something with which to hit him, and her hand fell upon her candle which she had left carelessly on the table. It gave her an idea. She quickly took the belt from her britches and, after a struggle, bound her husband's hands together and then to the leg of the table. He fought hard but, with her training and her anger, she had a new-found strength. When he was well secured, she pulled down his britches to reveal his bare bottom.

It was surprisingly smooth.

"In God's name, what are you doing?" he begged, fear sounding in his voice, but, curiously, also something like desire.

"Call me 'Master'," she commanded, remembering the junior footman's pleading.

"I'll call the guards!" he said. Elizabeth doubted it. No captain of a ship would want to be discovered by his own men, having been overpowered and tied, bottom bare, to a table by his own cabin boy. However, Elizabeth thought she ought not to dally with him.

She grasped the candle and touched the tip of it to her husband's hole.

"What in the Devil's name is that?"

"This is for the footman. It is what he would do to you." She pushed the candle in. Her husband gasped. "This is what it feels like," Elizabeth said as she slid it all the way in.

"Oh, God!"

"Do you wish for more?" She slid it half way out and, when he did not answer, all the way back in.

"Dear God," he said again, but this time it was a groan of pleasure, not pain.

"Do you wish for more?" Elizabeth asked again.

The captain was silent for a moment. Elizabeth paused. Then in a whisper he said, "Yes."

She felt elated. "Yes, what?" Her whole body tingled with the power she felt.

"Yes, Master."

She pulled the candle out and plunged it back in. In and out she rammed it, feeling only the power of having her husband under her and in her control.

"Yes," he cried, "oh, yes." He was moving his hips to meet her thrusts and, with her free hand, she stroked a little at his stiff manhood. His body suddenly became tense, as she had noticed with Peter and the footman, and then he reached a climax that seemed to explode from his centre.

Elizabeth pulled the candle out, and he groaned. She then unbound his hands, but he did not move for a moment. Elizabeth was suddenly worried what he would do, but he only pushed himself off the table, pulled his britches up, and walked over to the porthole and looked out, one hand leaning against the wall as if he still did not have the strength to hold himself upright.

Elizabeth busied herself by cleaning and wrapping up the candle in one of her neckerchieves. Outside, she could hear the town coming to life; shouts from the sailors, local merchants calling their wares. She thought that her husband would most certainly now throw her off his ship, and that she would somehow have to find a life there in that alien place.

For a long moment, the captain said nothing. Then, just when the tension in the cabin had grown to a point where Elizabeth thought she was going to scream, he turned to face her.

"You are never to do that again," he said, his voice low. Elizabeth nodded – she had not thought that she would.

"And I am sending you home to England on the next ship."

"No." Elizabeth looked him in the eye and held his gaze. "I need to find the treasure." She realised that if she returned to her old life in London she would die of the boredom of it. "It was my mother's dying wish."

"You cannot stay on this ship."

"Then I will find another."

"I will not allow it."

"You cannot stop me." Though Elizabeth thought he probably could.

"You are my wife."

"In name only!"

"I will tell them that you are a girl."

"And that you brought me aboard, knowing that?"

He stopped then, and their eyes locked for a long moment. It was Martin who looked away first, and Elizabeth knew then that she had won.

He took her ashore that afternoon, laughing at her unsteady gait on land, and showed her all the worst parts of the most sinful place on earth. Elizabeth gaped at the near-naked women dodging the whips of their masters in the muddy streets. She stared at the luridly clothed people of all different colours and mishaps and sizes. She gagged on her first taste of Jamaican rum, and felt it burning as it went down her throat, bringing tears to her eyes.

She watched a bare-knuckle fight, in which a man's nose was broken with an audible crack and another man's ear was bitten clean off. She saw a cockfight and a bear fight and monkeys dancing to tunes ground out on penny whistles. She saw a couple copulating in the streets and slaves chained together and kept in a filthy state, women being sold on street corners, drunks lying face down in the mud and others stepping over them as if they were not there.

Elizabeth had grown up in London and thought she had seen most of everything there was to see in the world, but that first night in Port Royal, her eyes were wide open and so, too, was her mouth. She went back to the ship a different person; all her new found strength seemed to have been drained from her by the savageness and barbarity of the town around her. She wondered if Martin had not been correct, and that she should return to London and continue her life there in the safety and comfort to which she was used.

She fell exhausted into her bunk and dreamed of cocks fighting with men's heads on them and monkeys leering at bears as they performed sexual acts on women in chains. She saw houses turned to rubble by a single shake of the earth, and the sea rise up in protest at what was going on and drown the whole evil town and all its inhabitants.

12

The Fight

Jack spent most of the next day in the crow's nest, watching the ships come and go from the port. Pip tried to keep her company, but she was not in the mood and sent him away. She wondered if this was to be her last day on the earth and, because of that, she watched with extra interest all that went on about her. Most of the crew were ashore, pursuing whatever particular pleasure was their fancy. This was a town that pandered to every taste. She wondered if people would take pleasure in watching her neck being broken that evening.

Harry was off somewhere, busy creating and concocting some miracle, Jack hoped. She could only sit here and pray that, somewhere in her life, she had done some good and God would chose now to repay that goodness. Captain Silk was with the Mountain Man's master, arranging the money for the wager. They went to and fro, not seeing Jack in her perch high up.

It was near sunset before Harry returned and called her down. He seemed most pleased with himself. She did not ask what he had been up to; sometimes she thought it better to not know. Pip was about the ship, and Harry called him too and, with Captain Silk, they set off for the tavern. It was still early when they arrived and Harry took Jack out to a yard at the back. He produced a foul-smelling ointment and proceeded to rub it on to Jack's arms and legs.

"'Tis to make you slippery, hard to get hold of."

"Like a greased pig." Jack made a face, and Harry laughed. "Just put an apple in my mouth when he is finished with me," she said.

Harry slapped her back. "You will be grand, my lad. 'Tis only five minutes. Keep moving, and if he grabs a-hold, protect your neck. Leave the rest up to me."

There were several fights before Jack's own, but she did not care to watch them. She knew how big her opponent was, his method of fighting, and what she had to do. She saw Harry put something into a glass of milk, and hoped he had gauged the dosage correctly. Captain Silk and Pip came out to wish her well. She smiled bravely at both of them and waved them away, claiming she was making preparation for the fight. In truth, she felt she was preparing to die. She prayed for forgiveness of her sins, knowing that all the good things she had ever done would not outweigh the lie she had been living for the best part of her life.

All too soon, Harry called her in, and she entered the fighting floor to a deafening noise; the customers, mostly drunk on expectation, were on their feet, stamping and shouting. She could see some staring in disbelief that she could even think to take on the Mountain Man. She saw more money change hands. Her opponent was sitting in his corner; she nodded an acknowledgment to him and he nodded back to her. She wanted the noise to stop, so she waved and flexed her muscles for the audience. This only caused more whistling and stomping, which did not subside until the landlord called for the fight to begin.

Jack's plan to stay out of the reach of the giant man was more difficult than she had thought in the small space allowed them. She knew punching and kicking would be of no use, her being so much smaller, but she put her stature to advantage by ducking and diving as he followed her about the floor. She managed to land a kick upon his shin, which he barely seemed to notice, and herself received a knock to her shoulder when she did not duck quickly enough. It was the smallest of knocks but, even so, it gave her an idea of what a full blow from his hammer-hand would feel like.

She heard someone call that one minute had passed; she was

already exhausted and wondered how she would ever last even one minute more, let alone four.

The man seemed to be slowing in his movements; she hoped it was because the sleeping draught had started to have its effect, until she saw Harry still had hold of the glass of milk. She weaved about some more, and took a blow upon her upper left arm while landing one, a love-tap to him, upon his back, before he had time to turn. She dived between his legs, shaking her left arm to lessen the numbing pain as she straightened up. Each blow she landed was greeted with a roar of disapproval, and each time she was hit, the crowd shouted even louder. She was sure only Captain Silk would have wagered money upon her.

The blow she landed angered the Mountain Man, and he came at her quickly, using his massive girth to try to prevent her from escaping him. She was quicker, however, and, with a side step and a kick high into his stomach, danced away with nothing more than a grazed shoulder. Someone called two minutes.

The crowd were growing wilder, screaming and rabid. Jack could hear nothing above their noise except her own breathing. Her opponent came at her again, and again she evaded him. His chest was heaving from the exertion and his face was fierce. Most of his fights lasted only half this time, and he seemed not to understand how someone as small as Jack could not yet be beaten.

He threw himself forward as if to crush Jack; she jumped aside but the Mountain Man caught hold of her right foot. Thankfully, the grease Harry had applied did its work, and she slithered away. Three minutes. She thought this might be her only opening and jumped with all her force upon his back. It appeared to have no effect; he reared up and sent Jack flying across the fighting floor. She landed awkwardly and twisted her left ankle. He was up again and coming at her. Fire shot up her leg from her ankle when she put any weight upon it, but she had no choice but to ignore it. She dived out of the way, but he managed to grasp an arm and twisted it hard up Jack's back. Jack could see the crowd, their faces frozen in front of her. Then she saw Pip running across the edge of the space towards Harry. The Mountain Man loosened his grip for a second, and Jack pulled herself free and stumbled out of his reach.

The Mountain Man roared his disapproval and so did the crowd. Jack was cheating them, not only of their money but of the satisfaction of seeing blood. The bigger man charged at Jack, his fists flailing and his eyes burning with rage, but he was easy to get avoid, and Jack remained out of his reach. She heard someone calling four minutes.

The crowd were on their feet. Their mood had changed. Having bravely lasted this long, they were now calling for Jack, wanting her to be victorious. The Mountain Man's master was screaming at him, purple in the face. Jack felt an up-surge of energy; she suddenly thought that it might be possible to come out of this alive. She could see the Mountain Man was having trouble breathing, and though it was painful, she could stand upon her ankle and could feel none of her other injuries.

For the first time, she stood her ground as he came at her and bent low, sending him crashing over her back. She turned quickly and before he could rise again, struck him on the back of his neck with both hands. The blow appeared to have no effect, and she was close enough to him that he was able to take both of her ankles and pull her to the floor. All he needed to do was lower his weight upon her and she was done for. But in his anger, he tried to hold on to her ankles and stand himself. He lost his balance, and had to release her. She scrambled to her feet and moved to the far side of the floor. She had no energy left; if he came at her now, she knew she could not move to save herself.

They stared at each other. The giant was gasping for air now, his face quite pale. He looked as if he must fall. Jack prayed that it was not Harry's draught having this effect upon him. The rowdies were howling their disapproval that the fighting had stopped. Jack moved around the space, but her opponent made no move to come after her. She realised that he had more to lose than she did now. He was the champion, undefeated; she was a mere newcomer who had no intention of staying. All she had to do was wait out the final minute.

The mob had started throwing things; they had come to see – and win money from – a fight, not a stand-off. Jack decided to try a little trick Harry had taught her. She approached the big man and made as if to strike him on the chin but pulled her punch up short, so that she made no contact. He reacted as if she had punched him, snapping his head sideways and staggering backwards. The crowd went wild. The Mountain Man regained his balance and took a swing at Jack; thankfully, his reach fell short, too, but Jack slapped her thigh to make it sound as if contact had been made, and flipped over backwards. The crowd rose as one, thinking this must surely be the end of the fight, but Jack sprang back on to her feet. It sounded as though the whole of the island had roared.

Jack tried several feigned punches to the giant's stomach, slapping her chest to approximate the noise; the man doubled up, groaning. He took hold of Jack's arm and flipped her over. She landed awkwardly, and felt her already injured ankle collapse under her. She rolled out of the way as her opponent threw himself upon her. The crowd were screaming at the fighters. Jack could no longer tell if they were for her or the Mountain Man, and she wondered if they themselves knew anymore. Somehow through the noise she heard the bell ringing to announce the end of the five-minute fight. It had lasted an eternity

The tavern erupted. She got to her feet and helped the Mountain Man to his. She wanted to bow like an actor after a play, but thought that would give the game away. Captain Silk leapt on to the fighting floor and gathered Jack into a rough hug. When she had untangled herself, she saw the Mountain Man being dragged out by his irate master. Jack started after them, having to fight her weary way through the congratulatory, boisterous mob, and followed them outside. There, she found her late opponent being beaten by his master with a large stick.

She rushed over and wrestled the stick from him.

"Stop it," she shouted.

"He is mine to do with what I will," the man answered. He kicked his slave, who made no move to retaliate.

"Then I will buy him." Jack placed herself between the two men.

"You?" The master looked her over with contempt in his eyes. "With what?"

"With this." Harry arrived with a purse full of coins and clubbed the man over the head with it, causing him to fall to the ground, unconscious.

"Come." Harry took hold of Jack. "The captain has had news that the Governor's men are about to take the ship. We must get back onboard." He bent as if to pick up the purse.

"Leave it," Jack said. "It is payment for his slave." Then she turned to the black man. "You are free to do what you will now." She hobbled after Harry.

The giant came after them. Jack stopped him. "I gave you your freedom. I have no need of a slave."

"Let us decide this later –" Harry interrupted "– when we have rescued the ship."

As it was, the freed man proved very useful. Jack could not run at any speed, and the former slave carried her most of the way to the ship, where Captain Silk and his men were fighting to rid the ship of its unwanted boarding party and readying to set sail.

Harry ran up the gangplank to join the fighting. Jack longed to join in, too, but she could barely stand unsupported so she allowed the Mountain Man to lift her out of harm's way into the riggings, from whence she could watch.

She was impressed by the crew, who were remarkably sober and well organised. She realised she had not seen them fight before, and was impressed by their discipline and efficiency. The ship left its mooring and sailed out into the harbour, a few of the Governor's men still onboard. These were soon over-powered and taken to the brig. There had been no damage done to the ship that Jack could see, nor had any of the crew been seriously injured, though a few had been left behind in the port.

Jack learned from a shamefaced Harry that, in their rush to leave, he had left their winnings behind. He had been entrusted with some of it, which he had used to secure the freedom of the slave, but the rest had not been collected. Captain Silk, however, was jovial at its loss.

"An excellent evening's entertainment," he laughed, and helped Jack down from her perch. "I hope your new servant does not eat too much."

"He is not my servant. He is free." Jack, unwilling to make much of her fatigue and injuries, strode purposefully off towards the crew's quarters. However, the pain in her injured ankle was so intense that she blacked out.

When she came round, she was in the First Mate's cabin. It was day outside the porthole; her ankle was heavily bandaged and throbbing painfully. Harry was at her side, and so too was the Mountain Man.

"Ah," Harry said when he saw her eyes flutter open. "You have finally awoken."

Jack sat up and gasped as the movement sent shivers of pain through her leg.

"While the rest of us have been up since dawn scrubbing and mending, you have been lying here like Lord Muck."

"Hush," the Mountain Man said, not understanding that Harry was merely jesting.

"Where are we?" Jack worried that if they were being pursued, then they should be on deck ready to fight.

"We make for Negril to holiday on the sandy beach there until the Governor recovers from his righteous indignation."

"Then we are not presently in danger?" Jack lay back and closed her eyes.

"Not presently." Harry laughed. "There will be time for your ankle to heal before our next fight."

They left her there, and she slept on and off for most of the day and all through the night, courtesy of one of Harry's sleeping draughts, put to its proper use for once.

The next morning, her ankle felt better and she ventured up on to deck. They were sailing close to the coast, and she wondered again at the beauty of the island; the deep green of the land and the blue of the sea, with cliffs and small beaches dividing the two. The colour was so intense, and in such sharp contrast to the greyness of London that she had to close her eyes and open them again to ensure she was not dreaming.

The Mountain Man and Harry saw her and made a fuss over her being up and about. She sent Harry off to find her some food, for she had missed several meals and was most hungry. The big black man sat at her feet as she ate.

"You are a free man," she said to him.

He nodded but did not say anything.

"Free to do what you will, go where you will."

He nodded again, as though he did not believe her.

"When we reach Negril you may leave the ship." At that, he gave her such a look of panic that she checked what she was about to say. "Or not, if that is what you wish."

His panic subsided a little.

She realised that he had never been free, and knew not what that entailed. Every moment of his life until now had been controlled by someone else. It would take him some time to become accustomed to freedom.

"What is your name?" she asked.

"The Mountain Man," he said as if it was a stupid question.

"No, your real name."

He looked at her as if he did not understand.

"What did your mother call you?"

His face fell. "I knew not my mother."

Jack felt bad, but she could not call him 'Mountain Man'. She knew that slaves were given names by their masters, like John or Robert, English names that suited them not at all. She would not do that; if he wanted a name, he could find one for himself.

As if reading her mind, he said quietly, "When I was young they called me Blue Boy, for when I was born, they said that my eyes where not like a slave's at all, but blue like a white man's. Perhaps you could call me 'Blue'." The big man was silent for a moment, then he smiled. "I would like that."

Pip arrived with some fruit for her, and seemed cross for no reason Jack could think of. He sat and fidgeted and cast dark looks at the former Mountain Man.

"He is to be called 'Blue' from now on," Jack said. Pip ignored her.

"Is your ankle recovered?" he asked at last, but as if he did not care to know the answer.

"It is much improved," Jack said, and then she remembered something. "And thank you," she added.

"For what?" Pip asked suspiciously.

"For distracting Blue during the fight."

"Distracting?" He clearly did not understand.

"When you ran to Harry."

"He asked me to fetch water for you, but you did not drink it."

"Sorry," Jack said, then, "Thank you anyway."

The three of them sat in silence for a time until Jack could not bear their brooding presence any longer.

"I am weary still; I think I will retire."

153

"I will help you," Blue said and stood, too.

"No, I will help." Pip pushed him aside.

"I am his friend," the big man said.

"And I am his best friend," Pip answered, looking near to tears. "Or, at least, I was."

"And you are still." Jack tried to calm him, realising now what the trouble between them was. "You must both help me, for I can scarcely walk." She put her arm around each of their shoulders. They were of such different heights that the trip below was awkward and uncomfortable for Jack, but at least they seemed happier.

Once in the cabin, neither showed any signs of leaving.

"I wish to continue what we began in the crow's nest," Pip whispered urgently in her ear. "I know you are ready for it," he said, patting Jack's thigh and feeling for the phallus. "Send him away." He nodded his head sulkily towards Blue.

"I, too," the big man said, having overheard the conversation, "I, too, would have you use me for your pleasure."

Jack was shocked – she wanted them both to leave her alone.

"Is this what your last master did to you?" she asked, angry that one man could force himself upon another.

Blue shook his head sadly. "He beat me only and kept me from other men, knowing it to be my inclination."

Jack did not know what to think. "You like men?" she asked. He nodded without looking at her. "Do you like Pip here?" The big man kept his eyes fixed on the floor. Pip started to protest, but Jack silenced him.

"I will not be angry if the answer is yes."

"Jack, what are you saying?" Pip slapped at Jack's thigh.

"Hush," Jack said. "Do you like him?" she repeated.

Blue nodded his head as if ashamed to admit it.

"Pip, do you like Blue?"

"Jack, how can you ask that?" But even as he was saying it, Jack could see Pip looking Blue over, his eyes wide with something that was not unlike longing.

"It would please me to see that you do," Jack said, hoping to give Pip a way out of his obvious quandary.

She thought that they might not understand her, but both men knew only too well what she was asking of them.

"And you would watch?" Pip was clearly excited by the idea and so was Blue, who had stopped looking at the floor and was gazing upon Pip.

Jack nodded, although the thought brought her no great pleasure.

"We will do it for you," Pip said, even as he was reaching for the ties of his britches.

"For you," Blue repeated, his excitement now evident in the bulge in his trousers. He looked at Jack as if for final approval. Jack nodded. Blue lowered his trousers and produced a penis in proportion with the rest of him. When Pip saw it he gasped in amazement; Jack thought he might be worried by its size but it soon became obvious that he was delighted by it. He took it in his hand and stroked it as if it were a cat and, indeed, it did seem to purr under Pip's attentions.

"Sweet Jesus, 'tis a beauty," Pip whispered and bent his head to kiss its dark length.

Blue took Pip's small member in his hand and stroked it. Pip looked up into his eyes and Jack thought she saw a spark of something rare and beautiful pass between them. Pip dropped to his knees and took the large penis in his mouth and started sucking noisily on it. The big man closed his eyes and rested his hand gently on Pip's head. Pip tugged at his own member as he sucked and licked, groans escaping his very full mouth.

Jack watched, caught between excitement and guilt at witnessing this very personal scene. She could feel her woman's parts swell inside her and wished that she could be touched as she had touched other women. That she could feel someone's soft tongue against her dark opening or even the hardness of the phallus inside her to relieve the loneliness that dwelt there.

Pip had now stood up and turned his back to Blue, bending over the bunk to present his bottom. The black man moved closer and very gently pushed his penis into Pip. Pip cried out in pain but also in pleasure, for when the big man stopped, Pip begged him to go deeper.

Jack was barely aware of them, so lost was she in her own desire. Each thrust of theirs reminded her of the times she had spent with women, and how much she longed for one now. Each groan took her back to Anne and her alabaster thighs, or Nell's perfect breasts. Jack crossed her legs and pressed her hand hard between them. She found the soft round mound of her woman's parts through the rough material of her britches and rubbed it with her thumb. She rubbed in time to the thrusts of the men, getting faster and faster as they did, until all three reached their climax at the same moment. Their cries cut across each other until they were as one.

Then, in the silence that followed, Jack felt the tension disperse that had been there before. She knew that now they could, all three, be friends. She also guessed that Pip would require her less for the service of her rather modest phallus now that he had found a larger, more willing one.

13

The Chase

Elizabeth woke to shouting so loud and urgent that she wondered if her dream had in fact come true. There were men running on the deck above her and the sounds of the ship setting sail. She sat up in her bunk and saw Port Royal slide out of view through the porthole. She wondered if Martin was so keen to be rid of her that he was sending her back to England already.

She dressed and went above. Her husband was at the helm, his cheeks red and his eyes bright with excitement. When he saw her, it was obvious that he had completely forgotten her presence and was only then reminded of it.

"Get below," he shouted at her as if she were a naughty child, "And stay there."

She had no inclination to follow his instructions and went, instead, aft to where Peter was in conference with the boatswain.

"Where are we heading in such a hurry?" she inquired of him.

She had not seen him since their encounter in his cabin and he could scarcely bring himself to look at her. He dismissed the boatswain and took her by the elbow to the most distant corner of the ship, where they could not be overheard.

"You will not breathe a word of what passed between us." His grip on her arm was painfully strong. "It is not my custom to... go with boys; I was excited by the thought of... what awaited me in the town."

She removed her arm from his grasp. "If you tell me where we are headed, and with such haste, I will consider your request." She had no intention of telling anyone, but thought she could use his fear to her advantage.

"Ah." Peter's eyes took on the brightness she had seen in her husband's. "We have a commission to capture William Silk."

"William Silk?" Even Elizabeth had heard of him, the most notorious of all the pirates.

"He was in Port Royal even as we docked. They had kidnapped the incoming Governor but, not knowing it to be he, put him ashore unharmed. Now the same Governor wants Silk's head and is offering a handsome reward for it." He took out his sword and brandished it in dramatic fashion. "And I think I am the man to deliver the rascal's head."

Elizabeth felt excitement rise in her. All thoughts of returning to her quiet life in London were now banished. To be chasing pirates – how could that compare to an afternoon with the other captain's wives, swapping gossip and cake recipes? To be in a real fight, to put to use the skills that she had learnt from Peter. All of her body seemed to tingle, and she now understood the gleam in her husband's eye.

They sped along the Jamaican coast on a good wind. Elizabeth gazed at the passing scenery; it was impossibly green and rugged. The island seemed to rise as one piece from the sea rather than roll out of it, as she had seen the coast of England do. Every now and then they passed golden beaches fringed by dense undergrowth and surrounded by small islands, miniatures of the main island.

Navigation was difficult so close in to the shore, but there were many places for a ship to hide and the captain did not want to overlook any of them. The crew were active and alert as Elizabeth had not seen them before. Her husband, also, looked a different man, more in command, issuing orders with a calm, steely authority that Elizabeth had not known he possessed.

She stationed herself in the foremast crow's nest to be out of the way of the rest of the crew and to stand lookout, warning of hidden rocks and peering into the many coves for any sign of the pirates' vessel. By sunset, they had seen no sign of Silk's ship, the *Revenge*, and weighed anchor in a small natural harbour. They set a night watch and ate heartily of the fresh food bought in Port Royal. Elizabeth fell into her bunk exhausted from the days watching and the excitement and, although she thought she would never rest, she no sooner touched her head to the pillow than she was asleep.

She woke in the morning full of energy. It was another fair day, though the winds were lighter and they proceeded more slowly. It was thought that the pirates were heading for Montego Bay where Silk had known associates. It would take two days' sailing, longer if the winds were not strong.

Peter was on deck, taking some of the crew through their sword practice, and Elizabeth joined in. The men fought harder than Peter, though with less skill, so Elizabeth never found herself in any danger. There were a number of cuts and bruises amongst the fighters where one or the other had been over-enthusiastic, so Peter called a halt early for fear that someone would truly get hurt.

The tension onboard boiled over into several fights that day, one amongst a group playing cards, the other in the captain's cabin. Elizabeth heard raised voices as she approached the door.

"I do not run this ship on superstition," she heard her husband saying.

"But the runes have not been wrong before."

"Well, they are now." There was the sound of something being thrown to the floor.

Elizabeth entered, interested to see what was going on. Her husband was standing above the boatswain, who was on his knees collecting something from the floor.

"Get out," her husband said when he saw Elizabeth.

"We have the commission," the boatswain said without standing up. "Let us take it and say we could not find him."

The captain had been glaring at Elizabeth, but he now returned his gaze to his crewman. He had gone quite red; Elizabeth did not think she had seen him so angry, not even with herself.

"Get out of my sight before I have you locked in the brig." The poor man scrabbled to his feet but, before he could leave the cabin, the captain grabbed him by the shoulder. "And if you breathe a word of this to any of the crew, I will have you whipped and then thrown overboard, do you understand?"

The man nodded, and Martin threw him from the cabin.

Elizabeth stood and watched her husband. She realised that she cared not at all for him, and on realising that, felt strangely and wonderfully free. She smiled broadly and lay herself upon her bunk. She no longer felt slighted by his lack of interest in her; she rejoiced in it. She owed him nothing and he was still reliant upon her and her locket to find the treasure. She laughed to herself.

"What is so amusing?" Her husband turned upon her angrily.

"You cannot hope to beat William Silk."

"What would you know of such matters?"

Elizabeth knew what she had heard from the crew. "That they overpowered the *Golden Sun*, a frigate of ninety guns, with only sixteen of their own, and killed every last man onboard. We are but twenty guns, and the half of them do not function."

"The *Golden Sun* was taken by surprise; this time *we* have surprise on our side."

"And you think that they will not expect pursuit?"

Her husband slammed his fist down on the table, sending maps flying. "I will not be lectured by a girl. If I hear another word from you, I will have you lashed." Elizabeth could see the steel in his look and decided not to provoke him further. The prospect of a fight with the pirates seemed not so exciting as it had done before.

She left the cabin and climbed back up to the crow's nest. It was by now late afternoon and the sun was lost behind the mountains. They anchored for the second night in another small cove and she would have liked to go ashore and sit on the golden sands, feel their warmth and texture, but it was forbidden. The crewman who had stabbed his card-playing companion was to be flogged – twenty lashes – and they had all been ordered to watch.

Elizabeth did so from the crow's nest. She saw the unfortunate fellow being led out and tied to the main mast. The Captain himself was to carry out the punishment; he took off his jacket and rolled his sleeves up. There was a pause while the First Mate read out the accusation and order; she could not hear all of it but she did not need to. No dissent would be tolerated; this flogging was a warning to them all.

She spied the boatswain standing to one side; at any other time it would be his job to administer the punishment, but the flogging was a warning to him as much as anyone else. The captain lifted the whip and brought it down sharply on the sailor's back. Elizabeth heard his cry of pain and, even from her great height, could see a red welt forming across the bare skin. Martin cracked the whip again and, again, lines formed random patterns, red against white, on the man's back. He cried out each time the whip caught him. It seemed to go on forever. Elizabeth watched in horror, not able to tear her eyes away, until at last the man slumped, unconscious, against the mast. Even then, her husband seemed set to continue, until Peter stepped in and took the whip from him and led him away to his cabin.

Elizabeth stayed where she was, although it was nearly dark; she could not bare the thought of going back to the cabin but did not know where else she could sleep. She did not relish sleeping in a hammock down in the crew's quarters, nor did she think she could share with Peter. The evening was still and warm, and the ship quiet now. She would stay where she was and sleep under the stars.

She had never slept out of doors before, and wondered at how much her life had changed in such a short space of time. She thought of Mary and hoped she was happy in her new position.

She hoped also that her father was well and happy, and that neither of them was missing her too much.

Yet she felt very alone up there above the ship, and she wished there was someone to whom she could be close. She wondered if there was anyone out there for her, someone as lonely as she. She sighed and settled herself more comfortably. There were so many stars in the sky, more than she had ever seen or even imagined when she lived in London. She lay back and tried to find shapes and constellations that were familiar but could see none. She did not even begin to count them; there were just too many.

Instead, she closed her eyes and imagined that she was being rocked in the arms of a loved one. She imagined that she was being gently caressed by warm hands and lips. She lay still until she could actually feel the imaginary lover, the warm hands cupping her breasts, the lips sipping at her own, stroking her stomach, feeling her thighs, and tracing the curves of her whole body. There were lips sucking at her breasts, a tongue licking its way down her body until it found her mound and, in amongst the hairs there, her soft centre. She gasped at how real this imaginary lover felt, and she began to touch herself, wetness lapping at her and building the tension in her until it was finally released with a long shudder.

She fell asleep then, and dreamed of that imaginary *amour* who wore a face faintly familiar and slightly disturbing for its familiarity but who took her hard and fast with a tool something like her candle until she was feverish with pleasure and reached peak after peak of high passion.

She woke in the morning, drenched in dew and her own juices. Below her, the ship was stirring; her husband was on deck, shouting for the crew to raise themselves and get underway. They should reach Montego Bay by late afternoon and there they would find William Silk. He seemed impatient to have the day started for, by the end of it, his and the pirate's fate would be sealed one way or another.

Elizabeth climbed down from her lofty bed and went to the cabin to find dry clothes. It smelt strongly of male odour and she wondered who amongst the crew her husband had found to take out his frustrations upon.

Back on deck, the crew *en masse* were more excited than ever. There was much shouting and running about; Elizabeth returned to her post as lookout. It was another beautiful day, and she found herself wondering if rain ever fell on this paradise island. The winds were fair and they made good speed.

Elizabeth stretched out her arms and noticed they had taken on a brown glow; she noticed, too, how they had changed in shape, become stronger and leaner from her sword practice and climbing the rigging. The whole of her body had changed, she realised, and she liked it. She thought that few would recognise her as being a girl. Where her height and broadness of shoulder had appeared unattractive in the dress of a gentlewoman in fashionable London, it suited perfectly her guise of a sailor boy.

The morning turned into afternoon without the sighting of a single ship. Elizabeth found herself growing more agitated by the passing hour. She often touched the stout sword at her side and the dagger. She had heard the men talk of killing others and had listened with interest. They described it as she had heard them describe sexual intercourse, their talk full of thrusting and cutting, reaching a climax with the death blow.

She looked forward to the prospect of a real fight with very mixed feelings. She had enjoyed her practice fights, marvelling at the speed and dexterity her body achieved. There was a certain joy in outwitting an opponent, making them think you were about to thrust one way and then striking the other. But in a real fight, when her very life was at stake, would all wit and reason desert her? Would her body obey the commands of her mind? Elizabeth did not know the answers to these question and knew that she would only find them out when it might be too late.

They were passing long golden beaches. Elizabeth was lost in her reveries when she heard the shout – another ship had been spied in the distance. She saw the captain put his eyeglass up and shout, in a voice hoarse with excitement and fear, that it was the *Revenge*. The crew sprang into action; the guns were manned ready for firing, swords were drawn and daggers clenched in sweating hands.

Elizabeth watched the preparations with a loudly beating heart. She had no duty in this fight. Her only instructions had been from her husband, who ordered her below every time he noticed her about the ship. She wondered if that might not be the best place for her, but she stayed where she was. She saw Peter and a band of the better fighters collect on the deck below her. She could join them, and help as she was able, but her arms and legs refused to move. She was sure that she would be of no use to anyone if she was so afraid before she had seen any fighting.

The *Revenge* had seen them and its Jolly Roger flag, which showed Silk's distinctive white devil and skull mark on a black field, was raised. She had been sailing on the same tack as them, and now slowed in preparation for the fight. It seemed to take an age before the two ships drew level. The pirates fired the first barrage from aft with two guns. The shot fell short by some distance, and the crew cheered in derision.

Another shot was fired, and this one landed closer, causing waves to rock the ship. The pirate vessel slowed and came about, to close the distance between them even more. Yet another shot was fired, this time from portside, and this one came perilously close. Martin gave the order and the cannons on the *Juno* finally fired their first shot. It landed just short of the bow of the pirates' ship, sending it rocking wildly. The two ships drifted closer together; Peter was readying the men with grappling irons for boarding. His face was pale, but his eyes glistened with excitement.

A shot from the *Revenge* hit their port side with a thunderous crack, and there was the sound of wood splintering. The two ships were close enough now that Elizabeth could heard the pirates cheering and see them waving their swords. A shot from Elizabeth's ship hit the cromster close to the waterline, and the cheering stopped. It was very noisy now; the air was filled with shouting and explosions, the smell of gunpowder and burning wood.

Elizabeth was suddenly aware of her own smell, for she was shaking and sweating. She found that she could no longer sit and watch. She climbed down out of the crow's nest and joined Peter and his men on the deck. If there were going to be a fight, and it seemed certain that there would, then she wanted to be in it, not watching.

Grappling irons were flying between the ships; the first of the pirates flew across and was rapidly dispatched by Peter's sword. He dropped howling into the sea. Elizabeth felt a shiver run down her spine at the sound. Another pirate came across, and then another and another, and the fighting started in earnest.

The men in front of Elizabeth jostled for position, trying to be the first to reach the pirates. The cannons had stopped firing, for which Elizabeth was grateful; the noise and the smell was making her head spin. Instead, the air was now filled with the grunts of men fighting hand to hand and the smell of their fear.

A space cleared in front of her as one of the crew slumped to the deck in a pool of blood. Elizabeth had her first clear view of the pirates. She was surprised to see they looked no more nor less frightening than her own crew. She had expected them to be demons of some sort, only half human, deformed or evil in some obvious manner. To see them there, ordinary men fighting the ordinary men of her crew, she was taken aback.

But only for a moment. A slim man of middle years lunged at her and she parried with her sword a little late. He caught her sleeve and scratched her arm. He came at her again, smiling, as if he thought he was in for an easy kill. She blocked his thrust and flicked her sword as Peter had showed her, so as to trap it above his head – and, with her dagger, she found the soft flesh of his belly. He sank to the deck, with a look of surprise on his face. Elizabeth pulled out her dagger and stared at the blood on it and her hand. She would have stood like that, forever in shock and horror, realising she had just killed her first man, but for Peter shouting a warning. She looked up to see another pirate lunging at her.

This pirate was older and rougher, looking more as she had imagined a pirate would look. He was not so easy to dispatch; having seen her kill his mate, he knew her not to be an easy fight. They locked swords again and again, the pirate using his superior weight to push her backwards towards the far starboard railings. She was aware of the noise around her, other men fighting, engaged in duels. The ship moved slightly under her, gulls wheeled above her. It was as if all her senses were heightened, her sight, hearing, smell, touch, even her taste, but focused on the man in front of her who was lifting his sword and bringing it down over her head. She spun out of the way and his sword landed heavily on the ship's railing, biting into the wood. As he fought to extract it, Elizabeth threw herself at him, tipping him over the side, and watched as he fell shrieking into the calm sea below. She did not have time to see if he rose again to the surface, for another pirate was upon her. As she fought with him, she wished she had someone to fight alongside her, and she remembered the strange dream she had once long ago in London. Never had she believed it would come to pass that she would be fighting pirates, although, in the dream, the sea had been rough and the lad from the tavern and the docks had been at her side – Jack.

Just as she thought that, as if her thoughts had conjured him from the very air itself, he appeared in front of her, fighting furiously with Peter. The pirate she was fighting noticed her distraction and lunged at her; she jumped out of the way in time, but he caught her a heavy blow on the arm. Pain seared through her shoulder and down to her hand; her fingers lost their grip on her sword, and it fell to the deck.

The pirate grinned and swung his sword and dagger over his head in a taunting dance. Elizabeth could feel her warm blood pumping from the wound. She dared not look at it, for fear that she would faint at the sight. Along with the blood leaving her body, she could feel her strength draining away. The pirate danced in front of her, twisting his sword and dagger in an elaborate fashion about him.

Elizabeth had heard tell that your life flashed before your eyes just before you died. All she could think of was the servants dancing at her wedding, Mary being guided around the room by the junior footman. It seemed a long time ago in a very different life. She knew she must gather her wits, or the mad pirate would slit her throat and then dance, grinning, on her dead body.

With the last energy she could summon, she kicked out at him, catching him between his legs where she knew it would hurt him most. He bent double, his sword slipping away from him on to the deck to lie beside hers. Senseless, he fell upon his own dagger, causing an avalanche of blood such as Elizabeth had never seen before. It rained upon her and everything around her. The pirate's body continued to twitch and jerk in a cruel parody of the dance he had just performed – his own death dance, it seemed – then he collapsed in a pool of his own blood and finally lay still.

Elizabeth, too, sank to the deck; she looked for the first time at her wound and saw that it was deep and long. She looked about the ship and found it to be suddenly, ominously, quiet. She could see no one else, nor hear any sounds. She knew that the fight must be over but not who had won it. She wondered if she had imagined the lad from her dream; it seemed unlikely that it could really be he, so far from London. She was suddenly too tired to wonder about it any longer, too tired to keep her eyes open. She drifted off into pain-free unconsciousness.

14

The Sea Battle

They made good speed around the coast, so Captain Silk was
surprised when a following ship was spotted. Yet it was only a small
ship, no more than twenty guns. Jack watched from the crow's nest
as sails were trimmed to slow for engagement. Her ankle was almost
healed, but she could find little comfort in that. In fact, in the past
few days, she had found little comfort in anything.

Pip and Blue had formed a fast and deep friendship and, at
every opportunity, engaged in sexual acts of one form or another.
Jack tried to excuse herself from witnessing these, for they made
her feel her own lack of female companionship so sharply it felt
like a cut. This, however, seemed to worry the two men, who did
not want her to be left out, and no amount of reassuring from Jack
could convince them that she was happy for them to do whatever
they liked to each other, but that she did not need to see them
doing it.

It was almost a relief to consider that there was about to be a
fight. Anything to distract Jack from thoughts of love. As the
distance between the ships narrowed, Jack could feel her
heartbeat quicken. She wondered at this; it was natural to feel
enervated before a fight, but this was different. It seemed to her
that something more important than a mere fight was about to
take place. She looked over the approaching ship to see if she
could find some clue, and saw that it was the *Juno*, Captain's
Luther's ship.

The ship, a naval merchantman, was small and ill equipped to fight them. The crew appeared willing enough, but unused to fighting. She knew the ship by reputation and, seeking out her captain, saw that he was, indeed, Luther. If she had not had to leave London so speedily, she might well have been on that very ship. It was an odd thought, which did nothing to quell the feeling of immense excitement that was building inside her. She could now see faces of the men on the *Juno*, and she fancied she recognised a few. Then her gaze happened upon a figure perched, like herself, in the crow's nest. The face was familiar, each angle and line she felt she knew, even better than her own. The boy was the spitting image of the red-haired lady from the tavern and the docks. He could only be her brother.

The excitement in her was at a fever pitch now, and she knew that the young boy in the opposite crow's nest was the cause of it. She was amazed, stunned even. She had had feelings like this before for Anne and Nell, though never as strong and never for a boy. Being raised as a boy, it had seemed the most natural thing in the world for her to be attracted to girls. She wondered, if her life had been different, if her father had lived and her mother not been driven to such extreme measures, whether her passions might have been different. She doubted it. While she liked men well enough, the form of women – the lines of their bodies, the way they moved and sighed and laughed, *everything* about them, in fact – held her in rapture.

She was roused from her thoughts by the report of a cannon. The shot fell short of their pursuers. More cannon fire followed, backwards and forwards, with much shouting and waving of swords. Jack ignored all of this; she could only watch the boy in the crow's nest. Coiled like a spring, he sat looking about himself as if greatly afraid. Suddenly, he got to his feet and, with a swiftness and grace that surprised Jack, climbed down to the deck.

Jack was afraid for the boy's safety for, although he had a sword and dagger, he looked so green and gentle he would surely have no idea how to use them. Grappling irons were now flying between the ships, and Jack decided it was time to descend. She would be excused from the fighting because of her ankle but she knew she could not stand by while her fellow crewmates fought and died around her. She thought, too, that she could keep an eye on the boy for the sake of his lovely sister, and see that he came to no harm.

Blue was waiting at the foot of the mast. Jack had discovered that he was scared of heights and could not bring himself to follow her up to the crow's nest. While she enjoyed his company for the most part, she was secretly delighted with this discovery, for it meant she could take for herself some hours of solitude without offending him.

The fight was already underway. The pirates had taken the initiative and boarded the *Juno*. Jack jumped across to join the battle, Blue following close behind her. With him at her back, she was able to take on and beat several assailants. Then, she encountered a man better dressed than the others and of military bearing. He was good with his sword and obviously enjoying himself. They fought backwards and forwards across the width of the ship, evenly matched. Around them was much fighting, and a fire was burning aft. Jack had hoped to look out for the boy, but the fight was too absorbing, demanding every ounce of her concentration.

Before either had a chance to dispatch the other, the signal came that the fight was over; Captain Luther had surrendered. Jack was almost sorry – she had been enjoying the duel. She raised her sword and saluted her opponent, who bowed and then threw himself over the side of the ship into the water. Jack ran to the railings and peered over. The sea was calm and clear, and there was no sign of the man.

Jack turned back and saw a large pool of blood. She wondered what terrible thing had caused a man to bleed so, and looked around to see who it was who had been so emptied of their life.

She saw old McTavish in a crumpled heap, his own dagger lodged in his neck. Near him was the boy; at first, Jack thought he, too, was dead but, when she touched his face, it was still warm. She also detected a faint pulse in his neck.

There was a deep wound in his arm that was still bleeding. Jack tore a strip from her shirt and bound up the wound. The boy groaned, a sweet sound even though it bespoke pain, not unlike the noise a woman made when she was near to her climax. Jack felt her heart quicken at the sound and wondered at its reaction. She lifted the limp body and Blue helped her carry it across to the *Revenge*.

On the ship, they had Captain Luther bound hand and foot and looking sorry for himself. Not such a fine gentleman now, Jack thought. He was pleading with Silk for his life, offering all his riches and his house in London. Silk laughed; what did he need with a house in London? The captain promised him the Governor would pay a high ransom. Silk laughed more.

Jack looked around and was pleased to see Harry and Pip unharmed. Pip ran over when he saw Blue, though he was obviously annoyed when he saw him carrying the boy so tenderly in his arms. Between them, they found a safe place on the deck to stow the boy. Harry treated the wound with iodine, rebandaged it and gave the boy a sleeping draught to ease the pain. Jack watched with her heart jumping wildly in her chest.

The others were called away to help strip Captain Luther's ship of any valuables, but Jack stayed where she was. She took the boy's head and rested it in her lap; she stroked his soft, flame-coloured hair and smooth cheeks. Never before had she seen such a pretty boy, such clear skin and high colour in his cheeks, just the image of his sister: they must be twins. Such a lovely neck and throat. Jack had to stop herself reaching inside the rough shirt to touch the skin. She had never felt this way about a boy, and even the girls she had bedded had not stirred as strong a passion in her as this sleeping lad was now doing.

Her hand fell upon the lad's chest, to mark his breathing, and she felt a lump. Curious, she reached under his shirt and came upon a chain. She gently pulled, and brought out a locket. It took her a moment to realise why the locket looked so familiar; it was an exact match of the one she wore around her own neck. She held it in her hand and felt the weight and warmth of it. Never before had she seen anything even close to resembling her locket, and here she held one that was an exact copy, except, as she looked at it, she realised it was not exactly the same.

She took her own out and compared them. The boy's locket was the opposite of hers. She held them next to each other and saw that they fitted together, the two halves making a whole, shaped like a heart. Jack pushed them together. How was it possible that this boy had the mate to her locket? When her mother gave it to her, she mentioned nothing of there being another and, although she had wondered at its odd shape, it had not occurred to her that it might be because it lacked a mate. Jack wanted to shake the boy awake and demand of him an answer. She also wanted to kiss those rosebud lips and see the eyes flicker open and discover what colour they were behind their pale lids.

But she did neither of these. Instead, she unclasped the two halves and slid the boy's locket back inside his shirt and noticed a bandage there, as if binding some previous wound. The bandage was clear of blood, though, and under it Jack noticed a swelling of flesh. Her heart tripped over itself. She looked around to see if anyone could see her and, deciding no one could, she lifted the shirt and peered under it. Despite the bandage she could see the unmistakable shape of two small but perfectly formed breasts. Jack let the shirt drop. No wonder her heart was in turmoil, no wonder her breath was catching in her throat and her hands wanted to touch and caress this boy. For the boy was a woman, the very same who had so beguiled her in London.

Jack knew not what to do now. All prisoners were to be given to Captain Silk for him to decide their fate. If he were to discover this boy was a girl, there was no knowing what he would do to her. Jack could not hide her for long; any number of the men saw her brought aboard, and Harry had tended her wounds. Jack looked about her. She would make a shelter to keep the hot West Indies sun off the unconscious figure, and then bethink what needed to be done.

She fixed a sail over some barrels and left the girl there to find Blue. He was hauling barrels of ale and rum from the captured ship – the crew would be very drunk that night. Captain Luther and the few of his crew left alive had been returned to their ship and bound to the masts, unable to do anything but watch as their ship was looted. The Captain was still begging for his life.

"I have treasure maps," he called across to Silk. "The cabin boy, he knows." He looked about him wildly as if to find Elizabeth but was unable to locate her. "Old treasure maps that only the cabin boy and I know how to read."

Jack felt almost sorry him. It was such a desperate plea, and it seemed most unlikely that the captain of a ship such as his would know anything of treasure. She hoped that if she were to meet her death in similar circumstances, she would meet it with more dignity.

Most of the pirate crew were back aboard, readying the ship for sailing; they needed to make some distance between themselves and the disarmed ship before more bounty hunters came after them.

Captain Silk was arranging the booty and looking very pleased with himself. Jack decided to wait before she broached the subject of her unconscious friend. She wasn't sure what he intended for the other captured crew members, and thought she would wait until he had done what he would with them before mentioning it.

The prisoners were a pretty sorry lot, some hardly fit to be sailors. It did not seem to be Silk's intention to offer any of them a place on his crew. He ordered all his men back onboard the *Revenge* and for the grappling irons to be released. Jack thought this meant that he was going to let them be, as did the men on the captured vessel. Another ship would be along in a few days and the men would then be freed. She breathed a sigh of relief.

She returned to her unconscious friend. The ship was underway now, the sails full-bellied with wind and making good time towards Negril, leaving the *Juno* adrift behind them. Jack took the sleeping woman's hand and felt her forehead. She was warm but, thankfully, not burning with fever. Jack was pleased she had hidden her away so she had not suffered the fate of her crew mates, but she was not out of danger yet.

Jack needed to bring the matter to Captain Silk, and soon, before they were discovered. She left Blue to guard the girl and went to seek out the captain. He had retired to his cabin and when Jack entered, was sitting behind a large chest full of coins, grinning broadly.

"Sir." Jack did not know quite how to start her tale.

"A good haul and a complete victory."

"Yes, Cap'n." Jack watched as he counted out the coins into piles.

"One of these is for you," the captain said, and nodded to Jack.

"One of their crew remains onboard, sir."

Silk looked at her sharply.

"I found her... him –" Jack quickly corrected herself and hoped Silk had not noticed "– amongst the barrels. He is wounded deeply, but having fought so bravely, I thought he might make a good addition to our crew."

Captain Silk stood, his red face redder and his eyes narrowed.

"I ordered all their crew adrift. I want no bounty hunters on my ship."

"I heard no such order." And, indeed, she had not. She thought hard and fast how she might remedy this. "But as he is here..."

"Not one left to hamper us, I said."

"It was Wild McTavish he slayed."

The captain blinked and lifted his gaze to the ceiling. McTavish was one of the longest serving of his crew, and Jack hoped he held

175

him in some esteem.

"And several more before that." Jack tried to play her advantage, but wondered if the mention of McTavish had been a good idea or no.

"Where is this stowaway, then?"

"On the fore deck." Jack knew there was no point in lying.

"Show me."

They went on deck and Jack led Silk to where her new friend lay. She nodded to Blue to stand aside so that Silk might see her.

"Small for such a good fighter." He kicked her none too gently but she did not stir. "And young, too. As good as you, perhaps?" He turned back to Jack.

"I know not; I was engaged in fighting their First Mate."

"And did you kill him?"

"He jumped ship when our victory was called."

"Let us hope he cannot swim, or that the sea monsters take him." He paused, as if in thought. "Very well then. When he regains his strength, we will have a contest, you against him."

Jack breathed a sigh of relief, but Silk was not finished. "To the death." With that he left, laughing.

Jack sat down on the deck and gently stroked the smooth cheek of the unconscious woman. At least it gave her time to think what next to do. She hoped the woman remained unconscious for some time yet, because it would give Jack time to come up with a plan.

That night, the ship anchored at the west end of Montego Bay. None of the crew was allowed ashore; they would be given leave when they arrived at Negril, and they could not yet be sure if any other vessels were chasing them; best to have a full crew aboard. Jack settled down to sleep beside the woman and Blue stood watch over them.

Pip resented Jack taking up Blue's time. Although he had not been much involved in the fighting, hearing tell of it excited him immensely, and he wanted to know every bloody detail. He was greatly disappointed when Jack refused to tell him anything, which added to his resentment.

Under the canopy of the sail and between the barrels, Jack set up a bed as best she could. Her jacket she folded for a pillow and brought up a blanket for them to share. It was a warm night and the sea was calm. Once the crew had retired below to drink their plundered rum, it was blissfully peaceful.

Harry gave Jack another sleeping draught and after she had slipped it between those soft pink lips, the woman seemed to sleep more easily. Jack curled up beside her and fell asleep herself. In her dreams, she remembered another dream: the two of them fighting side by side. Some of the men they fought she now recognised. There was Wild McTavish, though she knew him to be dead, the Governor, then the First Mate who had thrown himself overboard, the captain of her first ship and the boatswain who had hated her so much. Then, in her dream, she turned to the woman, who stood a few inches taller than herself and was broader in the shoulders, and saw her face properly for the first time. In this dream, she took hold of the lady who she felt she already knew so well, and kissed her upon the lips and slipped her tongue into the willing mouth. Her hand felt under the calico shirt and the bandage and came upon two round breasts, their nipples already erect and demanding the attention of her thumb.

In the dream, she pressed her hips into the woman's pelvis and heard her groan with the pleasure of it. She kissed the soft skin of her neck and slid her hands to the top of the woman's britches and untied the rope cord. She felt the woman's warm breath in her ear, and fancied she heard her whisper her name and beg her to continue. She pushed up the rough shirt and the bindings and found the eager nipples with her lips and, as she sucked on them, her hands explored the soft thighs and downy hair of her sex. Still the woman whispered her name and held her head, seeming to urge it lower.

Her hunting fingers found the wet, warm opening and dived into the beckoning well. The woman groaned a long, low groan, like one reaching the shore after a long and dangerous swim. In the dream, Jack moved her fingers in and out of the well, pressing her thumb on the soft flesh at the top of its opening. She was thirsty to drink from this delicious source, and let the nipple she was still sucking slip from her lips to trace a line down the centre of the woman's body with her tongue. She paused at the opening and the woman pushed her body up to met the tongue, groaning her name still louder.

Jack lapped at the juices there, flicking her tongue so as to gather every drop, rubbing her thumb still into the soft flesh, feeling it swell and soften even more. Her fingers were in under her tongue, pushing in and out. The woman was panting now, her breath becoming shorter and shorter. Jack could feel the woman close to her climax as Jack was herself, her own breathing short and laboured, her senses overwhelmed by this woman, her smell, her taste, the feel and sound of her.

In the dream, they both reached their climax at the same moment, exploding into tiny pinpoints of light, flying out of themselves to join the stars in the sky. Little drops of bright dust fell over them, tingling where they landed, lighting up their bodies as if from within. In the dream, the woman sighed a sigh of complete contentment, and rolled away from Jack. Jack snuggled in behind her and, in the dream, they both fell into a blissful sleep.

Jack woke in the morning to the sun gently touching her toes. She yawned and stretched. It seemed that her body was more alive than she had ever felt it, as if the sun were filling her with energy from her feet up. She sat up and saw the woman lying next to her. She remembered the dream and wondered at how real it felt. She then remembered what Captain Silk had said about the duel.

She crawled out of the makeshift shelter and stood on the deck, marvelling at the beauty that surrounded her. The sea was the deepest blue she had ever seen and the land a dark green with just a sliver of golden sand separating them. She decided, in that very moment, that she had to leave the pirate ship and take the woman with her. A pirate's life was not for her, the running and hiding, the fighting and wrestling, the needless and cruel killings. She wanted more from her short time on this earth.

It was difficult to leave a pirate crew. She could buy herself out, except that she had no money. She supposed that she could use Blue but, having secured his freedom, she would not send him back into slavery. She could jump ship, but would risk being hunted down; with a wounded companion, that would be difficult. She wanted to leave and be free to start a new life in peace.

She needed a plan, a good one, but needed time to think it all out. She went in search of Harry: she needed some more sleeping draught for the woman to buy them that extra time.

15

Two Hearts

Elizabeth woke from the strangest of dreams. She looked about her and wondered where she was and how she had arrived there. Draped above her was white material as though she were in a tent in the desert, a picture of which she had seen once in a book, but under her were hard wooden boards, and the whole world rocked ever so gently. She was alone, although it seemed someone had been with her, for there was a warm spot in the blanket next to her.

She felt warm and satisfied, though very hungry. The dream clung to her body like a silk sheet, making her skin glow and her heart sing. Yet there was something troubling her. Why was she asleep on the floor and not in her bed, and where was Mary? She sat up and felt a shooting pain in her arm. She looked down and saw a blood-stained bandage wrapped tightly around it. The sight of it nearly made her swoon. Then she started to remember. Her shirt was of coarse material, and she was wearing britches like a lad, a poor sailor lad, and she was on a ship; she now recognised the rocking motion and the creaking sounds.

She remembered her husband and the deal and the fight with the pirates. She wondered who had won and on which ship she was. Not her husband's, she thought, for she would be in her bunk in his cabin. The pirates', then. She shuddered at the thought. She gingerly touched the empty space on the blanket beside her and wondered what sort of man had lain there and whether the dream had, in fact, been only a dream. She closed her eyes and tried to wish herself back in London, to her comfortable life with fine dresses, a bed and Mary to see to her needs. She should never have come.

When she opened her eyes again, a lad was kneeling before her. Even though she felt giddy from loss of blood and the sleeping draught, she recognised him instantly as Jack. Close to, he was a scrawny thing and none too clean, though he did not stink as much as some of the sailors she had met.

"Please, Mistress," he whispered urgently, "lie down."

Elizabeth was shocked by his request, and that he knew her real sex. What if her dream had not been a dream? What if he had taken her once while she were asleep? Did he wish to do it again, and while she was conscious?

"You must pretend to still be asleep." Jack pushed gently upon her shoulders.

Elizabeth would have slapped him, had her arm not pained her so much.

"That is enough of your impertinence," she said as sternly as she would have if she had been speaking to a street urchin on a London street, for he seemed to her to be no better than that.

"The captain must not know that you have risen."

"The captain is my husband."

"Captain Silk?"

"No," Elizabeth said impatiently, "Captain Luther."

"Oh." Jack bit her bottom lip. "Then I have ill news for you. He is set adrift, and most of his crew are dead."

"Then I am a prisoner?" She needed to question him about so many things but instinct dictated they must wait until she could establish her own plight.

"Well..." The lad looked nervous. "Not exactly."

"Then what, pray?" Her mind raced with all the other possibilities, none of which seemed at all savoury.

"I found you and brought you aboard before Captain Silk could set your husband's ship adrift. He was not happy with me and ordered that, when you are sufficiently recovered, we are to duel."

Elizabeth was much relieved. "That is no great thing." Jack looked so small and young, she could hardly imagine him to be a match for her and, even if she were to lose, what could they do to her?

"To the death," the lad added ominously.

"I am sure I could defeat such a pathetic specimen of the male sex as you," she said haughtily.

"Maybe," the lad said as if he doubted it, and as if that were not the point. But if it were not, then what was?

"Besides, I have no intention of remaining on this ship. I will inform this Captain Silk of my sex and rank and he will return me to Port Royal."

Jack waved his hands about. "No, no," he said in a urgent whisper. "The captain must never know your sex or your rank. If he did, he might well kill you, or worse."

"Worse?" Elizabeth could think of nothing worse than dying.

"Women are bad luck on a pirate ship. He might drown you, or flog you or..." She could not or would not finish her sentence.

"Or what?" Elizabeth inquired, although she was not sure she wished to hear the rest.

"Or let the crew have their way with you." He said it quickly, as though by saying it thus, it would not sound so bad.

Elizabeth sat back to think on this. It seemed she was at the mercy of this common lad, having lost the protection of her husband and his ship. He appeared a milksop; she wondered how he had survived amongst the other pirates. She would have wished for a stronger, more manly protector, but if he were the hand she had been dealt by the Fates, then it was he with whom she would have to live.

"I presume you expect me to be grateful?" she demanded of him.

"Well, I... No, not really, although..."

He was about to continue, when a burly older man and a huge black man appeared behind him. Elizabeth shrank back into her shelter, sure that they meant to do her harm, and that the lad would never be able to stop them.

"He be awake then," the burly man said.

"Shh." The lad took from him a small vial.

"That will knock him out for a good few days."

"Here." The lad pressed the vial to her lips, to get her to drink.

"I certainly will not!" She tried not to think what might happen to her unconscious body.

"Captain Silk needs to think you have still not regained your senses."

"Then I will pretend to sleep," she said firmly. "Now, I would like some food and drink, for I am very hungry."

The lad sighed and turned to leave.

"And English rum, not Jamaican," Elizabeth added, "for I do not like the taste of the Jamaican."

Jack left, but she noticed that he paused beside the black man, who had remained close by, and spoke to him before hurrying away, leaving the black man where he sat.

She lay down and tried to find comfort, but her arm pained her badly and her mind was in turmoil. What was she to do? Firstly, she must escaped from the pirates' ship, and for that, she would need the lad's assistance. Probably, she would also need his help to reach Port Royal but, once there, she could turn him over to the authorities and watch while they hung him from the city gates. She thought that would please her greatly.

She remembered the dream again, and prayed that it was but a dream, for she had to admit that she had enjoyed it in a way she had not enjoyed any other before. In remembering the dream, she also remembered the other, where she and an unknown – no, not unknown, for she realised, of a sudden, that Jack was the stranger from her former dream, beside whom she had fought. It had, it appeared, come true.

It also seemed that he had been following her, or she him, that the Fates meant for them to be together in some way. It was all so strange, and her head hurt to think on it, with the heat of the dawning day and the pain in her arm she found that she could scarce keep her eyes open or her mind focused on anything, and soon drifted back into sleep.

She woke fitfully throughout the day. Sometimes Jack was there, sometimes he was not. Once, she awoke to find him pouring liquid into her mouth, and hoped it was merely water, for she had not the strength to resist him. His hands felt cool against her hot skin, and his whispered words brought her more comfort than she thought possible. She found that she was pleased when she woke with him by her side, and disappointed when he was absent.

She woke again properly when the light was dim and the ship quiet. Jack was sleeping beside her, and she had an opportunity to look at him closely for the first time. She saw that he was quite pretty for a boy. His cheeks were soft and his skin smooth. He was small and his arms and legs, where they were visible, were tanned to a warm brown colour. His hair was fair, lighter on the top where the sun had touched it. In his sleep he had a slight half-smile on his face, and looked harmless enough. He slept with one arm behind his head and his legs sprawled wide, as if he knew of nothing that would harm him.

Elizabeth noticed around his neck a chain of good quality gold, which was strikingly similar to the chain of her very own locket, and wondered how a lad such as he would come by such an expensive item. She tried to imagine him stealing it from a lady in the street or lifting it from some dandy's pocket, but neither scenario felt true. Then she wondered if it might be a token given by a grand lady for some service, and found herself blushing as she imagined what that service might be.

Unbidden and unstoppable, her mind conjured up an image of

the lad leaning over the supine form of a naked woman, tenderly kissing her throat, and stroking her body with the gentlest of touches. Her mind's eye watched him rub and lick her, working her body into a frenzy with his teasing ways and then, when the woman could stand it no longer, entering her with a force and speed that brought the woman to a sharp and satisfying climax.

Elizabeth found herself to be quite hot and felt a longing to be once more amongst female company. She thought of Mary and her new-found friend, imagined their bodies tangled in a passionate embrace. She wondered about Rose and if she, too, had found a new friend. One of her patronesses, perhaps, who tingled at the accidental brushing of the neck with those soft hands, at the removal of an imaginary hair from the breast. These tentative touches turned to more urgent ones as the patroness responded, clothes were torn to find the flesh underneath, tension built up until it felt unbearable, and then the glorious release.

It was too hot under the shelter. Elizabeth could not breathe. She crawled out and stood slowly, feeling a lightness in her head. She was near to the railings and she leaned there, feeling the soft sea breeze ruffle her hair and restore her breath.

She thought over the events of the past few days as best she remembered them. Some things puzzled her as she thought on them: the lad knowing her to be a woman but his companion not; she knew not what to make of that.

She was distracted from her thoughts by the view before her. They were close into the shore and it might have been dawn for, as she watched, the world seemed to emerge from the dimness that had first been there. In the growing light, a long beach of golden sand first appeared and then, behind it, swaying palm trees and, behind those, in the distance, mountains. All thoughts deserted her, and she marvelled at the beauty before her.

While she was thus engaged, she heard light footsteps behind her. She froze, her body stiff with the expectation of a blow, or worse. There was a pause.

"It is very beautiful," a voice said, close to her shoulder.

She turned slightly. It was Jack; she nodded.

"You should return to the shelter immediately."

"It is too hot."

There was another long pause as they both stood and watched as the world took on more and more colour. The lad sighed and turned from the railings. As he did so, the chain round his neck slipped from his shirt and a locket swung free. He tried hastily to tuck it away.

Elizabeth grabbed his arm to stop him; it was *her* locket! He must have stolen it while she slept! But then she realised she could still feel her own, nestling safety between her breasts. She pulled it out, half expecting it to be a phantom, but it was exactly as it had been the day her mother had given it to her. She caught hold of the lad's locket in her other hand and compared the two, marvelling at their similarities and noticing their differences. It was clear they fitted together and, as she clicked them into place, she saw that they formed one perfect heart.

As she stared, her heart began to race. "Where did you get this?" she demanded.

"It was a gift from my mother." Jack was trying to pull away, but Elizabeth held her firmly.

"And from whom did she steal it?" It was incomprehensible to Elizabeth that the mother of a common lad could have come by such a locket through any other means.

"I know not how she came by it, but she was a gentlewoman, like yourself, and had no need for stealing." He snatched his arm angrily from Elizabeth's grasp and turned his back upon her.

"A gentlewoman?" Elizabeth had no doubt he lied, but she needed to know more about the locket.

He nodded, his back still turned to her.

"May I see it?" Elizabeth asked, not daring to believe the lad would let her see it, but he did, lifting the chain from around his neck and giving it to her without looking at her. She snatched it from him. Martin had said there had been two but thought the other lost. She knew not how Jack had come by it, but thanked the gods of chance that had brought her to it.

She pressed open the secret catches of the conjoined locket. There was a strand of hair inside the lad's locket; she pushed it impatiently to one side. Under it, she saw the completion of the treasure map. It was an island which she recognised from her hours of studying the maps on the voyage from England, and the island was not far from where they presently were, just off the western tip of Jamaica. There was even a cross on the map indicating exactly where the treasure was to be found.

She snapped the lockets shut; the secret therein would ensure her safe passage off the pirates' ship and to a new life, wherever she chose to start it.

"Your mother told you nothing of the locket?" she asked tentatively.

"No." He still had his back to her.

That was good; it meant she would not have to share whatever treasure there was with him. She handed the locket back to him; she had all the information she needed from it. Still, she was curious.

"And you know not how your mother came by such a fine piece of jewellery?"

The lad shook his head. "I had thought it came from her mother; she was a lady-in-waiting to the Queen."

Elizabeth laughed out loud, for it was a preposterous suggestion. Her own grandmother had been one of the Queen's courtiers; for the lad to think he came from such a grand line was ridiculous.

"And what was her name, this lady-in-waiting?" Elizabeth thought to prove how deluded the lad was.

"Elizabeth Bridlington," he answered without hesitation.

Elizabeth felt herself grow cold despite the growing heat of the day. "That is not possible."

He turned and looked at her for the first time. "It is not only possible but true." He looked angry.

"But..." Elizabeth was not sure if it was her wound or the news that made her feel so ill. She leant against the railings to steady herself.

"I was named Elizabeth for my grandmother's best friend at Court." The two women had died together in a terrible carriage fire. So badly burnt was the carriage that not one fragment of either woman survived to be buried.

"And your grandmother's name?" the lad asked.

Elizabeth was not inclined to tell him. She wanted – no, needed – to talk of other things. "How did you know me to be a woman?" she asked.

The lad blushed to the roots of his blonde hair. "When I was tending your wound, I noticed... Besides, I have seen you –"

"You are a rogue and a scoundrel." She made up her mind to have no more to do with him. "I will enjoy killing you in our duel. I am going now to the captain to inform him that I am fit and ready."

"No, please." He tried to prevent her from leaving, and she slapped him sharply across the cheek. She saw the big black man, whose presence she had not noticed before, now rise from the deck behind them.

"Call off your slave," she demanded, hoping not to sound as frightened as she was.

"He is not my slave," the lad said, "but he will not stop you going where you will." It sounded as much an instruction to the big man as an assurance to her. She walked past him, only half-believing he would not attack her. When he did not, she headed towards the bridge, hoping the layout of the pirates' ship was not dissimilar from her old ship.

The short walk made her head spin, and she had to stop for a moment and lean on the rails. She felt the lad move to help her, so straightened up again and moved on. She did not want to fight him, and hoped she would not have to. However, she did not want him to see any weakness in her still. She would tell the captain of the treasure in return for a share of it and passage to London, where she could enjoy her supposed widowhood in peace and quiet.

She selected the first and largest of the cabins, and entered without knocking. A large man was seated in front of a spread of food and drink. She remembered how hungry she was.

"What the devil?" The captain looked up at her entrance.

"If you are Captain Silk, I am here to tell you I am recovered and ready for the duel," she said, unable to take her eyes from the food.

"And if I am not?" he asked, but it seemed to Elizabeth he asked it playfully.

"Then I am here merely for breakfast," she answered, emboldened by her hunger."

The man laughed. "Excellent," he said. "Then join me at my feast." He was mocking her, but she was beyond caring. "A condemned man eats a hearty meal."

She did not quite understand his meaning but her legs took her to the table, someone placed a chair under her and she sat.

There was all manner of food that she did not recognize; fruit, vegetables, fish and meat. A sailor piled her plate high with a variety of the foods and she began to feast ravenously. Never before had she been so hungry, and never had any food tasted so delicious. She would have liked to ask after a number of the exotic items on the plate, but could not stop eating long enough to do so. After a time, she noticed the captain was eating nothing and was, instead, watching her.

"Captain Luther did not feed you well?" he asked, and grinned. Elizabeth did not know what to say; nothing in her upbringing had prepared her for a conversation with a pirate. Fortunately, he did not seem to require a response.

"You were his cabin boy?"

She nodded.

"And you killed Wild McTavish?"

"I killed three men, none of whom I stopped to inquire his name."

She marvelled at her daring in speaking thus to such a man as Captain Silk, but he seemed to find it amusing.

"He liked to dance," the captain said.

"Oh." She remembered the sailor with the dagger in his throat, and wondered if she could claim that as her doing and, indeed, if that were a good thing to own. "He slipped while doing his dance," she answered.

"Indeed." He seemed to think on that. "On to his own dagger?"

She nodded.

"He would have liked that," he said. He looked hard at her, and Elizabeth wondered if she should say anything more.

"Before the good captain departed, pleading for his life like a desperate nursemaid, he made mention of a treasure map."

"A treasure map?" Elizabeth learned so much about her husband in that one sentence. She knew that he had tried to trade her secret for his life.

"He said only he and his cabin boy knew of it."

"He lied," Elizabeth said. She knew that, without a ship, she would never find the treasure and this ship and its captain seemed as good as any, especially if the alternative was to fight a duel to the death. But she wanted to make sure this Captain Silk knew that she was in charge.

"I guessed as much." The captain seemed to lose interest.

"Captain Luther knew not where the treasure lay; only I know that."

He looked at her in surprise and disbelief.

"And I will show you for a half share and my freedom."

"I could just let Jack kill you in the duel."

"Kill me?" Elizabeth laughed. "What makes you so sure I would not kill *him*?"

"That slave of his," the captain said, "he won him in a fight."

"Indeed." It was a good purse for a fight, Elizabeth knew, but saw not its significance.

"The fight was against that same slave."

Elizabeth was amazed. The lad was so small and the black man so very, very large. The captain laughed at her confusion.

"But here, show me this treasure map and we will see if we cannot strike a bargain."

"The map was lost with the ship." Elizabeth was not going to show him the locket.

Captain Silk shrugged his shoulders and made as if to leave the table.

"But I will know the island when I see it for I committed its latitude and longitude to memory."

"How very fortuitous." Again, he looked as though he did not believe her, and she wondered if her fate was to die at the hands of a lad no taller than herself.

"Come, then, show me." Silk rose and went to a small desk on which his maps rested, but she did not follow him. She could still see him, though, as he rifled through the maps, and it was several sheets before she saw the island whose shape was engraved in her locket and Jack's.

"No," she said. "I know where it lies, its shape and appearance. If I were to tell you now, however, you would have me tossed overboard."

"Ah." His eyes twinkled. "I see my reputation as a ruthless cut-throat preceeds me. All fiddle-faddle and eyewash, my lad. Where would a Pirate King be without Fear following him amane? But you may trust me for, all in all, I am a gentleman."

He bowed, mockingly.

Though she still did not quite believe him, Elizabeth felt more calm. "Trust *me*, I shall know it when I see it."

16

Mermaid Island

"They say it is guarded by ferocious mermaids –" Pip looked ready to explode with excitement "– with tails of emeralds and eyes of rubies, who can crush a man with a look and sing so sweetly that men lay down and let them." He barely paused for breath. "And on the island, the huts are made of spun gold and decorated with diamonds and there are women who are so beautiful that to look upon them is to be driven mad. No man has ever landed there and come away alive."

Though she had not confided in the captain, Elizabeth confessed to Jack that their destination was Mermaid Island.

Jack had heard these stories and believed none of them, but Pip had not finished.

"They say that they keep the men who dare to land in caves and use them only for their own pleasure, and if any of the women gives birth to a boy child, they have a great feast and roast the babe like a sucking pig."

"We should send ye there, then," Harry teased Pip. "You are so small they would throw you back as being of no use to them at all!"

The men around laughed, and Pip looked affronted.

"Tell us more," Jack prompted him, for the island sounded a veritable paradise to her, and she needed cheering up, since the woman she had rescued now spent more of her time in the captain's company.

"And when the moon is full, the women dance naked upon the

sands while the mermaids sing upon the shores, and any man who sees them is turned to stone and thrown into the harbour to tear out the hulls of ships that try to land there."

Harry snorted. "Belay yer gaff, youngster. 'Tis more like so named because the island is shaped like a mermaid, is all. I have sailed the oceans, man and boy, and have never yet seen sight not sound of a mermaid."

This belittling of a favoured nautical myth started a heated discussion. Jack turned thankfully to her own thoughts. She was relieved that there was to be no duel, but also worried that this side trip to find the treasure was delaying her departure from the ship. Since she had decided to leave, she could think of nothing else, though it was looking less and less likely now that the woman would be going with her. When she saw the woman about the ship, she seemed pointedly to look the other way.

Jack also had a nagging feeling about this new adventure upon which they were embarking. Something deep inside her told that it was wrong but, more than that, that it was somehow her fault and she should be doing something to stop it. She knew not what she could do. Pip seemed not to notice her preoccupation, but Blue questioned her on her long face and seemed to guess its cause. It was all that she could do not to tell him of her peculiar passion for their new crewmate, for she knew in the telling of it that she would reveal not only the newcomer's secret but also her own.

So, over the following days, she stayed by herself, mostly perched in the main mast crow's nest, watching from a distance as the crew went about their tasks. Seeing the woman in close conversation with Silk and feeling a growing dread as they approached the rocky outline of what other pirates had told her was the fabled Mermaid Island.

"Jack." Pip broke across her reverie one morning when the island was visible. He scrambled into the crow's nest. "The captain wants to see you; they have a plan."

Jack wanted no part of any plan, but she climbed down to the deck. She did not want to anger Captain Silk any more than she already had. In his cabin sat the woman, now in dress and cap, looking much as she did the first time Jack had seen her. Only now, she was laughing and flicking her skirts about her. Jack was shocked; why had she been so foolish as to tell the captain of her true sex? He was not to be trusted. As she entered, he was laughing.

"If I did not know better," he said, "I would throw you over my table and take you as a dog would." Jack saw a cloud of anxiety cross the face of the woman, and then she forced a smile and laughed a little too hard.

"Ah, Jack." Silk saw her. "We have a plan, as you can see."

The plan – to Jack's relief, she had not revealed herself after all – was for Jack and the woman to row ashore, dressed in female attire, and claim to be passengers from a ship seeking safe harbour from pursuing pirates. Once the island's women were distracted, the pirates would then land and loot the treasures said to be there. The plan filled Jack with a sickening dread, not least of which was the thought of donning dress and bonnet. She had not worn women's garb since she was three years of age, so she had little or no memory of what such clothes felt like to wear. She was terrified that when others saw her in the dress of a woman, they would know her to be one.

There was a dress laid out for Jack, made of a fine soft fabric. It had come from the captain's trunk, a souvenir of some port or another. It was too big for her, but the woman set to work to fix it with pins. Jack stood still while the woman worked around her. The captain was called away by one of the crew.

"Put your arms up," Elizabeth commanded, but Jack would not move.

"You are the last person on this ship who I would wish to take with me, but it was considered yourself or Pip who would best pass as a woman, and Pip is needed here. As far as I can fathom, you do nothing on the ship but sulk in the crow's nest." Jack did not say anything, but it warmed her a little to know that the woman had at least noticed where she had been.

"In truth, I would rather have your slave than you, but I do not think this dress would go round one of his legs, let alone his waist."

"He is not my slave," Jack said quietly.

"As you wish." She tugged at the dress and then stopped. "You will wear it unaltered if you will not let me fix it."

The dress was left unaltered. Jack could not bear to have the woman so near, the smell of her, the feel of her hand when she accidentally brushed Jack's skin. It was all too much, and Jack threw the dress to the floor and stormed out of the cabin, bumping into the captain on his way back in.

"My two fine ladies had a spat?" Silk said, and laughed. "Or was it more fishwives at dawn?"

Jack did not answer.

"You will do this, Jack my lad." He put his arm around Jack's neck, his grasp a little tighter than was comfortable. "That is an order, for there is more at stake here than the proving or not of some paltry sea dogs' myth."

He let Jack go, and she retreated to the crow's nest, where she stayed until Pip came to fetch her just after dawn the next morning.

The woman was already dressed and looked almost radiant in the dawn glow. How the rest of the crew could not know she was a woman on seeing her dressed thus, Jack could not believe. She took her own dress into the dingy with her, determined that no one should see her in it. As it was, most of the hands were still abed; only Blue, Pip, Harry and the captain were up to see them off.

"'Til the next high tide," Silk shouted after them as Jack began to row away. "Then we come ashore."

The words filled Jack with such foreboding that she was

scarce able to row.

"Oh, for heaven's sake," the woman snapped when they were not progressing as fast as she thought they should. "My maid could row better than this."

"Then perhaps you should have brought her along."

"Indeed, I should have."

Jack knew then that she was trying to keep up her courage, for something in her eyes looked sad and the woman spoke no more for a long while. The physical effort of the rowing should have steadied Jack's fears, but every stroke that took them closer to the island made her all the more afraid. The silence between them unsettled her further.

"Then is your name Elizabeth, truly?" she asked eventually, after she noticed the woman casting at her a furtive glance.

"My name is Eli," the woman said, as if Jack were stupid and, indeed, Jack had heard the captain call her by that name.

"Your *real* name. Were you truly named for my grandmother? For her name was indeed Elizabeth." Jack paused in her rowing, for her arms and back were starting to ache.

"Keep going," the woman ordered. Jack sighed and returned to her rowing.

"Elizabeth, yes," the woman said after a few moments.

Jack smiled.

"What amuses you?" Elizabeth demanded.

"Nothing," Jack said, and rowed all the harder to gain the island and get this terrible thing, whatever it might be, over all the sooner. Before they reached the harbour, Jack stood and put on the dress and cap, while Elizabeth steadied the boat. She could not help but smile at Jack's woebegone expression at the ill fit of it, but had not the time to take her revenge with a 'told you so', for the tide was swelling, and they must go on.

They reached the entrance of the harbour, which was surrounded by high cliffs and scattered with rocks. It was easy to see why so many ships had foundered there. There were no mermaids that Jack could see, though she imagined she heard voices floating across the water.

"There are people on the shore." Elizabeth sounded both excited and scared. "Let me be our ambassador, for it is my map and my treasure."

Jack was only too pleased to leave everything to her, wishing to keep out of mind of anyone they met.

"Should I wave?" Elizabeth asked, as though checking some point of etiquette. Jack had her back to the shore and could not see it.

"Are they waving?"

"No."

"Then 'twere best not."

"You have your dagger?"

Jack nodded; it was tucked into her britches that she still wore under the dress.

"I *will* wave," Elizabeth said firmly. "We want them to think we are friendly," and she waved her arms about, nearly upsetting the boat.

"They are waving back."

Jack turned her head and saw five or six people on the beach looking in their direction. It was hard to tell from that distance if they were men or women. Jack felt dread rising again like a wave of nausea. Something was very wrong; something terrible was about to happen, she could feel it.

"I do not think they are women," Elizabeth whispered. "For none of them is wearing a dress." She sounded worried. "I hope they will not overpower and ravish us."

"It is a little late to think on that now," Jack said and arranged her dagger so it would be easy to reach in a fight.

"Oh, be quiet," Elizabeth snapped.

They were well within the harbour proper by this point, its

steep walls rising above them on two sides. Jack noticed several small ketches anchored behind an outcrop of rocks. They would be no match for the *Revenge*. She wondered if there were cannons concealed in the cliffs, and hoped that there were.

They reached the shore and the six figures watched while Jack beached the dinghy and helped Elizabeth out. She seemed to expect Jack to carry her ashore, so Jack hoisted her over her shoulder and dropped her none too gently on the sand.

"Well, really." Elizabeth was about to tell Jack off, but the approaching figures stilled her sharp tongue. Elizabeth had been correct when she said none wore dresses, but they were all certainly women. Jack noted that Pip would have been disappointed, for the stories were untrue; while none was hideous, they were neither of such beauty that they would strike men mad. Though, not being a man, Jack could not tell for sure.

One had on baggy pantaloons and a turban such as Jack had seen in pictures of Eastern pirates. Another had britches like her own, and third had a skirt made of what appeared to be straw; yet another had on a ragged soldier's uniform.

They stopped a few yards from Jack and Elizabeth and stood, as if waiting for them to speak first.

"We come from a boatful of women, and we are fleeing from fierce pirates," Elizabeth began and, even to Jack's ears, it sounded false. "We seek shelter here in your harbour."

One of the women near the back of the group pushed her way forward. She was a black woman of middle years.

"Jack?" she asked, and then, "Jack!" she said, smiling broadly.

Jack recognised her; it was Martha, one of the Carib women from the carver's village.

"Jack!" Martha ran to her and lifted her up, twirling her around. In the process of so doing, Jack's dress, which they had not had time to properly fasten, fell momentarily to the sand.

"I swear by the Devil's dame, you are skinnier every time I see you."

"Martha." Jack hugged the woman, delighted to see her.

"You still have the object?" Martha laughed, and nodded to Jack's crotch. "I hope you have learned to use it properly now."

Jack felt herself start to blush, and she was most glad when Elizabeth interjected loudly, "As I was saying..."

"Yes, yes, being chased by pirates, we heard you," Martha cut across her. "I wish to hear what Jack has to say about this."

Jack found everyone staring at her. She looked about her. Beyond the beach was a flat, green area with huts scattered over it. Straw huts, none made of gold, spun or otherwise; the women wore no jewels. If there were treasure here, it was not, she thought, that which the pirates were seeking.

"Have you treasure here?" she asked the group. She heard Elizabeth beside her hiss in exasperation.

"No." It was the woman in the uniform who spoke. "Not gold, not jewels," she said it with a sigh, though not as if she regretted the lack of those things, but as if she knew the rumour of them had caused no end of trouble.

"Look." The woman in the straw skirt approached Elizabeth. "She has the locket."

This brought squeals of delight from the group, and they surrounded Jack and Elizabeth and enveloped them in a group embrace. Elizabeth struggled to extract herself.

"It has a map; I know there is treasure here," she demanded of the group.

"She must be Miss J's granddaughter; she has the look of her," one woman said.

"And the temper." All the women laughed.

"I know you have treasure..." Elizabeth started again and then stopped. "Miss J? I... she..." She looked about her in confusion.

"That was her locket to mark the way here for those who might come after her," the woman in the uniform said very sadly. "But I am afraid you are too late. She died just this past winter."

"Eighty-five years she was, though, and happy to the very end," Martha added on a lighter note.

"We all miss her," the woman in the grass skirt said, "Especially Lizzy."

Jack's head was spinning. She could barely follow what was being said. Her own grandmother had been here? And the locket had something to do with it. She took her own out from under her shirt. The women all stared at her.

"The other locket," someone cried. "They have come as a pair, just as Lizzy and Miss J did."

"If you look closely –" the woman in the turban peered into Jack's confused face "– I think it is indeed true. Come, come, we must take him to Lizzy." She tugged at Jack's arm.

"Wait." Jack stood her ground, not sure where or to whom they were taking her, but knowing that they only had until the next high tide before the pirates would sail in and plunder the peaceful village.

"There *are* pirates out there, waiting for our signal."

"The ones chasing your ship of women?" Martha asked and laughed heartily. "You can do better than that."

"No," Elizabeth said, "I lied."

This brought more gales of laughter.

"Please listen; there *is* a pirate ship." Jack could not bare it.

The women wandered off towards the huts, still laughing amongst themselves.

"The excuses some women use," Jack heard one say.

"Do they not know that all women are welcome here?"

They left Jack and Elizabeth standing on the beach alone.

"What are we going to do?" Elizabeth demanded, as if the whole thing was Jack's fault.

"We have to stop Silk."

"Of course," Elizabeth said. "But how?" She stood biting her lip, and Jack felt a warm upsurge of feelings for her.

"I have been so stupid," Elizabeth continued.

Jack nodded.

"If only my mother had explained. I thought the locket pointed the way to the whereabouts to real treasure."

"It does," Jack said quietly, regarding her warmly.

"I know that." She looked at Jack, her eyes wide. "You... were in my dream, you see. I had a dream we were fighting side by side..."

"... against the pirates," Jack continued.

"On a ship..."

They finished the sentence together: "In rough seas."

"What does it mean?" Elizabeth grasped Jack's hand.

"I do not know, but we have until the next high tide to find out." Jack noticed Elizabeth's eyes for the first time. They were blue like the sea, clear and bright, and they seemed to Jack to be inviting her to dive in and swim in their glorious coolness. She wanted to kiss her more than she remembered wanting anything in her life. Elizabeth still had hold of her hand.

Jack knew this was neither the time nor the place, but she could not stop herself. She pulled Elizabeth close and planted her lips upon hers. Elizabeth was momentarily surprised, and Jack wondered if she had made a terrible mistake but, even as she broke off, Elizabeth pulled her back into the kiss, and they melted into each other. Their lips flowed together, their tongues touched and retreated like teasing children, their arms entwined and their bodies were drawn together as though they were irons around a magnet.

Jack wanted to feel Elizabeth's skin under her hand, she wanted to kiss the soft flesh along her collar bone, feel the weight of her breasts, one in each hand. She wanted to spend the rest of her life exploring the body she now held so tightly, but she knew she could not. For if she did not find a plan for deterring Silk and his cut-throats, the rest of her life might not be very long.

She broke off the embrace, pushing Elizabeth gently away, out of her reach so she would not be tempted to kiss again. Elizabeth looked confused and a little annoyed, as though she had been awoken from a wonderful dream.

"Why?" she asked, and Jack could not tell if she were asking why she had stopped kissing, or why she had started.

"We must warn the women of the danger we have wrought for them."

Jack ran up the beach after the women, who had not noticed they were not following. Elizabeth came after more slowly. The island's denizens were already in amongst the huts when Jack caught up.

"Please," she said, "You are in great danger."

"The pirates?" Martha asked with a twinkle in her eye.

"Yes."

"They pursue you."

"No," Jack said, trying to impress upon them the importance of her information. "We came with the pirate ship. They mean to plunder the village. We were sent ahead to help them gain ease of passage."

The women kept walking, as if she had said something of no more import than she thought it might rain. They stopped in front of a hut and knocked quietly upon the wooden door, then waited in silence.

"Yes?" a weak voice called from within.

"We have a visitor for you," the woman in the uniform called out.

"A visitor?" The voice was obviously surprised. The door creaked open and an elderly woman emerged. "A visitor?" she asked again.

Jack watched the old woman. She was small and wizened, but upright in posture. She looked exactly as Jack's mother would have looked had she been able to live out her full number of years. The old woman turned her gaze to Jack and stared at her very long and very hard.

"It cannot be Henry," she said finally. "He would be much older by now, but I know of no other lad who could look thus, unless it is..." She took a faltering step towards Jack.

"Jacqueline." She grasped Jack to her in a fierce hug. "You were no more than a babe in your mother's arms when I left, and how I longed to see what had become of you." She pushed Jack out to arm's length and looked at her again. "I see the way has not been easy, but that makes for a strong heart." She put her hand to Jack's heart. "I believe yours is stronger than most."

Elizabeth had joined them. She stared at Jack. "Jacqueline! You are also a girl?" The old woman, in her turn, stared at Elizabeth, her hand to her mouth as if in disbelief.

"Oh, Miss J, if only you were here to see this."

Jack did not understand. The old woman went to Elizabeth and hugged her warmly.

"Your grandmother, Jacqueline, was my life-long companion, and you are her spitting image, born again into my life."

Elizabeth stood awkwardly, not returning the hug. "My grandmother was a lady-in-waiting to the Queen," she said haughtily.

"Indeed she was, as was I. Elizabeth Bridlington then." She smiled.

"She died in a carriage fire," Elizabeth said sharply.

The old woman laughed sadly and shook her head. "The best way, we thought, to slip away with no hue and cry after. No bones to bury."

"You falsified your death!" Elizabeth sounded outraged.

"It may seem cruel, but your mother was happily married and you were born healthy."

"She grieved her whole life for my grandmother."

"As a daughter should." She dismissed Elizabeth with a nod of her head and turned back to Jack. "As, indeed, I see you grieve, and I am sorry." She took Jack's hand. "You must tell me all."

Jack shook her head. "First we must decide what is to be done about the pirates. They cannot be allowed to plunder the island."

The old woman sighed. "Will they never leave us in peace?"

"We have called everyone to the Council hut for a meeting," the woman in the turban said.

"Oh, granddaughter." The old woman took Jack's arm. "It is good to see you finally. I wondered if you would ever find this island, but we never gave up hope, Jacqueline and I. We knew in our hearts that you would find us. I am sorry she is not here to see it." She took Elizabeth's arm, too. "And to see you come together, it is as if I were watching my own life played out again before my failing eyes." She looked from one to the other and sighed a deep, contented sigh.

"Let us dispose of these pirates of yours and then you must both tell me your tales of how you came to be here. I am sure they will make most entertaining listening."

17

The Battle of Mermaid Island

Elizabeth could not concentrate on the talk around her. She knew she ought to, for it was her fault that the pirates were here at all. But she could feel neither concern nor guilt, for she was more taken with a feeling she was quite unused to, a feeling she could barely name. But if she were to be honest with herself, she knew that feeling to be lust.

She watched Jack as she sat and listened to the women, and watched the look of concentration upon her face. Jack's hands moved as she explained something, her head inclining as she considered a point someone else put forward. How she had not seen before that Jack was a woman, she did not know. Everything pointed to her sex, her lack of stature, the softness of her skin, the lightness of her voice, the way she moved and the way she kept still. Now that she knew Jack to be a woman, Elizabeth could not doubt it.

The kiss on the beach had been like lightning passing through her body. It left her knees weak and her heart pounding. It had been so unexpected, yet it seemed to be what she had been waiting for her whole life. It was like no other kiss she had ever had, reaching parts of her body that she had not known existed. She wanted very much to repeat the experience, but all these other women were taking up Jack's time and attention. It was enough to make her want to scream.

She had read a poem once on the subject of love – "Shall I

compare thee to a summers day?" – and thought it to be fanciful in the extreme. She had been very fond of Mary, but never thought to compare her to a flower, nor kneel beneath her window and compose odes to her beauty. She had never been much distracted from the routine of her normal life.

But now, though her life was far from normal and although the most important battle ever was about to take place, she could think of nothing but Jack's soft lips. She watched them as Jack talked; such a waste of movement, when they could be upon her lips, kissing her, whispering in her ear all the endearments Elizabeth so longed to hear. She marvelled that she could feel such strong emotions for one such as Jack, so small and rough, so...

Elizabeth sighed.

... so wonderful.

Then, she started to worry that Jack might not feel the same way. She had kissed her on the beach, but here amongst these women she could talk and listen, help as they planned the defence of the island, as if there were nothing else upon her mind. To have such a fever as Elizabeth felt and for it not to be felt in return, that would be worse than death.

The women around her began to move away, and she was left wondering what had been decided. She got to her feet and sought out Jack amongst them, her heart beating widely for fear that she had lost her. Someone touched her shoulder and she turned in fright to find Jack standing behind her.

"Are you not well?" Jack asked, with such a look of concern in her eyes that Elizabeth's worries left her. "We are to return to the ship, but if you are not well..."

"No." Elizabeth would not be left behind; she would stay by Jack's side at all costs.

"Then we must hurry."

They returned to the beach. Elizabeth could see that the tide was already turning; Jack stopped to tie up her dress more tightly.

"What are we to say?" Elizabeth asked to distract herself from staring.

"That we saw no weapons."

"Why that?"

"Because we want them not to ready the cannons."

Elizabeth wished now she had listened more closely. She helped pulled the dinghy to the water's edge and climbed in while Jack pushed it out into deeper water and then clambered aboard. Jack settled on the middle bench and took both the oars. Elizabeth slid on to the bench beside her; she could feel the heat of Jack's body through the material of both their dresses.

"Jack," she said, but was too afraid to look at her.

"Yes?"

"I know I have not always been very nice to you."

"It doesn't matter." Jack prepared to start rowing, but Elizabeth stayed her hand.

"It does matter, for now I find that I..." She could hardly bring herself to say the words. She looked up into Jack's brown eyes and there she found the strength to continue. "... that I am in love with you. If you find it strange, a woman loving another woman, that is well." She hurried on in case Jack interrupted her. "It is a peculiar passion, and one I have felt all my life. If you find it so, I will return to London and manage my husband's estate. You need not fear for my future..."

Jack stopped her speech by laying a hand on hers. "I have loved you from the moment I first saw you in 'The Jolly Sailor' in London but never dreamed I would have the privilege of you returning my love." She kissed Elizabeth lightly on the cheek. "When this day is through, and if we both survive it, then we can speak more of love." She picked up her oar and Elizabeth the other, and together they rowed back to the ship in silence.

Harry was waiting for them, and threw down a rope ladder.

"What ho, fine ladies?" he called cheerfully. "Be the island awash with treasure and beautiful maidens, ripe for the plucking?"

Jack climbed up the ladder first. "There is none of either that we could see," she said, divesting herself of the hated dress as she spoke.

Pip was there to help him aboard. "You are not mad, then, nor turned to stone?" He felt Jack over but stopped when he saw Elizabeth climb aboard.

The captain appeared, and Blue stepped up beside Jack.

"No treasure, eh?" He looked at Jack and laughed. "They hide it away, but we will seek it out."

"There is nought but a few old women and straw huts." Jack tried to dissuade him.

"All the better for burning, then," Silk said, and laughed cruelly.

Elizabeth returned to her cabin and changed back into her britches, pleased to be out of the dress; she had forgotten how restrictive women's attire could be. She retrieved her sword and dagger and by the time she returned to the deck, the ship was being readied to sail into the harbour. Jack was nowhere to be seen, nor were Harry, Pip or Blue. She wondered if Jack were telling them of the women's plan and, if so, could they be trusted? Pip she had never taken to, nor he to her, and the black man terrified her, although he had done nothing but watch over her.

Row boats were being prepared for the landing party and as far as she could see none of the cannons had been prepared. She wondered what she was expected to do and suddenly felt alone and vulnerable. She realised that if the women's plan failed, then it would be certainly be the death of her. She hoped that she would die bravely in the battle if she had to die and not suffer some terrible, slow death at the hands of Captain Silk.

She spied Jack forward with her little band of men. An odd bunch they were, too, Harry being broad and heavy, the black man huge, while Jack and Pip were both small. She wondered if the five of them had any chance against the rest of the crew and doubted it. Somehow, despite all these thoughts of death and battling against the odds, Elizabeth's heart felt light. As if the love in it for Jack let it rise above the fear. With a smile and a light step, she went to join them.

They were in a tight huddle and stopped talking when she approached. She thought Pip looked at her oddly.

"All right," Jack said. "Everyone knows what they are doing." The men all nodded and dispersed.

"And what am I to do?" Elizabeth asked, thinking of all the things she would like to do with Jack.

"Stay by my side," Jack said. "And pray, if you believe in God, for it is a miracle that we need."

The ship weighed anchor and set sail for the island. Jack and Elizabeth stayed forward and watched as the tall cliffs drew nearer until they towered over the ship. It was so calm and quiet, and felt almost unreal. Elizabeth found herself holding her breath, waiting for something to happen.

All of a sudden, a boulder the size of Elizabeth's head whizzed by her and embedded itself in the deck. Noise exploded from the cliff, high-pitched screaming and whistling, as though all the banshees from Ireland had settled on the rocks and were all singing at once. More boulders rained down upon the ship, landing with timber-splitting crashes.

The crew were running about, many with their ears covered, obviously fearing that this was the song of the mermaids and to hear it would drive them mad. Silk was bellowing orders, but was having trouble making himself heard above the racket. He did manage to order some men below to man the cannons.

"They will destroy the cliffs," Elizabeth whispered hoarsely to Jack.

"Do not worry; we have taken care of that."

"Jack!" Silk bellowed from the helm, "You said that they were unarmed."

"We saw no guns," Jack shouted back.

There was a scream as a boulder felled one of the pirates. Elizabeth could see the women on the cliffs loading the large stones into what appeared to be giant slings. They were remarkably accurate. Then, she heard a shot ring out and saw one of the women fall. She turned to see Captain Silk with a pistol raised and smoking. Suddenly, Jack was no longer at her side; she sprinted down the deck towards Silk, and threw herself at him to disarm him. Elizabeth raced after her. Harry and the others, too, were nowhere to be seen. In the chaos, it was a moment before the rest of the crew noticed the tussle between Jack and Captain Silk.

Elizabeth was sure Silk would crush Jack, so great was their size difference. She held her sword ready to strike but they were rolling about, so closely intertwined that she could not land a blow on one without risking hitting the other. Suddenly, there was a loud report and Elizabeth smelled gunpowder and burning flesh. The pair stopped rolling and, for a moment, it seemed the whole world had stopped. Then the two bodies fell apart, and Jack scrambled to her feet, thankfully uninjured. Captain Silk lay still, a rosette of blood growing upon his chest.

The crew who had gathered to watch the fight stood for a moment, looking at the prone figure, as if willing him to rise. When it was obvious that he would not, they turned upon Jack. Elizabeth flew to her side and, together, they raised their swords. At that moment, the weather suddenly turned against them. From perfect calm, a strong wind sprang up, and the ship began rocking about.

The first pirate threw himself at Jack, lunging with great force; Jack stepped to one side and caught him in the back with her dagger. That was the start of a long fight, and it was the fight, almost blow for blow, about which they both had dreamed. Man after man threw themselves at the two women and, side by side, they fought them off, helping one another where they could or fighting their own opponents as the swing of battle dictated.

Elizabeth was surprised by Jack's skill, and pleased with her own. If she were to die there and in that moment, she would die a happy woman, fighting as she seemed born to do and beside the woman she realised she loved more than anything else in the world.

Through their fighting, Elizabeth became aware of another sound. The boulders had ceased to rain down upon them, but off in the distance, there was a sound like thunder. After a time, the crew heard it too, and a great shout went up.

"Cannon fire!" one pirate shouted.

"A ship!" cried another.

The men fighting Elizabeth and Jack scattered as a cannon ball from the newly arrived ship landed close to the *Revenge* and set her pitching even more wildly.

"Come." Jack took Elizabeth's hand and ran to the railings. Below in a dinghy were Harry, Pip and Blue.

Jack waited while Elizabeth climbed down the ladder and then came after her.

"What is happening?" Jack asked.

"It seems the Governor has arrived," Harry answered.

"The Governor?"

Elizabeth did not know if this was a good or bad thing, except in that it had shortened their fight and, for that, she was grateful. "Was that part of the plan?" she asked.

"No," Jack laughed, and hugged her, "but his arrival could not be better timed."

"You are pirates, you four – will you not be hung?"

Jack looked at her. "I hope not." And she laughed again.

Elizabeth realised how beautiful she was when she laughed; she also realised that she had never before seen her do so.

They rowed ashore, the five of them cramped in the small dinghy. A small group of women met them on the beach.

"Who was hit?" Jack asked even before she was out of the boat.

"Martha," one of the group replied.

"Does she fare well?"

The woman shook her head.

"May I see her?" Harry asked. He had with him his bag of potions.

The woman looked doubtful.

"He is a good healer," Jack said.

"Come, then." The woman led him away.

"And we must hide you," another woman said.

"No." Jack stopped her.

"But the Governor?" Elizabeth could not see how Jack could be so calm when the Governor had vowed to hang every last pirate in the Caribbean.

"I have a plan," Jack said mysteriously, and smiled again.

The pirates' ship was even now being pounded with cannon fire and in danger of sinking. Elizabeth learned that Pip and the giant had disabled the cannons on the *Revenge* so that they were unable to return fire. From the beach, they saw the Governor's men board the stricken ship with very little resistance. Without their captain, the crew had had, to put it nautically, the wind taken from their sails.

Once the pirate ship had been secured, they watched a small boat come rowing ashore. Elizabeth could see six or seven men in it. She hoped they did not come to fight, for she was quite exhausted. As the boat neared, she recognised one of the men; it was Peter, the First Mate from her husband's ship. She was surprised to see him, as she had thought most of the crew of the *Juno* had perished or been abandoned. Jack recognised him, too, but she was more interested in two other of the men onboard.

Pip nudged Jack. "Are they not the sailors we rescued with you?" He asked.

The two men in question were dressed in smart uniforms.

Jack nodded. "The Governor and his manservant."

"But we..." Pip started and then stopped.

"Put them ashore, yes."

"If Captain Silk had known..." Pip clearly could not believe it.

Elizabeth did not understand, but the boat was landing and Jack strode off to meet it.

"Governor," she said, as he helped the older of the two men from the boat.

Elizabeth marvelled at Jack's confidence; she was such a small, untidy figure beside the Governor but he seemed not to notice. He grasped Jack's hand and shook it firmly.

"It is good to see you again," he said. "We have often wondered what became of you."

The younger man had jumped from the boat while Peter and the other crewmen dragged it up on to the beach. He joined the Governor.

"And here we find you –" said the Governor "– having already defeated the infamous Captain Silk and his crew, stamp me!"

"Pardon me, sir," Jack said and laughed, for it did indeed sound as though the man was disappointed at having missed the battle. "It is good to see you recovered," she continued, and he looked a little embarrassed.

"There is a reward." The younger man had noticed the Governor's awkwardness and stepped in. "For Silk, and for our own earlier rescue."

"Then let us see if we can find you refreshment and shade and discuss these matters."

Elizabeth wanted to hug Jack. She seemed so calm and confident and in control. She wanted to chase everyone else away and have Jack all to herself, for the two of them to be nestled in one of the huts, listening to the sounds of the sea and exploring each other's bodies, with all the time in the world in which to enjoy it. She knew she would have her chance soon enough, but with every passing moment, the waiting became more difficult.

The women from the island led them to the large hut where they had held their meeting earlier. Peter fell into step beside Elizabeth.

"Well, well, young Eli – or may I call you Elizabeth?" he said with half a grin. "And how did you happen upon this island?"

"I was captured by the pirates," Elizabeth answered, not knowing how much he knew and not wanting to give too much away.

"I heard that all the crew were either slain or set adrift. In truth, I have some ill news on that account. The *Juno* was discovered in the shipping lanes off Port Royal but two days ago. Your husband was suffering from exposure and lack of water. Though he was treated for his condition, I fear he died. My deep condolences, Madam."

"Oh," she said, and wondered if she should feel some guilt perhaps for her dead husband, though, in truth, she felt none. "I was injured in the battle, and fell into a faint. I knew not of my husband's plight. But how did you know he was my husband?"

Peter blushed. "I was his... First Mate. He took me into his confidence." He recovered his composure. "You appear to be now in good health, Ma'am."

She wondered if she should show him the scar on her arms, still not fully healed. "How come you here?" she asked instead, hoping to redirect the conversation.

"I jumped ship when the battle was declared lost and swam ashore. I made my way to Montego Bay where the Governor was setting sail in pursuit of Silk, and offered my services. I was hoping for revenge on Silk, but found instead he was already dead and his crew a poor enemy without him." He, too, sounded disappointed.

"I am sorry we denied you a fight."

"Oh well, there are plenty more pirates at sea. The Governor has offered me my own commission." He was very proud of himself, and Elizabeth found she was pleased for him.

They had reached the hut, and the women sat them down and produced cakes and a sweet drink tasting of vanilla and honey. Elizabeth found she was very hungry and ate a great many of the cakes, which seemed to amuse the elderly Lizzie greatly.

"Just like her grandmother," she said, shaking her head and laughing. "Oh, how I wish she were here to see it."

Jack talked in a huddle with the women, and then spoke to the Governor and his men. Elizabeth could see she had everything shipshape, so she went and sat on the verandah of the hut and watched as the sun slipped behind the high cliffs of the harbour. The sky was full of birds, and all around her she could smell the warm aroma of spices. She leant back against the wall of the hut and closed her eyes.

Her body should have felt fatigued after such a hard day. Instead, it tingled as though she were waiting for something to happen. Her heart began to pound faster and more loudly, and all her senses were heightened. She ran her hand along the bench and marvelled at its smoothness, worn that way by endless generations sitting upon it over time, as she was doing now. The thought delighted her; she was sitting where any number of women had sat before, helping in the process of polishing the bench to a perfect finish.

The wood felt as warm as the body of a living woman, as if there were heat coming from a beating heart within. The whole island had that quality about it. Elizabeth had not thought much about the earth upon which she walked before, but this island seemed to pulse around her as if it were a living thing. In fact, it seemed to buzz around her head – she opened her eyes and saw a large insect fly around, and then alight upon her arm; it sucked at her skin. She slapped it away with a scream and saw a small hole begin to form.

Lizzie came out to see what the noise was. "Te Namu," she said when she saw the hole. "You had better come inside; this is their time of the day."

In the hut, it appeared that the negotiations were nearly over, and more food was being served. The Governor and his men were to stay the night as guests. Elizabeth joined Harry, Pip and Blue, who were sitting to one side.

"I think it is a liberty," Pip was complaining as Elizabeth sat down. "The money should be split four ways, not five." He glared at her. "For what did she do, but lead us into trouble?"

"I am sorry," she said, not quite meaning it, for everything had turned out well for her, and then realised she did not know of what he was talking. She asked, "What money?"

"The reward for Silk's head," Harry said, smiling broadly. "Enough to set up my own tavern in Negril."

"Oh." Elizabeth knew not how the rest of her life would go, but felt sure she would have little need for money. "You may have my share, if Jack does not need it."

Pip's eye lit up, and Elizabeth thought how like a rat he looked.

Jack had finished her discussions, and came to join them. She looked tired.

"The Governor will take you back to Port Royal, and you will each receive your reward there."

Blue was very upset. "You do not come with us?" Jack looked at Elizabeth; there was something of a smile in her eyes. "I think I will stay here awhile, for there is a sweetness about this island that I like."

"Then I will stay, too," Blue declared.

"You cannot." Jack took his large hand in her own. "Harry will need help in running his inn, and Pip is too young yet to be let loose on this world. You must look after them both for me."

"I wish to look after you," Blue persisted.

"I will need no looking after here." Again, Jack caught and held Elizabeth's gaze in something like a promise. "This is an island for women only."

"But you..." Harry and Pip both said at the same time. They all stared at her. After a moment, Harry started to laugh, loudly and deeply.

"Oh, my poor Sweet Anne," he said, and laughed harder.

Elizabeth looked at Jack for an explanation.

"She accused me of getting her with child." Jack laughed too.

Harry slapped her on the back. "The story of you losing your manhood, I believed that." He wiped his eyes. "No wonder all the ladies found you to be so good." He continued to laugh until he had no breath left and even Pip had joined in.

They were shown to their huts. The Governor and his party remained in one with Harry, Pip and Blue. Elizabeth had hoped they would have one to themselves but, instead, she was made to wait one more night before their life together could begin properly. She and Jack shared a mattress, though, and a blanket and the warmth of Jack at her side carried Elizabeth into a slumber sprinkled with tiny glimpses of what that life together might be like.

Epilogue

The Governor and his ship sailed just before noon the next day on the outgoing tide, taking with them Harry, Pip and Blue, as well as the disabled pirate ship and its captured crew. Jack stood on the beach and watched the ships disappear from view. The day was sunny again, but the wind was fresher, and in her heart she prayed for a safe journey for them all.

The women of the island were glad to see the men go and danced in circles on the sand at their departure. Jack, though, knew she would miss them and worried for their future. She was aware of Elizabeth by her side; more than just aware, for there was a burning in her body that needed to be quenched and she knew that Elizabeth felt the same way. They needed time together away from all other company to tend to these fires, but that time was not quite yet.

She took Elizabeth's hand, raised it to her lips and kissed it.

"Soon," she said to the question in Elizabeth's eyes. "Soon and then forever."

They walked back up to the big hut. There was to be a meeting to decide if she and Elizabeth could stay, and upon what terms. She knew her grandmother would support them, and Martha, who was recovering from her injuries but might not walk again. The fact that she had secured the women the legal ownership to the island as her reward from the Governor, a step that some of the women thought was unnecessary but gave them such protection as the Governor could offer them; these things would all count in her favour. But she knew, from seeing the other discussions, that it could be a long and drawn-out process.

The women were all gathered and seated; she was invited to speak, putting her case forward as to why she should be allowed to stay.

"For all my life, I have lived amongst men as a man and felt myself an outsider. Here, I feel I belong and with all my heart I wish to stay, living amongst women as a woman with the woman I love."

"And what have you to offer the community?" a woman asked, in a tone none too friendly.

Jack would do anything to stay and told them that she would help with the boats, fishing, crops, whatever was needed. They seemed to accept that, and then it was Elizabeth's turn to plead her case. She stood and looked at Jack pleadingly; Jack's heart went out to her. She was such a strong woman and proud, yet looking so vulnerable. But there was nothing she could do to help; this was Elizabeth's time.

"I want to stay here –" she looked around at all the faces turned in her direction "– because Jack does."

Jack heard some murmurs of disapproval from the gathered women. Elizabeth heard them, too.

"I have searched all my life for love and found it neither amongst the men of London, nor amongst the women there. I have come half way around the world in great danger to find the treasure that this locket promised." She held it up for the women to see. "And now that I have found its treasure –" she took Jack's hand "– I have no intention of letting it go."

Jack wanted to applaud the speech, spoken so articulately and fiercely but it seemed not to be the fashion of these women to do so. She looked around to see how the women had received it, and saw some nodding in what she hoped was approval. Elizabeth, however, had moved on.

"And, contrary to what you may think of women such as myself, I have skills that I think will be useful here. Not needlepoint or the spinet, but accountancy, reading and writing. Skills I would like to share with any woman willing to learn them."

Jack and Elizabeth were sent outside while the women discussed their fate.

"I thought this was paradise," Elizabeth complained, as they sat on the same smooth bench she had sat on the evening before.

"It may be." Jack took her hand and kissed it again. "With you by my side, anywhere will be paradise."

"I hear there is a waterfall." Elizabeth wished to be as far from the muttered mutterings of the women discussing her fate as possible.

"Should we not wait here?" Jack said.

"No." Lizzie emerged from the hut. "They will be hours, if not days, in debate. I will tell them where you have gone."

"Are you not staying in there?" Jack asked.

"I am too old for all this; I have said my piece, and they know my mind." She sighed and eased herself on to the bench. "It has always been this way. It took them two full days to decide the fate of Jacqueline and myself. She was ready to leave after one; I made her stay. It is not paradise: most of these women have nothing in common except that they love women and want to live freely, expressing that love." She sighed again, and Jack wondered if she might cry. Instead, she smiled.

"But it is the closest thing on this earth to Heaven, and I love it. Now go and wash yourselves, for you both smell of unrequited lust."

She shooed them away. Jack took Elizabeth's hand and, together, they ran through the village, following the stream until they came to the waterfall. They heard it before they saw it and had to turn off the main path and take a smaller one down to the deep, green pool. They both stopped and stared at the beauty of it.

The water fell some eight feet down a sheer rock face and splashed playfully into the pool. All around it were large grey rocks, with ferns and all manner of plants growing between them. The sunlight fell on the pool and rocks, dappled through the leaves of the surrounding trees.

"It is perfect," Elizabeth said, brought near to tears by its beauty.

Jack grinned – to see her brought almost speechless was a treasure. She stepped to the edge of the pool and looked into it. It was deep, and as clear as any water she had seen. She took off her boots and threw herself forward into the blissful coolness. She surfaced, laughing and shaking her head. Elizabeth was at the edge of the pool, looking most concerned.

"Come along," Jack called to her, and swam back to the edge. She could feel her clothes dragging against her, and took off her shirt, throwing it over a rock to dry. She did the same with her britches, so that she stood naked in the water. The last thing she removed was the wooden phallus; she threw that on top of her shirt. Elizabeth stared at her as if she were mad. Jack laughed again and dived under the water, feeling it flow over her body. She stayed down for as long as her breath held and then burst back out of the water. Elizabeth was sitting on a rock, frantically trying to get her boots off. Jack swam to her and saw that she was crying.

"Oh Jack," she sobbed, "I thought..." Then she hit Jack hard on the shoulder. "I thought you had drowned!"

Jack took her hand. "I am a fish, born to swim. I will teach you, too; then we can be fish together. But first..." She climbed out of the pool and stood before Elizabeth completely naked. "You cannot be a fish with clothes on."

She took the lace of Elizabeth's shirt and slowly undid it. Elizabeth stood quite still and let her. When it was undone, she lifted the shirt over Elizabeth's head. Under it was the silk binding that she had mistaken for a bandage. She carefully unwrapped it, noting her hands were shaking. She barely dared look upon the naked body and, when she did, she could not stop looking. The breasts stood sharp to attention, and there was a delicate contrast between the tanned skin of Elizabeth's arms and the pale flesh of her torso. Jack reached out one hand and cupped a breast in her hand. It was so beautiful. She held it as she might hold a small bird, and fancied she felt a heartbeat against her fingers.

Elizabeth closed her eyes and sighed. Jack then undid the cord that held up her britches. She had never seen a woman completely naked before, but she longed to look on Elizabeth's body bare of every stitch of clothing. Her hands shook even harder as the britches dropped to the ground.

The triangle of hair at Elizabeth's centre was the same fierce auburn colour as that on her head, but in tight curls. Jack brushed the back of her hands against it and Elizabeth let out a groan of such longing that Jack found herself close to tears. Elizabeth opened her eyes and looked deep into Jack's; then, as one, they came together and began kissing. It was a feverish kiss, lips too long denied, tongues thirsty for the taste of the other.

They kissed hard and fast until they were both breathless and dizzy. Their bodies did not touch for fear that the fever that burned within each of them would turn into a fire so great that it would destroy them both.

"Oh, Jack." Elizabeth was the first to break from the kiss. "My legs can no longer take my weight." She crumpled into Jack's arms and the feel of her silky skin against Jack's sent bolts like lightning through her body. They crumpled together on to the rock. Jack lowered Elizabeth on to her back on the warm granite.

They started kissing again, but this time their hands joined the exploration, as if they could no longer be denied. Jack ran hers over Elizabeth's flat stomach and gently swelling breasts, lingering long and lovingly at the nipples. Elizabeth's hands were busy, too, stroking Jack's back, circling her small breasts as no woman had done before. Jack felt quite dizzy; she had no idea that the touch of a woman's hand could make her feel so much. She had seen what her touch had done to others, and now she began to know what they had felt. It was no wonder women had groaned so sweetly under her administration.

She moved her hands to Elizabeth's hips and thighs, marvelling at the skin's softness. She worked her way to the space between Elizabeth's legs, that soft, wet space she knew was waiting for her, where she could lose herself in its wonder and bring Elizabeth such ecstasy. Her fingers found the coarseness of the hair. Elizabeth sighed quick sighs, and arched her back as if to hurry Jack's fingers to their final destination. But Jack knew the pleasure would be all the greater if she were slow, so she teased Elizabeth a little, tracing the triangle of hair with the softest strokes. Elizabeth groaned in frustration and squeezed Jack's bottom, drawing her closer, twisting so that Jack's hip was pressed into her mound, grinding her hips into Jack's.

Jack knew the time was right; they had both waited long enough. She slid her fingers inside Elizabeth and found her wetter and softer than with any other woman with whom she had ever shared this. Elizabeth gasped at her touch; her whole body contracted as if to draw Jack deeper, and deeper Jack went, sliding her two fingers as far as they would go, resting her thumb on the soft part at the top of the opening. Elizabeth was gripping Jack's bottom with both hands, breathing in little gasps, raising and lowering her hips as Jack slid her fingers in and out.

Jack was hot and wet, too; each gasp of Elizabeth's made her groan. It was as if they were joined, and what she did to Elizabeth she could feel being done to her. Jack kissed Elizabeth's neck and throat, licking the beads of sweat from the skin. She worked her way down to the breasts and took one nipple in her mouth.

"Oh, Jack," Elizabeth groaned.

It sounded like a plea but for what, Jack did not know, so she moved her fingers faster and deeper, sucking hard on the nipple.

Elizabeth was clutching at her back now, opening and closing her hands, groaning and tossing her head. She was so close to her climax, yet seemed unable to reach it. Jack slid further down her body, licking and kissing as she went. She buried her nose in the coarse tangle of hair and breathed in Elizabeth's smell. It was like the forest around her, damp and sweet-smelling. She dipped her tongue in the opening without removing her fingers and thumb.

"Sweet Jack," Elizabeth groaned again, "I am in Heaven."

Jack lapped at the waters there, flicking her tongue against the swelling of flesh, rubbing it hard and fast.

"Jack," Elizabeth cried out. "Oh, Jack, Jack, Jack." Her body buckled under Jack; she threw her head back and squeezed Jack's fingers tight. Jack gazed down at her; her eyes were still closed, her mouth open and her lips the deepest pink. Her face had taken on a luminescence, as if she were alight from within. Jack had never loved anyone so much as she loved Elizabeth in that moment. With her arms thrown back, her face so open and trusting, she looked so vulnerable and yet so strong.

She gathered Elizabeth into a fierce embrace, tears springing to her eyes. Elizabeth, too, was crying.

"Oh, Jack," she said again, and kissed her forehead tenderly. "That was like a dream." And she smiled. Jack smiled, too. It was very like her dream.

They slipped into the cool water together, Jack supporting Elizabeth. She felt their skin touch under the water and wondered at how it made her want to start kissing Elizabeth all over again. Instead, she tried to show her how to float on the surface of the water, relaxing her so that her body let the water hold her up rather than fighting against it, getting Elizabeth to move her arms and legs to help her glide through the water. Elizabeth was a fast learner, and could soon paddle, but it would be some time before she could follow Jack along the floor of the pool, chasing after the fish that lived there.

It was tiring work, learning to swim and, when Elizabeth was too exhausted to continue, they both climbed out and basked upon one of the big rocks in the sun to dry off their bodies. Jack lay on her stomach and watched the gentle breeze ripple the surface of the water.

Elizabeth settled herself down beside her and rubbed her back tenderly, kissing her neck and shoulders. She started to roll over, but Elizabeth stopped her.

"Stay," she whispered in her ear, "For now it is my turn to take you to Heaven."

Jack felt a shiver run down her spine; she had never had anyone touch her in the way Elizabeth did, running her hands over her back, kissing and licking her ear and neck. Jack could feel her body absorbing all these new sensations. Her skin tingled with each touch, her muscles tightened, begging for Elizabeth to touch each of them. Elizabeth was so close she could smell the sweetness of her; she could feel the brush of her coarse hair against her hip. She lay still, willing her body not to move, to stay and let Elizabeth do what she would. From deep within her, she felt the heat rising.

Elizabeth's hands found their way under her to caress her breasts. Jack groaned as Elizabeth had done. She could feel her nipples harden under Elizabeth's ministrations and she could feel the heat within her start to blaze. Elizabeth kept one hand gently pinching Jack's nipple and, with her other, she explored her bottom, running her fingers down along the crack between her buttocks, occasionally letting them slip low enough to brush against Jack's two openings. These touches sent shivers all through Jack's body and caused her to groan louder.

"Do you like that?" Elizabeth whispered in her ear.

Jack had not the breath to answer her.

Elizabeth slid her hand under Jack and pushed the heel of it into her mound. Jack pushed hard into the hand, hoping the pressure would bring some relief to the tension she felt, but Elizabeth moved her hand and Jack groaned in disappointment.

She even wondered if Elizabeth had done this before, but only for a second because, in the next moment, Elizabeth was inside her, first one finger and then two.

Jack was dizzy from all the different sensations this caused in her body. The feeling was exquisite; she pushed her hips down into Elizabeth's hand, forcing the other's thumb against the soft bulb of her woman's part. This made Jack gasp, but still she wanted more.

"Jack, you are so soft," Elizabeth whispered hotly into her ear. "And so wet. I want to make you climax. I want to make you call out my name as you made me call out yours."

The words and the hot breath they were delivered on caused such a burning in Jack that she was not sure she could wait. But Elizabeth had barely begun. She let go Jack's nipple but kept her fingers inside her, moving them back and forth slowly, delicately, knowing that this would drive Jack wild, knowing that she would want more, harder and faster.

Then Jack felt Elizabeth lift her bottom, raising it off the warm rock. Jack tried to turn her head to see what she was doing but could see no more than Elizabeth's face smiling mysteriously. Then, suddenly, instead of Elizabeth's fingers inside her, she felt something hard and smooth. It took her a moment to realise that it was her own wooden phallus.

How often she had wished for someone to use it upon her as she had upon so many other women, and now her wish had come true. Elizabeth used it expertly, inserting it slowly, moving and turning it so that it slipped in easily and, once in place, drawing it in and out, slowly at first but then with increasing speed, while still rubbing her thumb on the soft delicate bulb.

Jack was overwhelmed by all the sensations that now assailed her. It seemed at once that all her body was being stroked by the phallus, yet at the same time it felt as though she could feel nothing but tight walls inside her. Each stroke brought her closer to her climax, each stroke was as the touch of a burning feather.

Within her, she felt the fire gather momentum until it was an inferno burning out of control, threatening to engulf her very being.

She heard herself groaning loudly and could do nothing to stop the noises issuing from her. The whole of her body was beyond her control. She had given it over to Elizabeth, who was now taking her to a place she had never been before. It was an unknown place, but Jack knew that, with Elizabeth as her guide, she would face whatever was there and become a stronger person.

Elizabeth leaned over her. Jack could feel her breath, as fast and ragged as her own.

"Jack," she whispered. "Does this please you? Is this what you wished for? Is it?"

Jack could not have answered then if her life had depended upon it, for the burning within had collected in upon itself to a point of such intensity that Jack thought she would surely die. Then it exploded from her along every sinew and muscle, taking with it every ounce of strength, leaving her drained yet delighted.

"Oh, Elizabeth," she whispered with the last of her breath, before she collapsed back on to the warm rock. She felt Elizabeth hug her from behind before she drifted off into sleep.

She woke to the sound of low voices and gentle splashing. She rolled over and opened her eyes to find Elizabeth still asleep beside her, the phallus lying at their feet. In the pool, there were half a dozen women, as naked as they. One couple were cleaning each other, another were locked in a passionate embrace. Around the edge of the pool were other women, sitting in the sun or drying themselves. Jack sat up. Lizzie was sitting near them, combing out her long grey hair.

"You are awake, then," she said to Jack.

Jack nodded.

"They talked themselves through this one quickly, and that is usually bad news."

Jack felt her heart sink, but Lizzie smiled and winked at her.

"They will meet with you after sunset."

"And we will know then?" Jack did not know if she could wait so long to find out. "Do you know their decision?" Jack asked in a whisper.

Lizzie smiled again and went back to combing her hair.

Elizabeth sat up and stretched, then noticed the other women and tried to cover herself. Lizzie saw and laughed.

"Oh, no one pays the least attention, my dear," she said. "You will soon grow used to it." She winked again at Jack. "You both will."

Jack hugged Elizabeth to her and, for the first time in her life, knew that she and her peculiar passions were where they belonged.